'A diplomatic genius'

Gordon Brown

'A very good novel... recommended'

Alastair Campbell

'A terrific read that blends fact, fiction and fantasy. And a call for all of us to reflect on friendship, family and trust. What do we stand for, and what will we do to defend it?'

Sir Graeme Lamb, former Commander of the SAS

'As one long convinced the truth is very often stranger than fiction I enjoyed Tom Fletcher's debut novel *The Ambassador*. The author can draw authenticity from a career spent at the coal face of diplomacy and intelligence, which is why it is a page turner'

Frederick Forsyth

'A week is a long time in diplomacy: intrigue, betrayal, comradeship and reconciliation! A great read'

Mark Sedwill, Former National Security Adviser

'Will thrill readers intrigued by diplomatic life. Packed full of zealous characters, plot twists, conspiracies and betrayals'

Dame Nicola Brewer, former British High Commissioner

'A compelling tale of cyber-crime, terrorism and
as

*Tortoise*

assassination ... A real page-turner.'

# The Ambassador

Tom Fletcher CMG is the Principal of Hertford College, Oxford. He is a British diplomat, a writer, and a campaigner. He was foreign policy advisor in No.10 Downing Street to Tony Blair, Gordon Brown and David Cameron, and from 2011 to 2015 was the British Ambassador to Lebanon. He is a Visiting Professor at New York University and author of two works of non-fiction.

# TOM FLETCHER

# THE
# AMBASSADOR

CANELO

First published in the United Kingdom in 2022 by Canelo

This edition published in the United Kingdom in 2023 by

Canelo
Unit 9, 5th Floor
Cargo Works, 1–2 Hatfields
London SE1 9PG
United Kingdom

A CIP catalogue record for this book is available from the British Library.

Ebook ISBN 978 1 80032 896 9
Hardback ISBN 978 1 80032 897 6
Paperback ISBN 978 1 80436 423 9

Look for more great books at www.canelo.co

Printed and bound in Great Britain by Clays Ltd, Elcograf S.p.A.

I

MIX
Paper from
responsible sources
FSC® C018072
FSC
www.fsc.org

*To Louise, Charlie, Ted, and everyone who makes life more of an adventure than fiction*

*'Et surtout, pas trop de zèle.'*

(Charles Maurice de Talleyrand-Périgord, French diplomat)

*'Everyone has three lives: a public life, a private life and a secret life.'*

(Gabriel García Márquez)

# Prologue

Her Majesty's Ambassador to Paris took a deep drag on the spliff and let his gaze roam, from the boutiques and embassies of the Rue du Faubourg St-Honoré towards the brothels and kebab joints of Chatelet.

On the roof, the heat of the day was lifting, and there was early evening sunlight on the upper-floor windows and chalky brickwork. The air smelt of June dust, mopeds and dying flowers. The ramshackle grandeur was fading, and the frisky beauty of nightfall in everyone's second city stood exposed once again.

This was the part of the day the *Parisiens* called the *cinq à sept*, the hours when duty gave way to pleasure.

This was the time for mistresses, secrets and lies. Two hours when the city's centre of gravity shifted quietly from the law courts and ministries of the Right Bank to the jazz joints and bistros of the Left. When the truth hid as the night fell.

The sound of chatter from downstairs grew as the guests arrived for the annual Queen's Birthday Party. Ed Barnes exhaled slowly and closed his eyes. There was weary disillusionment in the pop of a champagne cork, where once there had been wondrous anticipation.

On the other side of the river, Lady Emma Barnes paused as she left the bookshop where she worked part time. It was her refuge from life as an ambassador's wife. The French called their memories *souvenirs*. More tangible than the English version. Something to collect. Something you can carry. Emma's were

I

neatly compartmentalised like the chapters of a memoir, sepia tinged. On nights like this, with Paris turning from day to night around her, the souvenirs were better company than the mess in between them.

She tightened the shoelaces on her DMs. A line she had read that afternoon was playing in her mind: *We become what we pay attention to.* If she turned left, she could be back at the residence in half an hour, time to change into something less comfortable and join the end of the reception, the dutiful wife.

She adjusted the band that held in place her long, silver hair. Stood back up. And turned right.

As darkness fell in the embassy garden in Paris, the candlelight flickered on the jewellery and medals of the guests. Revolutionaries and government troops had fought through these trees during the 1848 uprising. Shells had fallen on the terrace during the bloodshed of the Commune in 1871. Always that tension between the privileged and those outside the gate. And tonight the Paris elite were engaged in another dance of power and intrigue.

The orchestra played Vivaldi's *Four Seasons*. Waiters topped up the crystal champagne flutes from magnums of Pol Roger. Churchill's choice, *naturellement*. The air was warm with the aroma of candle wax, expensive perfume and cherry blossom.

Beyond the back gate the Seine flowed darkly on, washing away the sins of Paris.

As he strode into the garden, General Max Crawford quietly enjoyed the weight of his medals on the chest of his military jacket. The ambassador had asked him to look the part, and Crawford had no intention of letting him down. There were three medals that he never spoke about. He took a sip of neat whisky and scratched his chin, missing the familiarity of the stubble. His grey-flecked black hair was cropped short and there was a punchy squareness to his jaw. As always he exuded a wiry, taut vitality. A champagne cork pop made him flinch for a second. Invisible scars heal more slowly. He glanced around quickly, pleased not to have been noticed.

Watching Crawford from the window of her guest room on the first floor of the residence, Foreign Secretary Lynn Redwood fastened a sensible earring. She had the kind of grey bags under her eyes that politicians took decades of ambitious overwork to accumulate, and years of sulky retirement to fail to get rid of.

She had always hated Paris. A city built on raised expectations. All those love stories that started here. What happened to those people when they ended? Did anyone come back to the starting point and realise that it had all been a hoax? This place was too full of itself, self-satisfied. It made her think of Edward Barnes, the man who had once taught her, inadvertently, to assume the worst. She would play the dutiful guest tonight but stay as far from his exhausting enthusiasm as possible. Just occasionally she saw a flicker of the fire in him that she had once found attractive. But maybe he too had suffered from achieving his ambition. She watched the guests in the garden below, like dead carp circling each other in a stagnant pool. Redwood had come to loathe the dehydrated elegance of it all.

Aurelie Lafont, on the other hand, was waiting to ambush the British ambassador once he joined the throng. The Elysée Europe adviser was the French president's confidante and *consigliere*. Of Algerian origin, she had passed out at the top of her ENA cohort before becoming a spikily ambitious lawyer. She had an aggressive, pinched face. Despite her size, her physical presence and charisma sliced through the flabby massed ranks of French officialdom like a sharp knife through a ripe Brie. They called her The Sparrow, but only behind her back. Smiling to herself, she inhaled the cooler air of the evening. Toying with Ed Barnes over the years had been

3

fun, trying to coax some steel from behind all that eager charm. Tonight, she was confident he would finally understand the game was over. The Brits had centuries of baggage here, that sense of entitlement to France. She enjoyed the thought of how conflicted the nationalists would feel that she – an immigrant – would be the one to remind the English that they were just guests.

Aurelie nodded at Alem Nigusie, the deputy ambassador, who had taken up her position near the entrance to the reception. Her short black hair was held back in a neat hijab, pushed away from her forehead, which matched a skirt that fell just below the knee. A trim black silk blouse covered her arms. She scanned the garden efficiently. In one corner the NGOs reliant on embassy projects yet seething at the stale privilege of it all. By the tennis court the journalists, waiting like vultures to catch an off-guard comment and ruin a career. By the statue, businessmen were shovelling out business cards before checking if anyone wanted them.

Alem's job tonight was to ensure everyone got what they wanted. And to keep Lynn Redwood moving quickly enough not to offend anyone or take offence herself. Probably an impossible mission. She glanced up towards the ambassador's private apartment on the second floor and looked at her watch.

Lenny Goddard waited for the second hand to reach the top of the clock in the residence kitchen. The boss needed to exude confidence tonight. He glanced at the photo of his son on the noticeboard and felt a pang of fear and love. Lenny was now heavier than when he had first started as a junior butler, back when there were still enough butlers to have ranks. His moustache was whitening, but he retained the swagger that had made him a favourite of many of the excellencies he had worked with. Or worked *for*, as Lenny preferred it. 'He sees us all in, and he sees us all out,' the last envoy, Sir Angus, had said during his farewell speech. Sir Angus had also needed someone to see in his Ukrainian masseuse while Lady Georgina had her weekly Pilates class. Every ambassador had an itch, and Lenny saw it as his job to ensure they could scratch it. He sauntered towards the lift that rattled its way towards the ambassador's apartment, trying to ignore the recycling bin where he had stashed the cardboard packaging beneath the champagne bottles. Something about this visitor gave him a deep sense of foreboding. But he had never been able to turn down a request from a residence guest.

Orla Fitzgerald, *Le Monde*'s Irish star journalist, had arrived at the reception early. A former psychologist, she had traded in the interrogation of patients for the interrogation of politicians. She now had the most fun job at *Le Monde*, sniffing out scandal and persuading statesmen – and she was known to be better at the statesmen than the stateswomen – to open up. *Emotion is everything*, she convinced them. *Find your authentic voice. Let me help you tell your story, help you connect with your future voters.*

She walked through the portrait room of the British embassy, pausing to admire the breast cup modelled by a suitor on Pauline Borghese, Napoleon's sister. Curiously small, she had once commented to a momentarily speechless Ed Barnes. She was tempted as always to bounce on Pauline's now ceremonial bed, in which the suitor had sought his reward. Orla relished this city of hidden passion and lost poets. And she loved going to the British embassy, a gilded cage that paid so much attention to its shower gel and so little to its Wi-Fi. Partly to tease Barnes, the reluctant ambassador. Partly for the history, but mainly for the canapés and conspiracy.

Tonight she felt different, though. Even the air tasted sharper. Everything was about to change. And she would be the one to tell the world. Breaking news needed something, or someone, to be broken.

In her room on the second floor, Amina Joshi – the most famous asylum seeker on the planet, the *Time* magazine Person of the Year, a warrior, an icon, a prophet, a fugitive and, most recently, the ambassador's unexpected house guest – was working on her latest article, a call for a global government in response to the pandemic of the previous year. Joshi had been an outsider before she became an insider before becoming an outsider again. An Indian who had taken up lacrosse to survive her English private school. As a junior UN official in Bosnia, she had been profoundly marked by the sight of the skull of a child as a trophy on a warlord's car.

She didn't hear the noise of the reception in the garden below as she hammered out the words on the keyboard.

> The Universal Declaration of Human Rights is not in need of a water-board workaround, but a roadmap for our flawed species to reach towards our better selves. The Age of Reason is not fake news. And fixing climate change is a long overdue reset of our collective contract with our descendants, not something to be toyed with like a tacky game show cliffhanger. It is time to act.

Within an hour she would be dead, her blood running along the grooves of the oak floor of the British embassy residence.

A week earlier, Magnus Pederson had been waiting by the candy floss stall in the Jardin des Tuileries, just three minutes' walk from the British embassy.

The gardens were a place of children's laughter and lovers' whispers. At one end, the Louvre, and the glass glacier that topped the halls where humans could wonder at the best of human creativity. At the other end, the Place de la Concorde, where the blood of tyrants had long stained the square, with its incongruous Egyptian needle reaching into the Paris sky and its ten-euro coffees and the mayhem of its mopeds. The solid arteries of Paris framed the beautiful chaos of its people.

Pederson liked to tell people he admired the unsung executioner. The attendant at the guillotine who diligently scraped the blood off the blade before going back to an ordinary, quiet baguette-and-Brie life. There was compassion in a clean cut. Decent executioners were underrated.

The Fat Russian was late again. Always playing his games. Never appreciating the risks that they were running. Pederson had felt suddenly nauseous at the smell of candy floss. It was sickly and fake. He was unshaven and pale, his hair matted greasy against his scalp. He looked more like a suicidal grunge artist than an urban guerrilla. *A Kurt Cobain for the internet age*, as one over-excited journalist had called him. What sleep he had been able to steal over the past month had been on the sofas and floors of the Paris suburbs, the grubby urban engine of the city outside the

Périphérique ring road. His was a Paris that those fortunate to live, work and play inside the ring road pretended did not exist. That would change now.

Waiting for the Fat Russian like an addict waiting for a fix, Pederson spat, and watched his saliva seep slowly into the dusty path. One more piece of filth in a filthy city. The tourists pointed their cameras up at the confidence and hope of the city's horizon. Pederson preferred to look down at the excrement flowing into the sewers of Paris.

Eventually the Fat Russian arrived, as he always did. The waddle. The cigar. The slightly apologetic sense of entitlement. He scanned the ground in front of him for dog shit. The rolls of fat on his neck were like uncooked pastry. There was moistness amid the stray hairs on his upper lip. There was a scream from an amusement park ride as it lurched skywards, but he didn't seem to hear it. His hair was like the moss in a derelict swimming pool. He was out of breath.

Magnus Pederson hated the Fat Russian and the Fat Russian hated him right back.

'What progress, young Magnus?' The voice was an incongruous falsetto. He no longer pretended to care about smoothing out the Russian accent.

Magnus flinched, irritated that he had been gently nudged off guard again. 'The only challenge now is choice. We have more than you can have ever imagined. You just need to be clearer about the real targets.'

'Above your paygrade. Even above mine.'

They paused as two businessmen passed, deep in discussion. A smile at the sides of Churkin's mouth. 'Never trust a man whose suit fits.'

Pederson rolled his eyes. 'And the money, Churkin?'

The Fat Russian was now observing him carefully. Pederson thrust his hands deeper into his jean pockets in an attempt to hide his edgy frustration. He was lankier and darker than in the file. He had a wiry intensity to him, a childlike otherworldliness that the Fat Russian had once mistaken for innocence.

Churkin shrugged unapologetically. 'Also above our pay grade.'

Pederson scowled and stepped towards his handler. 'You once told me that declining powers are more dangerous than rising powers.' He thought about repeating the line he had scrawled on the wall of the bedsit on the Périphérique that morning. *If they build a wall around our internet, we will build an internet around their wall.* But something in Churkin's demeanour made him hold back.

They both knew that something was no longer working here. And that was dangerous.

Pederson was thinking of Lennon and McCartney. With all the great double acts, the tension eventually stops being creative and turns into something destructive.

Churkin was thinking of Lenin and Trotsky. Moscow were right: Pederson had been an asset when he was pointed at their opponents. He was now becoming a liability. And under the current president, liabilities didn't last long.

Sooner or later, every field agent ran out of road. Sooner or later, every handler did too. There were not many colleagues left from Churkin's generation. This was no business for the sentimental. In this game, the only measure of success was survival.

Pederson had wanted this meeting to go better. The Copenhagen recruits were expensive. They needed better security at the warehouses. The new software kept breaking. The lightbulbs, condoms and tea bags that fuelled the revolution did not come cheap.

But the Fat Russian could see that he was in his own world. Like so many assets he had moulded, Pederson was hearing only the sound of destiny. He was already lost to them. He was already lost to himself. Churkin wondered whether either of them would last the year. He paused to consider whether to go hard or soft.

He tossed his cigar to the ground and pressed his chubby face closer to Pederson. He punched the words out like the jabs of a street fighter.

'Just. Do. Your. Job. *Pederson*.'

Even the faux informality had now been discarded.

The Fat Russian cast a final questioning look at Pederson, who avoided his eye. And then he bent down with a slight groan to pick up his cigar butt, wrap it in a paper tissue and place it in his pocket. *Leave nothing behind*, as he drilled new recruits in the bleak cold of the Siberian training centre where he pretended to be based. Own nothing, influence everything.

And then he turned and disappeared into the fairground crowds.

## 2

The spliff was precisely rolled. Suitably ambassadorial. I inhaled time and exhaled youth.

It is the unconfined horizon that makes Paris different to other cities. You can't look across London or New York in the same unfettered way. That's why I had wanted to serve here. Not for the ticking clocks, royal visits and coffee table books of my residence, the envy of the diplomatic corps. For horizon. To remind myself that there was a world beyond.

I'd started smoking eight years earlier, after an unhappy two-year posting in Afghanistan. The work had been hard. A disjointed team, the constant threat from IEDs, family far away, the constant life-and-death decisions. I had been called back to London earlier than expected. An internal investigation had concluded that I had held back too long before authorising a hostage rescue. We had saved others on my watch. But we lost the NGO worker while I hesitated to pick the right moment. Beheaded on camera. I had managed to watch it only once, the rusty blade catching on bone. The occasional joint was one way I tried and failed to stop hearing the sound, asking the questions.

From the roof of the residence I had one of the best views across the city to the Eiffel Tower. Tonight, it was illuminated light blue. Since the pandemic they had taken to doing that once a week, a sign of gratitude to the city's health workers. Before the virus, we had forgotten how much we needed them. But the illumination always reminded me of the people they couldn't save.

From the garden below I could hear the clink of crystal glasses being set out on a silver tray. And a stray, flat note from a trumpet as the band tuned up, out of place like a fart in an elevator.

There was time for one last song before I went down. A song of self-reproach, not taking the time to do the small things. Willie Nelson finds a level of sentimental nostalgia that Elvis didn't. As I listened, I lay back against the tiles and closed my eyes.

In those empty days of lockdowns and distance the virus had already brought out a deeper form of human solidarity than we had known before. There really was such a thing as global society. We had spent more time preparing and eating food together. We started waving to strangers. We listened more to birdsong. We called people we loved more. We damaged nature less. We felt our emotions more keenly. We discovered the silence between the notes.

For me, the strange mix of estrangement and proximity had also made me determined to do more to keep my family together. A sense that there were a finite number of those moments of genuine connection still left.

Em had always called me sentimental, and she was probably right on that too. But there is immense power in the sweet spot where meaning meets experience meets nostalgia. In the increasingly rare moments where she and I still truly connected, it was in that sweet spot. When I felt it, normally towards the end of the wine bottle, I would want her and Steph to stay with me, to feel it too. It was usually the moment they got up to make a call or clear the table.

Looking back now, I think I felt that night on the roof that my life had been mostly lived. In reality, it was just about to begin.

I took another drag on the joint and glanced at the speech. This one had been drafted by Sophie Rawlings, the eager new second secretary. She had replaced a piece of dead wood in a building rotting with it. Her job would be to eat, drink and gossip her way under the covers of French politics. She was fresh out of Durham university, via a year learning Italian and doing the dishes at a castle in Umbria.

I'd told Sophie she had high potential. I hadn't yet told her she was burdened by an exhausting sense of youth and certainty that I had long since given up. Change the names of the countries and it could be the same speech I'd heard, and given, for thirty years. So much diplomacy is tedious platitudes and woolly assertions. *Our bilateral relations are getting warmer.* I chucked the text to one side. What did any of this matter anyway? Vicars, travel agents, porn stars and diplomats: the world had changed around us while we were busy making other plans.

I took a deep breath to clear my head. I would flatter them and then fall back on a stock joke and a couple of anecdotes. That always seemed to work.

Was this all there was?

Tonight at least there would be decent champagne. I straightened the knot of my plain navy-blue tie, reminding myself of the sense of intrigue I used to feel at people yet to be discovered.

There was a gentle knock on the door. A polite but firm cough. Lenny could clear his throat better than anyone in the business.

Like the best butlers, Lenny could multitask. He had procured my weed from a wiry, worldly Tunisian with a scruffy falafel joint five minutes from the Louvre. But he chose never to see me actually smoking it. Maybe he still wanted to believe that his ambassadors were different to everyone else.

Lenny had been at the ambassadorial residence for over twenty years. His parents had arrived in London from Guyana in the Fifties and he had been raised among market stalls and pie shops, a short canter from his beloved Upton Park. 'A Caribbean cockney,' his dad had called him.

I reluctantly stubbed out the joint on the tiles and came back through the fire escape that led from the roof to the guest corridor. Later I would wonder if I locked it.

I looked at Lenny with a mixture of affection and irritation, blinking to clear my head. 'Is it really time?'

''Fraid so, boss. This lot can smell the Pol Roger from the other side of the Seine.'

I grimaced. 'Any sign of Emma?'

Lenny avoided my eye. I waited for him to look up again. A shared moment of complicity and disappointment. Had he noticed my shoulders fall slightly? When you live in such close proximity to staff, there is little private life to preserve, even in France. He was one of the few who actually saw me without my ambassadorial face. Emma knew that off-camera face too. She said it was 'weathered by decades of decency'. There were worse scars to bear.

'Very well.' I was determined not to be surprised by her any more. The ambassadorial façade. 'Let's crack on.'

There is no residence like Paris. But every room reminds you that you are just passing through. Duff Cooper, ambassador after the Second World War, carried out an affair among the bookshelves of the study with the wife of an American diplomat. Outside is the line portrait of his wife, Lady Diana, looking appropriately startled. To the right, the *Salon Vert*, where the dukes who owned the place used to come to die. One did so after eating fifty-one eggs for a bet, I would tell my guests at breakfast. All under the eye of an imperious Wellington portrait, the man who had lived here after Napoleon's sister had been ejected, systematically bedding Napoleon's mistresses.

I buttoned my jacket and tugged at my cuffs so that there was a frisson of cufflink.

And then I was out into the early evening shadows and evening gowns of the residence garden.

## 3

It was drizzling in Copenhagen as the guests gathered in the early evening sunlight at the ambassador's reception in Paris. But Magnus Pederson did not feel the damp seeping through his slept-in black T-shirt and jeans. He leant back against the slate grey wall of the warehouse. The silence of the night was broken only by the low rumble of the lorries as they loaded and unloaded their cargo. It was bitterly cold.

This was not meant to feel comfortable.

He scowled at the old Nokia phone in his hand, dark against the blue of his veins. At school they had made him draw another martyr's hands, nails piercing the arteries.

Pederson wondered if there was release in the moment where the kamikaze pilot turned the plane and tore himself away from thoughts of his family. Or when the rock star finally chose between the slow slide into joyless decrepitude and the raw beauty of the razor blade.

He found his left hand resting on his neck. For a moment his skin felt like his father's. Could he himself have been a decent parent? He chuckled for a moment at the thought. A parent couldn't make the sacrifices he was prepared to make. A generation of parents had made the world more dangerous through their selfishness and hypocrisy. It had been the Edward Barnes interview with *Paris Match*, gushing ludicrously about the importance of family, that had helped Pederson see where to aim first.

He might miss the anonymity in the years to come. There had been periods of camaraderie and shared zeal to the early days of revolution. They had at times a sense that they were building something together, not just destroying together. There were impressionable rich girls and beery debates in the early days, a feeling of reckless purpose.

But there was no turning back now. Pederson was not a man for pointless nostalgia. There would be no kids. No neat lines. No love. No camaraderie. No boring life. No boring death.

For what could be less boring than the truth?

The call to Amina Joshi had been typically unsentimental. She was stronger than people thought and would be stronger still in death. Pederson always assumed – maybe hoped – that others would be listening to his conversations, recording and analysing them. Perhaps his few defiant, staccato words might one day be seen as the beginning of something extraordinary.

He flicked his lighter, the flame sparking and then fading. A colder wind swept through the empty street, bringing the stench of the docks. It seemed a shame to destroy the innocuous-looking device and its grenade of a SIM card. It would be a piece of history lying among the decaying fish and used condoms in the sludge of the waterfront that marked the edge of the meatpacking district.

But he threw it out into the darkness, listening for the splash. Sometimes this did not feel like much of a revolution.

Pederson trudged back to the warehouse. He tapped the code on the security lock and went down to the basement. Each time he typed her name she mattered less. They buzzed him in. Inside, the two girls with the black lipstick and the hangovers had printed two hundred hacked internet searches and private email accounts for him to sift. The first and most obvious rule of their work was to do it offline when you could. And in any case, he liked the fragility of paper. He stretched his arms above his head to get the blood flowing. He hadn't eaten for days.

16

Two hundred lives.

Two hundred decisions.

Were they sleeping now? Did any have a moment of prescience on what was coming their way? Death by the internet, a more civilised but no less painful way for the mob to destroy. He chewed hard on his lower lip. For every sin there had to be retribution. Truth was not meant to be easy.

No time to waste. Three piles, evenly and precisely stacked.

The saved. At least for now.

Those in purgatory.

And the damned.

Pederson picked briefly at the long pink scars on his arms, felt again the deeper wound, that twinge of loss behind his chest. It was time now for others to feel the pain.

The German judge with the small hands and the Bavarian walking holidays whose internet searches were dominated by graphic teen pornography. Nothing technically illegal, but surely enough humiliation to force a resignation, in the middle of one of the showcase international criminal court cases of the century. Would guilty men walk free as a result?

There was no smoke without fire. Damned.

The American politician in regular email contact with a distant ex-girlfriend. Both were now married, happily it seemed. There was no suggestion yet that they even met any more. But the intimacy of the messages, the shared confidences, the music recommendations, suggested this was a correspondence that neither would want shared. Was it enough to break a career? He seemed a pretty decent guy. A credible voting record.

Pederson's lip curled. A pause. Purgatory. For now. Until a more convenient moment. When the congressman had made a more visible television appearance or claimed a patch of moral high ground. For everything there would be a time.

The Iraqi interpreter working for the Brits who was being paid by both the Russians and Americans for information on what he was translating. Sending the money every month to his family behind Islamic State lines. His wife forced into slavery as a 'bride' of the caliphate.

Pederson hesitated. He scratched the rash behind his beard. The truth should not hide. So much hypocrisy, so little time. Damned.

The formidable French charity head had worked for twenty years with the survivors of humanity's inhumanity. But in an email, she had told her sister that she was putting a little money aside from an aid project for a retirement house by Lake Annecy, for the ageing mother she had never really been there for.

Not enough hypocrisy quite yet. Saved. For now. One for the next time the pillar of the community made a speech about corruption and transparency.

The popular Scottish football presenter who was sending a monthly payment to a single mother in Brighton. A childhood friend of Edward Barnes. Pederson looked at the smug smile on his Twitter profile, the jaunty tweets. The perfect tan, the perfect teeth and the perfect life. Not any more. Back of the net. Damned.

These were people who stank of hypocrisy. The UN official who liked to text his female staff during meetings. The diplomat with wandering hands. The journalist fiddling his expenses. The feminist who liked to be dominated. Edward Barnes.

Damned. Damned. Damned.

For Pederson it was about exposing the deceit, the hypocrisy of it all. Could the public really trust these people in authority when they had so much to hide? Nothing more complicated than that. Sometimes he wondered if it would be easier to simply release the whole lot in one go, the ultimate act of transparency.

But where was the drama in that? The modern public preferred a cliffhanger. Swipe left, swipe right. Like Romans screaming for blood in the Colosseum, they needed a moment of jeopardy. Thumbs up, or thumbs down, the gladiator gazing up in terror at the emperor's hand.

They would all feel the terror now. Pederson recalled the Latin teacher with the moist hands, quoting Cicero on the sword of Damocles. *There can be nothing happy for the person over whom some fear always looms.* Those he spared in the first wave would still feel that fear. Barnes included, for now.

He got up to stretch his legs and find another scarf. It was too damn cold. But today they would light the fire. He urinated against the wall, feeling a sad weariness come over him as he inhaled the tangy warmth and watched the puddle spread around his heavy black boots. The room was getting dark, but there was still so much to do. And who knew how many days they really had left? This was not some drive-by act of terror. This was their Pearl Harbor.

Pederson pushed the pile of papers to one side and sat back at his screen. He scowled as he shook the mouse to locate the cursor, and then moved it with a quiet deliberation over the word 'upload' and clicked. The unsung executioner. Only the victims did not yet know that the guillotine was slicing noiselessly through the air towards their necks.

A lightbulb flickered and went out. He sat back on the seat, looked at his companions, slouched grumpily in heavy coats in front of their screens. Pederson preferred to work only with women. He allowed himself a rare smile. For a moment he wondered whether some kind of speech was called for. This was the culmination of months of work, after all.

He paused.

'Girls. Do you think this moment will be written about in the future? Will people be talking about me a century from now?'

They carried on typing.

Was there somewhere an actor who didn't know that the role of his life was about to be written?

Pederson thought about continuing. But a wave of boredom and exhaustion washed over him.

Was this all there was?

He decided instead on just one word, softly articulated, but with playful menace. Behind the grin his teeth were stained with nicotine, cheap red wine and instant coffee.

'Boom.'

Pederson no longer needed instructions, from Churkin or anyone. He, too, would leave nothing behind.

## 4

Being an ambassador is theatre. I used to try to walk into the throng of the reception like the guy in the Carly Simon song walking onto a yacht. People who didn't know me said that I was energetic. That night, my job was to be as visible as possible and to shake hands with the maximum number of guests. But not to be trapped by the failed visa applicant, special interest lobbyist or ambitious businessman wanting an internship for his uniquely gifted daughter. Stay low, move fast.

Lenny took up his usual position by the door. He gave me a hint of a wink as he handed me a sparkling water, disguised as a gin and tonic. Normally I never drank before a speech. It was part of my code, a superstition almost. Lenny would be there once I was done, with a suitably robust gin and tonic, disguised as a sparkling water.

I scanned the garden, placed the water back on the tray, and took a gin.

By the bar, the head of my MI6 station, Harry Parkinson, was holding court with a small group of fellow spies. He was my eyes and ears into the intelligence world, and theirs into mine. Judging by the heels and cleavage of their wives, the group were mostly Eastern European spies, his speciality. Harry nodded grimly towards me. He looked to be well past three doubles, the amount of alcohol at which he claimed to be at his peak. I preferred him at two, and ideally not at all.

Diplomacy is the only business that elevates the handshake to the evidence of success and not just the start of a process. But since the pandemic there was often an awkwardness in its place, and I exchanged a series of nods with several eager English language teachers, all keener to take advantage of the champagne than to meet their host. One made the usual Ferrero Rocher gag. 'With this reception, Ambassador, you really are spoiling us.'

I smiled back as though it was the first time I had heard it.

One advantage of being ambassador is that people wrongly assume you have somewhere more important to be. I made for my deputy, Alem Nigusie. She was surrounded as always. In the office, she wore sober, serious colours, but at these events she always looked like she had just walked off a film set. I had always sought out colleagues with empathy, the ability to see the different perspectives, the different motivations, to read people from every angle.

'Hi, Alem. You look smart.' My generation of men no longer knew how to compliment a woman. When I joined the Foreign Office, the only diversity we had was whether the aging white men wore white or blue shirts. Had I already looked at her for a moment too long? She smiled back, with a hint of sympathy.

'Not so bad yourself, Edward.' A half smile.

I grinned. 'All under control? Your other half not here either?'

Alem shrugged. 'No. She's working late in the surgery. Emma?'

I pretended not to hear. 'The speech is crap. Churchill ignored every other page of Foreign Office advice because they alternated between "on the one hand" and "on the other hand". I need to share that thought with Sophie.'

'You have.' Alem sighed and drew me quietly away from the group. She put a hand on my arm. 'Just do your usual thing. Throw in some French. A clean joke. *Clean*. They love you, mostly. Short and sweet. Okay?' A wink.

'Keep a close eye on Lynn Redwood tonight, Alem. She wants you to chaperone her. Says that I should be free to do "my thing", whatever she thinks that is. She didn't say it like she approved.'

'I don't get the impression you're looking for her approval, Edward.'

A large hand gripped my right elbow, and another pumped my hand enthusiastically. 'Evening, squire.' I tried to suppress a shudder. Peter Kane, my neighbour and American counterpart, knew that his mock English accent caused my soul to wither.

Kane was a big donor to President Hoon, nothing to do with the genuine career diplomats at the State Department. He had bought the Paris embassy and was determined to get his full money's worth in prestige and interns. A loudly self-proclaimed 'digital diplomat', he was always looking for the next way to promote himself, and occasionally his country. Never knowingly undersold. Like many men of our age, we circled each other with grumpy mistrust and back-slapping camaraderie. A decade or so younger than me, his shock of blond hair always contrasted with mine in the official photos.

Salt and pepper, Emma had used to reassure me, back when there was still some pepper. And back when she still reassured me.

Kane smirked and looked me up and down. 'How's the low-carb diet going, Barnesy? Work in progress?'

I smiled wearily back, reaching in my mind for that last drag on the spliff.

'Kane, what a pleasant surprise.'

Gandhi had said, 'I know no diplomacy, save that of the truth.' He was wrong.

Kane's eyes darted around the garden. 'Tweeting tonight? Or still more an ink and papyrus man?'

He was wearing Converse trainers. I looked down at my own black brogues. Proper shoes, well shined by Lenny. Twenty years earlier, I had once worn brown shoes in the embassy. My last act of sartorial rebellion. Maybe my last act of rebellion.

'Isn't all that transparency a bit, well, undignified?'

Kane was leering at the calves of the new Finnish ambassador. 'But Barnesy, that's your problem. Social media is like some huge reception, much bigger than tonight. You wouldn't delegate it to your pretty new comms girl with the tits and teeth. Everyone else is there, but I don't know where you are. Another century?'

He was getting to me. Alem always said that she had never started a sentence that Kane couldn't talk over. I noticed she had melted away, timing her departure before he got into his stride.

I jabbed back. 'Diplomacy existed long before Facebook and will exist long after Facebook.'

Kane guffawed. 'Name me three British diplomatic successes since the Second World War. My lot are just as bad. All those summits, the protocol, the communiqués, the credentials. "Never mind your warm relations," didn't Churchill say, "what do you think they're for?" The emperor has no clothes, Barnes. No one is listening to you all any more. You're just too pompous to notice.'

I hoped he couldn't see the blood in my cheeks. 'Surely, Kane, we learnt from the pandemic that we need *more* global cooperation?'

His mock startled expression was replaced by a scowl. He was present for the first time. 'That really your takeaway? We learnt something very different: we won't lose the next one.'

Kane was the incarnation of the decline of a once great empire. Much like me, he would probably say.

I plunged gratefully into the next group. The European ambassadors were hunting in a pack. The EU ambassador fixed me with one of her Viking stares. 'We are all looking forward to your speech, Sir Edward. I'm sure it will be constructive.'

'Indeed, Excellency.' The sliding scale for diplomatic encounters is: *excellent, productive, constructive, practical, warm, good, busi-*

*nesslike, cordial, full and frank, difficult.* Once you get to *full and frank* it is probably a dust-up. 'In this case, I'm assuming you want something nice about Europe, and I should go easy on the nationalist stereotypes? Neither one is my forte.'

'There is still no collective word for ambassadors,' the dull Greek chipped in, as I pumped their hands, asked after their spouses and thanked them as sincerely as I could for coming. The Irishman, street savvy hidden behind a folksy bonhomie, offered, 'A pomp? A gossip? A smug?'

And then alongside me was my Danish counterpart. He had the intensity and jawbones of a man who spent too much time on a bike. 'Edward, we need to talk now.' His wiry body jerked from side to side to cover the escape routes, holding eye contact so that I could not feign sudden interest in another invitee. 'It's urgent, Ed. It's about Magnus Pederson. And your diplomatic baggage: Amina Joshi. We think it's going to get rough. You need to protect your daughter.'

I tried not to flinch. What had Steph got to do with any of that? I had read some of the stories about Pederson, a grimy internet guerrilla. But never in the same context as Amina. I needed to get Emma's sense of what Amina really wanted, where this chapter ended. Sometimes Emma's absence became like all habits: something I no longer noticed. But despite it all there were still moments when she was the only person I needed.

I had spent a career avoiding unwanted conversations. I introduced my Danish colleague to a passing businessman and caught the eye of an imaginary guest. Amina Joshi and this Pederson misfit could wait.

## 5

Amina Joshi was not used to waiting. Two months earlier, I had known mercifully little of her aspiration to restart the world. But then she had upended our lives on an otherwise normal Tuesday morning.

The embassy receptionist had believed she was a standard caller, probably a consular case. Amina had asked to see me, with characteristically stubborn persistence. The receptionist had checked with my PA, Penny Rainsford, who – unaware of our previous relationship – had been as firm as ever that I was not to be disturbed. I was already trying to get the new Japanese ambassador in and out in twenty minutes flat, with translation.

Amina had demanded an audience. Security was called. Five minutes later, they had sat her in the office of Alem Nigusie.

Later I had watched the CCTV. Alem had ticked efficiently through the process. 'What do you want here, and why were you so rude to our people?'

Amina's brown eyes narrowed. 'I want justice. I want refuge. Where's Ed?'

'The *ambassador* is indisposed. Just give us your name, please, and tell us what you are doing here. You're not British?'

'No, thankfully. But are you?'

Amina stood as she spoke, shoulders back. The two security guards stepped forward behind Alem, who waved them to one side. She had heard this a thousand times.

After a brief pause, Amina spoke without expression, mechanically, staring at a point on the wall above Alem's head. Her voice was expensively educated, the accent of the Davosphere. She was used to a bigger audience.

'My name is Amina Joshi. I demand asylum from Her Majesty's government under the terms of the Geneva Convention. Here, on British soil.'

She pulled back her copper-coloured veil. Her face was more lined than in the photos. Her eyes deep set but striking, exuding a complete and absolute confidence. She looked tired but defiant.

And when she straightened her back there could be no doubt that this really was the Amina Joshi who had been on the front pages for months.

Amina Joshi who had quit the UN to campaign for its replacement. Amina Joshi who had made the front cover of *Time* magazine, calling for an end to nation states in the face of pandemics, climate catastrophe, migration and global economic crises.

Alem never swore. She prided herself on being a role model to her team, and to the wider embassy. Her school friends had joked that she was the Muslim Mary Poppins, practically perfect. We put her on the front page of every FCO brochure.

She had looked from one security guard to the other. Then to the warrior campaigner in front of her.

And slowly, but with great diction and with one hand on her throat, she had mouthed, 'Oh for fuck's sake.'

Amina smiled back at her. It was a smile that *Time* had said could still 'open any door and inspire any activist on the planet'. But Alem saw for the first time the hint of menace in the narrowing of Amina's eyes.

'But, Ms Joshi, why do you need refuge? Who are you running from?'

Alem told me she had felt Amina reading her as she stared back at her for a moment. Then the smile again, but this time with a sadness in place of the megawatt charisma. 'This is just beginning. They will come.'

And then the recriminations and the long videoconferences with London and the calls from every capital from Delhi to Washington. We had tied ourselves in knots explaining the legal context, the Geneva Convention, the rules of asylum. We weren't allowed to turn her away. International law was clear on that point if nothing else. But no one was listening. This was simply too juicy – a prophet of liberty trapped under the protection of the British ambassador to Paris. Living under his roof.

My roof. And I didn't want to turn her away either. I'd known Amina since Oxford, mainly through Emma. They had been close friends for years, drifting apart for periods, but theirs was a load-bearing relationship. Over the years, I had the impression that the regular drinks had turned to occasional calls and from there to a line in a Christmas card. But I felt that Amina's choice of refuge was as much about Emma as any residual faith in British decency and respect for international law. And if Amina thought she was in danger, I was happy to offer that. Maybe Emma might see that there was some benefit to my work, to living in this place. It might be gold plated, but it was still an asylum centre.

It did not take long for me start to questioning the decision, though I got there more slowly than London. Amina started to broadcast. Orla Fitzgerald profiled her for *Le Monde*, describing the lines on Amina's face from 'bearing witness to the worst of humanity'. Orla had written that the weariness was also some-thing deeper: this was a woman watching her worldview come under relentless assault. 'Amina Joshi was a global citizen before the idea was fashionable. And she is still one now that it is not.'

'Drain the swamp?' she was quoted in Orla's piece. 'Let's start with the governments that weaponise intolerance in tabloids, places of worship and during political campaigns. That sell the snake oil of hatred of difference as a panacea for globalisation. That allow easy access to deadly weapons and lack of justice for those who use them. That hawk quick fixes for a complex world. That tolerate the inequality of opportunity in which extremism festers. That's the swamp.'

She had become increasingly critical in public of the Hoon administration's energy policies. 'Those hit hardest by Elizabeth Hoon are the hordes that will migrate, fight or die because of climate change. They are not yet born. And make no mistake – we will all be held to account by them.' The quotes had led to increased complaints from the White House to No 10 that we were harbouring 'a deranged critic'. The president's chief of staff had carpeted the PM's sidekick, James Sherriff, who had taken pleasure in blaming me.

In one interview, Amina had also attacked the UK foreign secretary, Lynn Redwood. Lynn prided herself on the backing of the *Daily Mail* and its belligerent allies. Amina called her out for her very deliberate use of language like 'plague of migrants', 'swarm' and 'infestation'. Every day, the Amina Joshi rhetoric was hardening and her legend spreading.

When I had challenged her on this, half-heartedly, her eyes had lit up with zeal as she developed her argument. 'Power is about more than just how many people you can kill, or the size of the trade deal. People write too many books about war and not enough about how wars are avoided. Or the periods of coexistence between the conflicts. We must defend the place where ideas, ingenuity and cultures interact and thrive. That space humanity built with such patience and sacrifice is now being tested, maybe to destruction. It is what you call diplomacy, but it is now much bigger than that. Protecting it requires sacrifice.'

She had begun to sound like she thought she was a prophet. I had countered. 'But diplomats have been defending that space since the first caveman persuaded another Neanderthal to stop clubbing him over the head and go hunting together. We try to get people to collaborate for resources, not just compete for them.'

But she had no patience for it. She would rattle off long lists of diplomatic failures – the Middle East, Afghanistan, Africa – in response. And return to the danger of politicians like Hoon and Redwood. 'Diplomacy is dead. The only thing tyrants understand is strength. We are going to remind them that our ideas have more power than they ever imagined. Just like we reminded the tyrants of the past.'

Again and again, I asked her who she was hiding from. I asked London the same question. Amina would just sigh. Colleagues who had known her in Delhi and New York would speak of an iron fist in a velvet glove. But there was no obvious threat to her personally. She was an irritation to national governments, but not one who faced imprisonment or – as she would mutter darkly to Emma – assassination.

Whatever else she was, Amina Joshi was now a diplomatic nightmare. Yet somewhere in between the attempts to bring down the nation state, she had brought some colour and life to the embassy. Her steely charm consistently knocked many of us off balance. She once teased me that 'there is nothing a white man fears more than an eloquent woman from the former colonies in a headscarf'.

And more importantly, I felt at first that she was bringing colour and life back to my family. Steph adored her, and Em was around more. We argued more, but about ideas rather than the attritional cumulated irritations of a life together.

Old and new power were to make uncomfortable bedfellows. But there was such vivacity, such life in Amina Joshi. She had a sense of graceful invincibility.

Despite everything, I still miss that.

30

## 6

As the shadows lengthened, I continued my diplomatic theatre at the reception. I was relieved to see Stephanie. How could I have helped to create such a daughter? I remembered her looking up at me from a pram with the wheel we never got round to fixing. She had always known where she was going, despite her parents.

We had somehow persuaded her to live with us at the residence while she finished her art course. Tonight she was in a white dress, her long black hair swept back from her face. She moved as always with a sense of time and place. Not too much make-up, I reminded myself not to mention later. She smiled in a way that straightened me out.

One day I would have to tell her that.

'Pops! Where you been?'

'Up on the roof. Getting the speech ready. Where's Mum?'

Steph looked awkward. 'Pretty caught up at the shop, I think.'

She knew enough of her father to see that I was momentarily crumpled, but also that it would quickly pass. Every child discovers at some point that parents need their help more than they now need their parents'. She'd got there faster than most of us. She stroked my cheek and tightened the knot of my tie. My shoulders relaxed again.

But I still wondered whether we needed to have a more honest conversation about her mother and me.

Emma Barnes was not a typical ambassador's wife. She was not even a typical wife. She had made clear from the beginning that her role was not to be Lady Barnes. 'Why should I sit through hours of embassy small talk? Why should I attend events where the main discussion point about me is my dress or my weight? Or you?' Instead, she resolved to discover the real Paris. And she had.

Em was the Left Bank to the Right Bank of my diplomatic life. And she was there now working late at Hemingway and Company, a bookstore full of nooks and crannies. Full of hiding places. Her haven. I suspected that her relationship with the owner was a growing additional incentive. I had once watched them through the window as I waited for her to finish. He was a heavily built man, with wild hair, a silver beard and big hands. There was an intimacy to the way he had stroked her cheek as she said goodbye.

I suppressed a sigh, but it didn't fool Steph. This was the embassy's biggest night of the year. 'After the pandemic, after all the media crap over Amina Joshi, it's even more important that we keep calm and carry on. Like we always do.'

Steph rolled her eyes. 'I heard you losing that exact argument with Mum all weekend...'

Something else had changed between us all since Amina's arrival: I was increasingly on the outside. After years of my work disrupting Emma's life, now her life was disrupting my work.

And now I was alone once again. I half-admired her.

Steph was watching me closely. I had kept my head down as they had argued, citing urgent papers in the study. She took my hands in hers for a moment. I wished I could tell her that I understood she too needed the freedom to fail. I had always tried too hard to protect her. Soon I would have to let her go.

Just not too soon please, and not too far.

'Steph, have you had contact here with the Danes? The ambassador was asking odd questions.'

But she had disappeared into the throng. Two minutes to the speech. By this point I was always on autopilot, my mind crafting

32

the words I would shortly say as I moved quickly through my guests. Maybe the Churchill joke about the best speeches being like a miniskirt – short enough to get the attention, long enough to cover the essentials. I didn't think I had used it all that much recently. That would work.

Onwards. The residence manager was giving me the signal that the moment had come, readying her usual look of icy disappointment. The band was looking on, ready for the nod. The microphone stand stood straight like a challenge. Or maybe a rebuke.

Then I spotted Orla Fitzgerald and swerved in her direction. She was wearing an emerald-green dress, a characteristically gentle provocation. Even I could tell that she had done her blonde hair differently to the usual functional tie back. A bit of Monroe curl in the way it fell over her shoulders.

Orla had been the Middle East correspondent when I had been posted in Beirut. I had come to learn that you always knew something bad was going to happen when she showed up in town. She had a nose for the next war and an instinct for danger. Once, after another of my uncertain efforts to compliment her, Orla had teased me that men always wrongly assume that women are making the effort for their sake. Orla would know whether we were still allowed to make jokes about dresses.

'Ambassador? Edward? Is everything okay?'

I stared at her. She exuded life and youth, but there was also a nervous edge to her that I hadn't seen before. Her senses were more alert: fight or flight. Then reality crowded back again, like a knock from Lenny on the door to the roof. I fumbled for an excuse to have come over.

'Orla, I'm sorry this is all so boring. What's now the least stuffy French word for miniskirt?'

She looked up at me with a mixture of compassion and amusement. Another one of those people who had worked me out.

'Some of this might be boring, Ed, but you're not as boring as you think you are.'

The marching band – bright red jackets and nutcracker-tight black breeches – had done its job. A passable 'God Save the Queen', and a slightly less confident '*La Marseillaise*'. The guests, well topped up, had applauded as loudly as is possible with one hand on a champagne glass and one eye out for the next canapé.

I stepped forward. I hate tapping the microphone before speaking – surely the fastest way to lose an audience. But something – nerves, drama, the bustle dying down after the anthems, a sense of foreboding, the nagging absence of my wife – made me do it that night. The last words hanging in the air.

*Marchons, marchons!*
*Qu'un sang impur*
*Abreuve nos sillons'*

March on indeed. Here we go again.

'Excellences, ladies and gentlemen, *bienvenue*. Tonight, we celebrate not just the Entente *Cordiale*. But the Entente *Formidable*. And, whatever our current differences over Britain's relationship with Europe, what a moment to treasure our shared values of liberty, equality and brotherhood. I am reminded of the time when Churchill was asked to speak, here in this very garden. He suggested that his speech would be like a *mini-jupe*. Aha, they said, what could the great man really mean? Well, he answered, with a characteristic grin, it means…'

The joke landed passably well, though I saw Lynn Redwood barely hiding her disdain, holding her iced sparkling water like a shield in front of her. The last time she had heard me speak she had told me pointedly that Churchill probably never felt the need to quote other people.

I continued. 'I want to tell you how important is the extraordinary – and *vigorous* – rapport between my prime minister and the French president.' The two hated each other. I glanced at Aurelie Lafont, hoping she would appreciate the *mot juste*. She was, as always, glowering at me with a mixture of rebuke and pity.

As so often at these moments, I was on my own. I couldn't see Max Crawford, my defence adviser. Or Harry Parkinson, the head of station. Lenny must be off preparing my emergency gin. Good man. There was no sign of Emma yet, and even Steph seemed to have ducked out – no doubt she would tease me later that she had heard it all many times before. I'd never anticipated that such a social job could be so lonely. But there was Alem in the middle of the room, giving me that familiar look of solidarity and gentle warning. And there was Sophie Rawlings, a copy of the speech she had written in her hand, looking slightly crestfallen.

The sweet spot of any speech is the moment when you feel the room and your voice slow down, and you can look into the eyes of your guests, knowing that they are with you. Night was falling now, and the firefly lights were in the trees.

As usual, several guests had their smartphones out. I had learnt to tolerate it. Sophie always told me that they just might be tweeting the best bits. Kane was of course glued to his screen. I very much doubted he was sharing any of it with a world that had better things to do. I dropped in an unplanned line.

'As we build back better after the pandemic, even our most powerful allies are looking inwards, and neglecting the international architecture that our grandparents constructed with years of such sacrifice and patience...'

I noticed that the EU ambassador liked this bit, and saw the Irishman glance across at Kane, who had of course missed the whole thing.

One of my predecessors had insisted on only giving speeches in English, 'to remind the French that I have the fleet behind me'.

But the fleet was long gone, and I switched languages to close, and to build up to the toast, 'to Her Majesty the Queen, and the president of the republic'. It was time to put them out of their misery, and to inhale another gin. Now where was Lenny?

I never got that gin.

## 7

It was Orla Fitzgerald who reacted first. She gasped, her eyes fixed on the screen of her smartphone. I caught her looking at me with pale, breathless horror. It was the look of someone whose life had changed in a moment.

I faltered but continued. 'And so, my friends, a toast...'

A scream from Sophie Rawlings, and she dropped her champagne glass, her face transfixed in revulsion on her own phone's screen. One of the bandsmen towards the back let out a loud curse. Even Kane was looking up from his phone now and into the faces of those nearest him, intrigued at the disruption but annoyed not to be part of it.

There was to be no toast.

Alem was at my side. She wrenched the microphone from my hand with none of her usual tact.

'I'm afraid there has been an incident. Please don't panic, and please stay in the garden. We will get you more information as soon as we have it.'

I looked at her in anger and confusion. She was pale, and her normally assertive voice was catching. She looked suddenly much younger.

Around the room, our guests were taking their phones from their pockets and staring at their flickering screens.

Then Sophie was with me, showing me her screen. At first I thought it was the NGO worker beheaded in Afghanistan. I tried to push the phone away, but Sophie insisted. This was not the grainy video that had haunted me for years, but something equally as terrifying, live and in high definition. Amina Joshi was fighting death as she had always fought through life.

Her back was against a wall. The gash across her neck oozed blood, almost terracotta against her skin. Eyes bulging and terrified, she slowly choked on her own blood. She stared at the world with a last look of ferocity and pain and closed her eyes. Her head stayed upright for a moment, and then rolled to the side, a deep gash visible across her throat. Above it there was a first small cut, jagged, imperfect. *Sang impur.*

And as the hot blood spread across Amina's white blouse, her face became the most famous on the planet.

Sophie wrenched the phone away from me again. Around me everything was in frantic motion. But the next moments were absurdly calm and ordered. Lynn Redwood's bodyguard swept her swiftly out of the way. Another security guard took my arm firmly, and, with Alem, we slipped through a side door, past the embassy grand piano, and into the kitchen.

We stood among the debris of the reception. Alem was regaining her composure, switching to the detached efficiency that the best diplomats find in the midst of a crisis.

'Are you okay, Edward? The French police are on their way.'

I looked at her. Time slowed for a moment. One of the staff was slumped on the floor of the kitchen, staring at her phone.

Whoever had killed Amina had to still be in the building. And Amina's bedroom was on the same corridor as Steph's room. The horror of what had happened to Amina was nothing compared to the fear that I could lose my girl. The Danish ambassador had warned me she was at risk.

'I'm going up to find Steph, Alem. We can't wait.'

38

I ignored the rickety lift to the residential wing, and instead took the stairs two at a time. Alem kicked off her heels and followed me up.

I pushed down the corridor towards Amina's door. And there was Lenny. His instinct must also have been to find the murderer before they escaped.

'What's going on, Lenny? Is Steph okay?'

He did not reply. Even he was speechless, gesturing back down the corridor towards the door. He tried to move to block my path, but then crumpled, his huge frame folding as he slumped against the wall.

I reached the door and tried to open it. At first it wouldn't budge. I leaned hard into the frame with my shoulder.

Amina Joshi's legs were twisted under her. Her white blouse was soaked in blood. A deep slash ran across her neck.

I looked around the room, expecting to see the attacker. In front of Amina on the floor, next to her right hand, was a long kitchen knife. Opposite her was a window, locked. The door to the ensuite bathroom was ajar. Trying to control my breathing, I pushed it slowly open. It was empty, save for her toiletries. There was no sign that they had been disturbed.

I felt her left wrist. No pulse but still warm. She had only just been killed.

Alem had followed me through the only door into the room. She turned away and began vomiting. A pool of blood had begun to spread on the floor around Amina Joshi's head, like a dark red halo.

We stood still as time slowed. There were sirens in the court-yard below. I called Steph's name.

I did not hear her enter, but I felt the force of Steph's body as she fell against me. In that moment she seemed to me like she had on her first day of school – innocent and vulnerable. Relief swept through me.

'Pop... oh, Pop.'

I wanted to take her away from this place, to protect her. I held her tightly, feeling the sobs well through her body and the resistance drain away. She was small again in my arms.

'I was at the party, in the garden, but I realised I'd left my phone in my room. I wanted to get some photos of the band, and your speech of course. After I saw you, I nipped upstairs. I checked in at the apartment to see if Mum was there. I wanted to tell her she should come down.'

I winced but appreciated the solidarity. Stephanie's cheeks had recovered some colour, her eyes a sharper blue. They were my eyes once. She seemed to need to speak.

'Mum wasn't there so I came back along the corridor. Lenny was just coming out of Amina's room. I guessed Amina had him running her errands. He's been treating her like he'd treat any of your normal guests. And all that on his busiest night of the year. I went back to my room and found my phone. I checked my hair in the bathroom. I knew there would be lots of photos. But I didn't want to miss your big moment.'

Steph hesitated. I felt an overwhelming responsibility for having plunged my family into this life. Into this death.

Steph was avoiding looking at the body. 'I listened at the door. It sounded like Amina was in pain.'

'Was she still alive? Did she say anything to you?'

'I don't know, Pops, it was such a blur. She always seemed so strong, and suddenly...' Stephanie suppressed a sob.

'Did you see anyone, Steph? Anyone or anything at all that can help us find who did this?'

But she was spent. I held her tightly. I told her again and again that I was sorry she had to see this. 'We'll get away. Just the three of us. I'm sorry I let this into our house.'

Stephanie was suddenly alert, staring back at me with a fierce intensity. I wondered if she had an image for the first time of my own death. A glimpse of my mortality. A day when she would look at my face for a last time, the light gone.

'Pops, whatever happens, this is not your fault.'

I looked from her to Alem to Amina's body. The only way to protect my daughter was to find the killer. Why were the police not here already? Where was the security team?

Even in those first terrified moments I also knew that we would have to find the truth. I did not realise then that I would have to find the truth alone.

Meanwhile, the internet silently distributed our images to millions, the next scene in a macabre piece of performance art.

And amid all the sound and fury I saw one thing so clearly that I never doubted it, even later when everyone else did.

The knife by Amina's right hand bore the embassy crest.

## 8

The first French policeman to enter the room looked with disgruntled weariness at the corpse, and then in disgust at the three of us. He introduced himself as Manuel Salins. He was thick set with dark hooded eyebrows and looked like he hadn't slept properly in years. His suit hung off him. How hard was it to buy a suit that fitted?

'Why are you in this room, Ambassador Barnes? This is a crime scene.'

He stepped over to Amina's body, felt her wrist and let her arm drop back to the floor. He opened her eyelids clumsily with his fat thumbs.

I looked at him with fury. 'This is my family's house. This is our guest. And whoever did this may still be in the building. My daughter is not safe.'

He rolled his eyes. 'We will take details of everyone who was at the reception. And it is necessary that I see everyone in the household, including your family. Tonight. Any other exits from this corridor?'

I showed him the fire escape. It was closed. But the attacker could have used it to get up on the roof. Salins drew a weapon and went through. Alem and Steph were comforting each other. Instinct made me follow him. It was dark but clear. Around us the lights of an ordinary Paris night. But below us in the courtyard flashing lights and panic. Salins glanced for a moment at the remains of the joint I had smoked earlier, picked it up and sniffed it. Then put it in his pocket. I winced at my carelessness.

Below us horrified guests were starting to process back through the embassy courtyard and out into the Paris night. Some were leaning on each other. Some glued to their phones, updating their profiles with the news that they had been there. That they had been participants. Survivors.

The roof was silent. My eyes slowly adjusted to the darkness. There was no obvious way down. If the killer was up here, he must be close.

Behind us we heard steps on the gravel. I swung round, clenched. But it was Salins's colleague. He looked at me with more disdain. We were in his way. He addressed us both:

'The camera continues to broadcast. In the room. There is footage out there of you arriving, checking her pulse. Shots of the daughter crying.' He turned to me. 'Ambassador, it is necessary that you inform us now. Was the camera placed there by your colleagues? Were you monitoring Joshi?'

I shook my head. This was not beyond Parkinson, but he would have had no reason to release the footage. Salins looked unconvinced. His suspicion of the Brits was clearly going to overwhelm any attempt to work together. But if Steph's face was now out there, she was at even greater risk.

Salins started back through the fire escape and to the room. I looked across the roofs of Paris and edged along the side of the ledge. It was dark and I struggled to keep my footing. I got to the end of the roof and peered out into the blackness. Was the killer watching me now? My shoe dislodged a handful of gravel and I watched it fall into the courtyard below. I felt my chest rise and fall as I strained to discern any sound.

Nothing. If the killer was inside the embassy, I needed to get Steph safely to her room. I took one last look around, retraced my steps and followed Salins back down.

Back in Amina's room it didn't take Salins long to find the camera, fixed to the top corner of a picture frame. He removed it and pulled the wire from the back.

'*Théâtre. C'est fini.*'

I asked Alem to take Steph to her room and get security on the door. I looked again around the room. Apart from the gash to Amina's neck, there were no signs of violence. The chair where Amina had been sitting was pulled back from the desk. The door had not been locked or forced.

Salins turned to his colleague. 'Suicide?'

I felt the anger rising. 'Who cuts their own throat?'

Salins swung round. 'I said it's finished, Mr Ambassador. It is for us to continue the investigation now. We will interview everyone, including your family.'

It was much too soon. The way in which Salins was already handling the evidence troubled me. He had seemed completely unshaken by the sight of the body, so uninterested in who might still be on the roof.

Max Crawford joined us in the room. I looked at him with relief. This was a man to have around. He was even still wearing his medals, though Salins pretended not to see them. Permanent five o'clock shadow. That curious blend of mischief and dash. Just William and Field Marshall Montgomery.

A former head of the Special Forces, Crawford was one of the most decorated soldiers since the Second World War. There were plenty of Crawford myths and legends, though he denied them all with an impish smile. I had only ever seen him in uniform or in a tatty leather jacket, jeans, trainers and no socks. He didn't seem to have any intermediate mode. Today, he looked like he was ready for battle. If we were going to be in the trenches at least I had some backup.

Crawford barely glanced at Amina's body. He took in the two policemen, looked back at me, one eyebrow slightly raised.

It gave me the confidence to take the leap. 'No, Salins, not tonight. This is sovereign UK territory. You have no jurisdiction here. This will be a UK police matter.'

He turned to me in fury. 'The world's most famous fugitive, under your protection, dies live on the internet. You tell us we must wait for a constable to arrive through the Channel Tunnel?'

A standoff. I lost my temper. The phones started to ring. My team consulting London. Salins angrily speaking to the Ministry of the Interior.

Crawford looked at me quizzically. 'What's next, Ambassador?'

I always insisted on not being called 'Ambassador', but Crawford chose this to be the one order he consistently ignored.

I was aware of a moment at a crossroads, and a memory broke back through. The smell of church pew and cassock, my mother's perfume, my father reading Frost at my grandfather's funeral, two roads diverging. That feeling of purpose among the grief.

Which was the road less travelled now that someone had brought death into my house, into my embassy, into my family?

I knew already in that moment that I could not rely on the French: Salins and his companion had no interest in finding out what had really happened.

I had no time yet to wonder why that was. But I knew instinctively that I had to find the truth, for Amina, for my family and for myself. This was my wife's closest friend.

For the first time in years, I could feel the adrenalin. I was where I was meant to be. And maybe, amidst the horror, I could show Emma that I was still the person who was where he was meant to be.

'Please show these gentlemen out, Crawford. And secure the building. No one touches anything in this room, including the body. We're going to find out what happened here.'

## 9

Crawford moved fast. Salins and his colleague, protesting loudly, were bundled from the building. I felt strongly that we needed them out of the way before they could settle on their narrative. Alem quoted obscure parts of diplomatic code at them to justify our actions, and then went to inform a surprised London of the situation. Crawford locked the front and back doors to the residence and went off to see what video footage we had.

I had very little time before the French secured whatever permission they needed to come back. London would not give me long. In the room I looked through the papers on Amina's desk. They were mainly scraps of draft letters and articles. The same themes – the failure of nation states to rise to the new challenges, the decline of American leadership under President Elizabeth Hoon, who had betrayed the world's women. A need for global governance. But one printed page caught my eye. It was neatly typed, unmistakably her rhetoric.

> Niemöller Revisited: Amina Joshi's Last Post
>
> First they came for Muslims. But I was not Muslim, so I just tweeted in solidarity. And did not speak out. Then they came for refugees. But I was not a refugee, so I wrote it off as campaign rhetoric. And did not speak out.
>
> Then they came for the Mexicans. But I was not a Mexican, so I watched Netflix. And did not speak out. Then they kicked

people of colour out of rallies. But I simply tried to understand grievances of those hit by globalisation. And did not speak out.

Then they came for the media. But I get my news from a Facebook echo chamber, so I wrote it off as beltway elites moaning. And did not speak out. Then they came for the sick. But I was not sick or American, so I did not speak out.

Then they came for the planet. But I was living comfortably in an air-conditioned corner of it, so I did not speak out. And who will be left to speak out for me?

I have sought refuge in Paris. Liberty, equality, fraternity. We lose when we lose that. Last century we nearly did. Yet those painful lessons are standing, blindfolded and arms tied before the wall, wondering if they will hear the first shot of the firing squad.

I have come to realise that it is not enough any more to be a commentator. We need a global uprising to defend the freedoms we have won at such cost. The struggle begins now. And I will play my part, pay any price.

I know the risks we will all run in the days ahead. 'You can stand up and fight only while you are alive. If they say I committed suicide, be sure that it was a murder.'

The quote was from Ulrike Meinhof, co-founder of the Baader-Meinhof gang, days before her death in the 1970s. And yet Amina had called the piece her Last Post. What was she really trying to tell us?

She had signed it in light blue ink. The fountain pen was to the left of the page.

I looked again at her body. The colour had drained from her face. But she appeared somehow serene in death, her anger gone. The knife was by her right arm. Would she really have had the strength to kill herself? Especially with her weaker hand?

I folded the page to place it in my jacket pocket. On the back was a telephone number, scribbled in her handwriting. An 01865 number. Oxford.

The door opened behind me. I froze, but it was Crawford. He had seen me flinch and his eyes darted around the room, alert for danger.

Once it was clear that we were alone, he joined me by Amina's desk, squinting for clues. I tucked the paper into my jacket pocket.

'Whatever happened in here, there's danger ahead. The killer could still be in the building. And the French will go ballistic that we chucked them out. My guys in the MOD are saying that No 10 are going to tell you to get back in your box.'

I nodded. 'But remember Shackleton's ad in *The Times* before the South Pole? Men wanted for hazardous journey. Safe return doubtful. Honour and recognition in event of success.'

Crawford grinned. 'Impossible to resist.' He turned to me. 'What next?'

'Just make sure Steph is safe.'

I had one ally. That might be enough.

This was a crime that no one owned or wanted. But I owned it now, whether I wanted it or not. And I was starting to want it.

## 10

The lights faded in the studio, and another highlights show was in the bag. As always, Scottish football commentator Ray Griffiths reached for his smartphone. He had joined Twitter only three years earlier, but it was now an irreplaceable part of his day. During a particularly dry interview with the Swansea manager his mind had been constructing a tweet on a speech given earlier that day by a far-right demagogue. The idiot had argued that refugees fleeing to the West should return home.

Griffiths loved the cut and thrust of social media. The best Twitter was a good argument. The tweet was almost fully formed in his mind. Something pointing out that the politician's grandparents had themselves come from Germany – should he also therefore 'return home'? What about Griffiths – those seventy-six goals for Scotland would have been scored for Sweden if his grandmother had 'returned home'. Empty Britain of anyone who had come from overseas and you would, well, empty Britain. Boom. He'd get a thousand retweets in the first hour, at least. He savoured the thrill of combat.

The transition from pitch to pundit had not been easy. His first few shows were nervy, stuttering. He had struggled to find his voice. But his childhood friend, now the prestigious UK ambassador in Paris, had told him to breathe, to feel his way into talking just as he had felt his way into taking a penalty. And since then, it had got better and better. It helped that he had read some books during those long coach journeys to away matches, enough to draw the jibes of his fellow players. Plus the spells overseas learning French and Italian. The seventy-six goals had also certainly helped, too. But he realised now that his success was mainly about emotional intelligence. He had found a way to connect with people.

And Twitter was all part of that. He tapped first on his notifications. There would be the normal bile from racists and their fellow travellers. Some solidarity, and a bit of adulation. But mostly banter. It was here that he found the material for those perfect intros and outros, the witty aside about a manager or player, the self-deprecating gag. How had pundits coped before social media?

It took him several seconds to fathom what was happening. He had millions of followers, but it was still highly unusual to have so many notifications. Thousands. The first few were vicious. Accusations of hypocrisy. Abuse. But then as he flicked through the timeline he found more disappointment, more sorrow.

It was only after having read several messages, increasingly mystified, that he found the link to the breaking news that they were reacting to. And the confidence evaporated. This was not a tackle to shimmy past with a trademark shake of the hips. This was a career-ending, brutal takedown. He was the victim. But the crowd were baying for his blood.

He stared for a long time at the headline: *Breaking: BBC Star Griffiths' Secret Love Child*. Beneath it the email from his Yahoo account instructing his bank to make the monthly payments to a single mother in Brighton, where he had spent an unhappy three months getting his coaching badge. The photo showed the mother, a Somali refugee, pushing a pram through the rain, looking miserable. Next to it was Griffiths' face grinning out of an advert for sliced white bread. 'Gives You Oomph!' They would have fun with that. They would have fun with all of it, the vultures and hyenas of the UK press.

The studio was suddenly quiet. The sound engineers and cameramen seemed to fade away into the darkness. He had never felt so alone.

And then he saw the missed calls. Three from his agent. Four from his brother. Five from his wife. Six from his daughter.

BREAKING. Breaking. Breaking.

–

Orla Fitzgerald was inevitably the first to file the basic elements of the story – Amina Joshi dead at the British ambassador's summer party, panic and terror among the excellencies, *sang* among the *sang-froid*, the scarlet-red lipstick marks on the glasses of undrunk champagne. The rapid arrival of the police, and their cool efficiency. The ambassador rushed away. The speculation.

It was, she wrote, 'a crime with too many possible culprits. A woman with too many enemies'. She quoted her last conversation with Amina Joshi, describing the woman's gentleness and flashes of humour behind the steel, but also communicating a sense of the danger she felt herself to be in. Anticipation that the failure of governments to contain the previous year's pandemic had broken the trust with those they governed. Hints of revolution.

Orla was still in the offices of *Le Monde* when the news of the first information dump broke. She had grey bags under her eyes and a tightness at the corners of her mouth. But her shoulders were alert. Fight or flight. Her assistant called through. 'Orla, it's happened.'

Her first reaction was irritation. Why had there not been more warning from Magnus? He had told her he wanted her to write the first story, set the media narrative. But he clearly wasn't going to make it *too* easy for her, that wasn't his way. She let the cardboard coffee cup fall, full, into the bin. She wouldn't need the caffeine.

As journalists everywhere were finding, the first hour analysing the leaks was overwhelming and frustrating. Pederson and the Dissenters had not itemised the cache of information. They had simply uploaded documents, seemingly at random. There was no index. No guide to where to look or what to look for. An overwhelming treasure trove of deceit.

Orla tore herself away from the screen. On the wall of the newsroom was the Benjamin Franklin quote that kept them hunting for the weak point, the human vulnerability that opened up every story. 'Three can keep a secret. If two of them are dead.'

They needed to find the needles in the haystack. But there was just too much hay. She gathered her team. 'We need keywords, folks. Something to navigate by.' They wrote them up on a whiteboard – Elizabeth Hoon, NATO, terrorism, Syria, UK, France. And the always high potential 'I' words – intelligence, Iraq, Iran, Israel.

After the first hour passed, Orla's team began to coalesce around the main trends.

First, as Magnus had warned her, the Dissenters had released decades of the browsing history of millions of people. It was not clear how they had been selected for this dubious honour. But a cursory look through the material was enough to know that marriages would be broken, jobs would be lost, conspiracies would be confirmed, and the police – apart from those about to resign – would be busy. It was a dry itemised account of betrayal and weakness. Millions were discovering that nothing they did online was really secret, let alone private. Millions were finding that they did not really know the people they loved.

–

Congressman Jonathan Cross squinted back at his reflection in the mirror. He looked better when he was winning. His stubble seemed somehow harder, easier to shave. His jawline was tighter, his eyes less hooded. In one more week, he would at last be governor. This was the culmination of years of fighting his way up, fighting for his people, the people without a voice. Until now. He splashed cold water over his face and let it drip down his neck.

Cross had run on opportunity and aspiration. How was it that a generation of Texans were denied the chance to compete? What did they need to take on the wave of automation and outsourcing that was ripping apart the local economy? Start small and build. We start here in our community. We fight back. We take control. Compelling messages for a population that felt under siege from the twenty-first century. These were messages and a messenger that pundits were starting to say could take him all the way. But this was no time for hubris. He had to stay focused on today, and now. Annie would help him with that. She grounded him. He pictured her at the door of the governor's mansion. Surely this would finally make her happy.

Breakfast was the usual chaos. That was how they loved it. The three kids in a riot of cereal, fruit, curiosity, spilt milk, arguments, lost bags.

As usual, his smartphone was not far away, and he stole glances at the news notifications as they crossed the screen. This was a reality of the modern family. Everyone felt the fear of missing out. Everyone craved the electrical charge that he felt at the word BREAKING.

He looked up at his youngest son. The day before they had been at the school induction, where the eager new head had discussed separation anxiety. This was a long way from the schooling Cross remembered, but these were different times. Either way, if James had any separation anxiety it was only for his Lego. A great kid. Five years old, and already they knew he would be fine.

A flash on the screen. *BREAKING*. Like an addict to the needle, Cross felt his eyes drawn back in. *BREAKING: Politician's Tawdry Porn Secrets Condemned*. A moment of sympathy for whichever poor bastard was about to have their day ruined. And of curiosity – few politicians need more than a few seconds to switch from concern for a destroyed colleague to wondering about the implications for their own career.

And then he reeled back, the room receding, the breakfast pandemonium suddenly silent. It was his face at the top of the story, grinning with ridiculous entitlement and overconfidence. It was his internet searches throughout the text of the article, made in hotel rooms on years-old campaigns. It was his career that was shattering into a thousand pieces before his eyes.

'What is it, honey? You look like you've seen a ghost.'

Annie was paused midway through buttering some toast, looking across the table at him. Her eyes were wide with concern. Cross tried to find the words but stuttered to a halt. He looked at the three kids, now falling silent and turning towards their father.

A voice for the voiceless who would never find the words to explain his shame.

BREAKING. Breaking. Breaking.

## 11

'Not our story,' Orla told those around her, as they grimaced at their own data. 'Football presenters and B-team politicians are just eye candy. Keep looking for the needles in the haystack, keep looking for the breaking news. The attention-grabbing trivia is the first category. But there are two more.'

The second category she had identified in Pederson's leaked material was telephone transcripts, mainly of calls between government people. These were not a classic leak – it was clear that they were not official government documents, or the sanitised records produced by officials. Barnes had once told Orla that official notes rarely represented reality; they were designed for posterity. He had made one of his usual clever expressions. 'Our jobs will be done when historians have read what I think he thinks he ought to have said.'

No, these documents were the real deal: the uncensored, genuine transcripts that were never supposed to see the light of day. The authentic language used between leaders – coarse and hectoring. The rush to judgement. Policies conceived as a means of spinning a media cycle. Just the French president's descriptions of his counterparts would fill weeks of columns and fracture his relationships with his fellow leaders. Magnus Pederson was out of the shadows.

Orla put two people onto specific search terms for the key leaders. What were they saying about each other? What did we learn about them that we didn't already know? Which political careers would be broken?

The third category was the compromising of counter-terrorism operations. This was harder to assess but looked massive. There were long lists of agent names – US, UK, French, even Russian. Their field agents in Syria, Iran, Iraq, Libya, across the Middle East. Numbers, addresses, family members. An immense cache of sensitive intelligence data. Pederson was calling time on espionage. No wonder the Brits and Americans had been so anxious to get hold of the material. What damage might this do to their efforts to keep people safe? Orla put another team on this. Check upstairs. Get the lawyers in. How much can we use? How much can we write? Where can we start to draw connections to Amina Joshi, tie the two stories together? How far can we go?

Dust, dust, dust. Inside the house they were using for the stakeout, Alison McNeil longed to taste some moisture in the air, for something green, for orange leaves in autumn. Only a few more days, and she would be back to normality. She glanced at Ahmed, her Iraqi interpreter. He looked tired. The month had taken its toll on both of them.

But at any moment, she expected to get the signal that Special Forces were ready.

She thought about their target, her target. Did he wake every morning wondering if today was the last time he would shave, eat, sleep, pray? Did he feel compassion for his victims as they bled to death on anonymous streets, bodies misshapen and limbs snapped by the force of the homemade bombs? Did he feel fear himself? She knew he felt love. She had watched him with his own child, pushing his wheelchair, ruffling his hair.

Was it right that she and the Australian government, or the rest of the coalition, were somehow playing God, choosing who should live, who should die, who should be orphaned? Alison was too tired for it all. She had long since found a way to detach herself from those she surveyed from beneath the safety of her burqa, silent as she moved around Mosul as Ahmed's 'wife'. It was a job. And she had seen enough of what Abu Mustafar was capable of to know that the world would be better without him.

She put the binoculars down and lifted the plastic bottle to her parched lips. The water was warm, almost undrinkable in normal circumstances. She thought of the beach in Sydney. Fresh fish. Salty surf.

The satphone vibrated. This was highly unusual, especially so close to a hit. Not in the protocol. Emergencies only. Immediately she pressed the green button and held the phone close to her ear. She exchanged a look with Ahmed and shrugged. He looked quizzical but went back to surveying the house opposite.

The timings mattered. When Abu Mustafar left, when he arrived, his routines and patterns. Understanding all this could make Ahmed's country safer. All this might one day mean he would see his wife, languishing somewhere in a jail as a former Islamic State 'bride'. Who knew what would be left of her once the *mukhabarat* had finished? He suppressed the sob. Her pain was his fault. His responsibility. And he was now doing the only thing he could to bring it to an end. He looked at Alison. This tough, determined woman. He admired her courage.

And the way her eyes laughed. He had always told her to stop – it was the one part of her that showed from under her burqa when they were on the move. But he longed for her to continue.

Now she was pale. Her eyes were flared, hunted, angry, exasperated.

She slammed the phone back down and was silent.

She looked at him hard and long. What was that look? It was anger, turning to pity, then to guilt.

'Ahmed, it's off, I'm sorry. There's been some kind of leak. We've been compromised somehow. I don't know. We need to get out of here fast. I have to go.' Her voice was urgent, unsentimental, the wrench of protocol kicking in.

Ahmed had known these moments before. One minute you were sharing your life with these people. The next they were gone. You never even knew their real names. He had once tried to find an American soldier he had worked with for six months in order to return a photo left behind in a safe house. But he had been told he had never existed.

They never got back in touch.

She stopped her frantic packing up and turned to him, gripped him by both arms. Now her face was fierce, almost warrior-like. 'Ahmed, your name, your identity, it's out there. You have to go. Anywhere. Start again, fast. You can't ever look back. I'm sorry.'

Ahmed sank to his knees. He gasped for air. His throat was dry. Was this fate? God's will? Did he have it in him to run again? Across the street Abu Mustafar was leaving the house, not knowing that a distant Danish god had just reprieved him.

As the door shut behind Alison, all Ahmed could see was his wife's face, bleeding and bruised, looking up at him in disappointment. This was just one more betrayal in a life that had known little else. Just one more betrayal of a region that had known little else. But what happened to a people when all these betrayals came together?

What had they done to her? What had he done to her? He reached for his gun and put it to his temple.

BREAKING. Breaking. Breaking.

–

It was not just Orla. In Cheltenham, at the 'doughnut', the UK's Government Communication Headquarters, they were working through huge amounts of Pederson's leaked data. They were doing it at the National Security Agency. They were doing it in Moscow. They were doing it in Beijing. They were doing it at the fake news sites and in the offices of the respectable media agencies. They were doing it in bedrooms, boardrooms and classrooms.

Officials were searching their own names and then recoiling in horror or relief. Politicians were searching for the names of their professional rivals. There was despair, schadenfreude, fear, remorse.

Orla knew that Pederson, citing the original Dissenters, had wanted one thing above all – to destroy trust in institutions and authority. Not just governments and leaders, but the entire edifice on which modern society was built. So she was not surprised to see the evidence of archbishops searching the internet for pictures of transvestite dwarves. Of Europe's judges breaking off speeches on European values to call Europe's leaders to ask which way a trial should go. Of newspaper proprietors threatening and black-mailing elected politicians. Of bankers getting inside information from Finance Ministry officials. And vice versa. When it came to the internet, no one was innocent. When it came to Pederson, everyone was a target.

These were all massive stories in themselves. But she was convinced from her conversations with Pederson and Joshi that there must be more. Magnus had told her not just that govern-ments would fall but that this was the start of revolution. He was just getting going.

Orla searched under Ed Barnes. Nothing. Yet. On that at least they had listened to her. Either way, she needed to talk to Pederson. She rose, picked up her coat and headed towards the door. Her assistant called after her. 'Where are you going, Orla?'

Orla Fitzgerald paused, one hand on the handle, the other scooping up her bag. 'I'm going to get my Pulitzer.'

## 12

Once we were confident that Steph was safe, Crawford and I secured the room, before he cleared the rest of the building. He covered Amina's body with a sheet. Alem confirmed that UK police would arrive on the first Eurostar and briefed Redwood, who was insisting on staying holed up in her room. We eventually agreed to sleep, and I was relieved to take up Crawford's offer to stay. I stood outside Steph's room, listening to her sobbing. Would she wear this experience like a scar? Or could she find the way to leave it behind? For now, though, I had a more immediate priority. As long as Amina's killer was still out there, they were a threat to anyone who had known Amina or might shed light on her death. That very much included Steph.

Was the Danish ambassador warning us that she personally was at risk, or just that they had picked up threats to Amina? Their files would presumably have more on Magnus Pederson than the rest of us.

And then, at last, Em came back. She went first to Steph's room. After twenty minutes she came to me and led me by the hand into our private apartment, where she poured us both a large drink. She was distraught but we held each other's shoulders as I shuddered through the story. After the chaos of the evening, she seemed somehow more quietly efficient, more in control.

Em rarely wore make-up and jewellery, especially since she had stopped attending official events. However much I wanted her to be more involved, I admired her most when she was at her simplest and most unspun. Too much of my life was spun.

We sat on the corner sofa. At the weekends this was where we did sudoku puzzles together. Her long grey hair was held back in a ponytail, lifting and toning the skin of her face. She had the outdoors skin of a walker. But there was tiredness in the eyes, behind the weeping. I had barely had a moment to think of the impact on her. Amina was a friend to her, not just a fugitive. *Was*.

I embraced her. For the first time that evening I could show some weakness, some uncertainty. She stroked the back of my head. My shoulders relaxed.

We sat in silence for a few moments.

'Where've you been, Em?' I meant tonight, not the last decade.

'I was coming back along the Left Bank, when I heard. Was a beautiful evening, a full-ish moon. I hadn't wanted to arrive halfway through your party still in my DMs, a rucksack on my back.'

I was feeling my strength come back. As ever, Emma had restored some balance and tranquillity. I breathed deeply. 'Are you okay?'

Em nodded. 'I just need a moment.' She pulled away from me and stood in the alcove, framed by the moonlight. There was an uncomplicated sadness to her. No theatre. We could rebuild when this was all over, not just the drama, but the job, the protocol, the non-stop hosting. Maybe this would bring us closer again.

She took the whisky glass from my hand, took a small swig and then placed it out of my reach. 'You're tired, Ed.' She waited.

We had first met at university. Her friend's pigeonhole was in the A–C section of the porter's lodge. A parcel had found its way in error to the neighbouring pigeonhole – Barnes. I had taken it to the room. She later told me that I had seemed chivalrous if slightly shy. Handsome but weathered, even then. My eyes were a brighter blue, the first thing she noticed. A sense of more fire in the belly. My hair was just about under control. I had, she later said, the sense of an engine in too low a gear. An eagerness to please. In those days she had found that endearing.

I would often say that it was love at first sight. For me I think it might have been. But Emma was never convinced of that. After the brief romance that followed, we had learnt to love each other, working through the patterns and rhythms of courtship. She had written the most wonderful letters, full of wit and adventures. She had always known that I had college flings, including with Lynn Redwood, and she never asked about them. Soon after we both graduated, we moved in together in London. I had wanted her to come with me to Beirut, my first posting. She was enthralled by the earthy glamour of it and visited twice. But it was too soon, and too far, and she needed to make her own mistakes. We drifted apart, but drifted back together in our late twenties, when the passing of time and lack of alternatives had worn her down.

It was never fireworks. I don't think she ever felt swept off her feet. It had just seemed to make sense. We married in the chapel at my old college, across the quad from the pigeonhole that had brought us together.

She had a sense of steely purpose to her. 'Ed, you've had a big shock. We all have. But we'll pull through. You always do. We normally do too. Just hold it together. Trust yourself. You're doing as well as anyone could. Surely even they recognise that.'

'They' was London. Emma had always had an instinct to protect me from the Foreign Office machine. A sense that 'they' were out to get me somehow. It used to make me laugh. Weren't 'they' after all my friends and colleagues? And as I rose through the ranks, hadn't I become 'them'? I wasn't laughing today. I was trying not to imagine the discussions in Whitehall. *Has Barnes lost the plot? We always wondered if Paris was a jump too far. He's never really gripped those staffing issues. Do the French really respect him?*

I ducked the moment of solidarity. 'Em, did Amina say anything to you about threats against her?'

Emma looked past me at the window, blinking. 'Amina was much stronger than you all thought. But she was also much more fragile than you all realised. She was getting more paranoid, especially after the interview with Orla Fitzgerald created all that blowback from Washington and Paris.'

'But surely that wasn't enough for her to think anyone would kill her? Just one more critic with a keyboard?'

'No. But remember that Amina had many layers. Saint Amina was just a character she had created to get her message across. I remember being shocked when the stats showed that the pandemic was killing more older, white men. She just said something like "every cloud has a silver lining". I don't think any of us really knew her, or what she was capable of.'

Maybe we would come through this stronger. The man I had become, worn down by reality and realpolitik, might give way to the man I had been, the man that Emma had loved. 'Let's get to the cottage in Snowdonia soon. Just the three of us. Get our chorus line back.'

She sighed deeply and looked back into my eyes. 'The chorus has always been fine, Ed. It's the verses that have changed. You can't fix that on your own. Let someone else worry about Amina. It's fine sometimes to just be, not to do.'

'I know, love,' I lied.

Eventually, I slept, my head full of nightmares. Years earlier, I had been posted to Jordan as a young diplomat. Hosted by a Muslim family for *Eid al-Adha*, the sacrifice feast, I had been invited to make the cut that killed the ram. Hoping that they would not notice my hand shaking, I had sliced the neck firmly and slowly from left to right, feeling every sinew and bone beneath the knife. The resistance and the release. And then my

64

host had stood on the beast's torso as it bled to death, halal style, hot blood oozing and spitting down the gutter. The blood had smelt sweet, like treacle.

I had held the knife tight, unable to tear myself away from the sight. My breath rose and fell with the ram. Again, the stillness at the centre of chaos.

The animal had not died for several minutes. Its blinking eyes gradually drained but would not close. It writhed and kicked briefly but then seemed to accept its fate. What I most remembered were its flanks, which had lifted and fallen with its breath, slower and slower. This was, my host said, a moment of recognition of its role in the ceremony, the spirit of sacrifice, the circle of life.

The same God of the Old Testament had given the same Abraham the ultimate loyalty test. Cut your son's throat. Prove that you obey me more than you love your son.

I woke sweating, my throat dry. When you thought about it, it was religion's most repellent story. What parent is ready to sacrifice their child for a test of loyalty? What vicious God asks such a thing?

Only a God preparing to do it himself.

## 13

It was, of course, Lenny who woke me the next morning. I was slumped over my desk after a few hours of fitful sleep. The Paris air was crisp. This was normally my favourite time of the day.

I scowled at my surroundings and then shuddered as I recalled the night before. I could taste the whisky at the back of my dry throat. It was six a.m., just enough time to clean myself up and get the senior team together before the UK police would arrive. I would need to address all the staff, keep Lynn Redwood onside but out of the way, rally the troops, start to rebuild, kill some rumours. Time was short: London would pull the plug, get the French back in, settle on a suicide. And the killer would still be out there, a potential threat to Steph and Em if they knew how close they were to Amina. There was footage everywhere of Steph in Amina's room with me. I took a deep breath. A nod to Lenny, who looked like he hadn't slept. I needed a shower and a shave. There was no sign of Emma in the apartment.

Lenny put a full coffee pot on the silver tray in the dressing room. Stronger than usual. I poured a second cup and looked out of the window at the courtyard below. The calm before the storm. There were some cameras outside the gate.

I looked at myself in the mirror. The natural unruliness of my remaining hair had returned. My face looked gaunter. There were darker bags under my eyes than usual. Weathered, but alive. Onwards.

I messaged Sophie to meet me in the office with the media summary. Her cheeks were slightly flushed. Unusually she avoided my eye. There was none of the usual eagerness.

'The BBC led with the death, quoting French sources that it was a suicide. Calling it a diplomatic nightmare. Saying no one knows whose jurisdiction it is. Website has photos of people gathering out the front. Reporting that it's all peaceful for now. People leaving flowers for her.'

Like some kind of Princess Diana. I gestured at Sophie to continue.

'But one protester is saying that the British government killed Amina. I think we'll get more of that. The BBC are reporting a new story that Orla Fitzgerald has done, saying that Amina was in contact with Magnus Pederson and the Dissenters. Apart from us, their leaks are now the main story everywhere. The Americans are trying to undermine it all, calling it fake news. There's a lot about this Pederson's character flaws – some unsubstantiated stuff saying that he's a blackmailer. No shortage of people lining up to put the boot in.'

I thought of my Danish colleague. The conversation we had never had. He had tried to warn me something was coming. I was clearly not the only one to have underestimated Pederson.

'And what about online?'

'That's where the action really is. Video from last night has been watched over nine million times. Embassy account is getting an overwhelming amount of hits. We can't keep up. A lot of abuse, a lot of conspiracy. A huge amount of stuff targeting us, well, you, Edward... umm, Ambassador. They have a photo of you from the party last night, with the US ambo.'

I peered at it over her shoulder. We looked suitably sinister.

Sophie was now in full flow. 'A Belgian site is claiming the French wanted Amina silenced because she was no longer able to control her supporters. Breitbart is saying the Russians wanted her dead, to cover up their involvement in leaks. And Russia Today is speculating that the Americans had the greatest motive.'

I frowned. I had learnt from years with politicians to assume cock-up rather than conspiracy. None of this yet added up to a motive. The internet gives everyone a hot take. Everyone's an expert. Everyone's a suspect. But I was troubled by Orla's speculation of a link between Amina and Pederson. Had Orla also got herself tangled up in his insanity? Surely they had nothing in common. Except their enemies.

Sophie continued. 'In the editorials, questions about how you ended up taking her in in the first place. Why weren't there better security measures for such a high-profile asylum seeker? No 10 is saying that this is all "a matter for the Foreign Office". The Foreign Office are saying that we are all focused on the crisis at hand, but there will be time to learn lessons later. They were asked by Sky if your position was secure and said, "Her Majesty's ambassadors serve at the pleasure of Her Majesty. Sir Edward is a seasoned diplomat with a reputation for hard work and integrity."'

I grimaced. 'A bit of a classic non-denial. Hardly reassuring. And what are the Press Office saying we should do? Are they putting ministers out to calm this down?'

'The line to take is that this is a matter for the French authorities and that we are doing everything to help them with their investigations. There was a strict order from No 10 to shut speculation down about who's running the investigation. They want us out of this story as quickly as possible. But the French are briefing this morning that we insisted – that *you* insisted – on handling the case yourself.'

'Keep me posted.'

'But are they not right that it was a suicide?'

While the governments seemed to need this to be a suicide, someone had clearly wanted Amina's death to look like a murder.

By the Brits. I was convinced that it was indeed a murder. But not by us.

'Just keep me posted.'

Penny Rainsford put her head around the door. Her grey hair was tied back and she had picked a trim trouser suit. She had been with me for years, moving with me from posting to posting. She could manage the mayhem, making sure that I turned up where I was meant to be, be who I was supposed to be and keep out the people who needed to be kept out. She worked into the schedule the evenings with Emma, the sudoku or film nights that I thought even then kept us ticking along, providing the rare overlaps between our lives. Left Bank and Right Bank.

'Do you want the good news or the bad news?'

I was too used to that particular rhetorical device, having regularly used it myself. 'How much more bad news can there be?'

'The foreign secretary is insisting on seeing you immediately.'

I went along the corridor to Redwood's room and knocked on her door. She was sitting, straight-backed, at the dressing table by the window. 'I think I am owed an update.'

'Good morning, Foreign Secretary.' I'm from a generation of diplomats who can make expressions of respect sound like disdain. 'I'm glad to see you looking well, despite everything.'

How easily we all lie. She didn't take my hand.

'What the hell is going on, Edward?'

She had always deployed a vocal range from husky to shrill. Why are the English so hopeless in talking about death? The euphemisms and awkwardness.

I glanced at Jack Fleming, her private secretary, who avoided my eye. The private secretaries were getting younger. How old could Fleming be? Late twenties? And why did they all feel they had to wear pinstripe? A tribe with its uniform and its codes and its secrets. Like mafia dons and their *omerta*. Power at that age corrupted faster than it corrupted the rest of us. Or maybe I was just jealous.

You had to be a control freak to survive in those jobs, while affecting a nonchalant lack of passion. Get too close to the minister and you were finished. Appear not close enough and the sharks would circle. I was now one of those sharks. The private secretary was not just bag carrier and consigliere. They were also therapist and punchbag. Fleming looked like he had taken a few rounds in the last twenty-four hours.

Redwood and I sat awkwardly for a moment, both caught in the moment of disappointed appraisal. We were getting older, and we saw it all too clearly in one another. Extra lines where there hadn't been. A lack of fire where there had once been a furnace. The slow process of decay. When we were young there had been a night together after a college dinner, during one of my breaks with Em. For me, potentially the beginning of something. For her the end of it. It was never to be repeated. Never to be mentioned again.

But then her face softened. 'Edward, I'm sorry this has happened.' For a moment the voice was slightly breathy, less controlled than usual. I could almost hear the Lynn Redwood I had once known, back when we had options, when we had uncomplicated hope.

'Thank you, Lynn.' I hadn't meant to use her first name. I had scrupulously avoided it since her appointment. Partly protocol, partly self-defence. She frowned.

Over the years, I had gone months, sometimes years, without thinking about her. But then she was suddenly there. In a doorway, at a table, and in some cities, everywhere. I saw her sometimes in the faces of strangers. Maybe it was a space we had been in together, her presence in the air of a street. Other times it was a song, Ray Charles quietly imploring a former lover if he ever crossed her mind.

Did I ever cross her mind as that undergraduate with a half-drunk bottle of Southern Comfort, libido and the swagger of someone who hadn't yet screwed much up? I had discovered in her then a connection that I had thought was not just physical. But those moments of brief abandon in Oxford, as the heavens opened, had been followed by years of increasing distance. Where had that girl gone, running through an Oxford quad in a flowery summer dress, soaked to the skin, vital and alive, laughing as she looked back at me? For a while I sent notes, but then stopped. I had cared about losing her. I had cared more that she had somehow lost herself.

I watched in trepidation as she entered politics, always worried that my world would collide with hers. We had both done all we could to avoid that. Now neither of us had a choice.

'We're all okay.' I tried to fill the gap. 'It's a shock, obviously.'

Again, that English inability to state the obvious: we will never be the same again. Being here with me, this life, this job, has stained us indelibly. My daughter in a room with a corpse. My wife's oldest friend killed in our house. We will always carry this. I will always carry this.

I thought again of my time in Jordan, and the ram, one eye fixed on mine as I held the knife, the sacrifice complete.

'Good, very good, I'm pleased to hear it.' There was another awkward silence. I felt again my daughter's sobs. She continued. 'But I know that this is all far from ideal. Are the French police handling it appropriately?'

Appropriate. A word I have always banned from my embassies. What did it mean, 'appropriate'? The vagueness of it.

'Well, the French are still saying they're in charge. But this is UK sovereign territory. A small corner of a foreign field that is forever England. This must be our investigation. I was not impressed by the French approach last night. They weren't asking the right questions. They want to close it down. They didn't seem curious about why the knife was by her right and not her left hand. Or who had the incentive to broadcast the death. And the killer's still out there.'

She was silent. I could hear the clock on the wall.

'Edward.' Her voice was firm again. 'As your foreign secretary, and as your friend...' I didn't feel a sense of much camaraderie. She cleared her throat. 'As your foreign secretary I'm asking you to think very carefully about what you do next. Discretion can be the better part of valour. You're not a detective. You're throwing everything away. Leave this to the French.'

I felt the blood in my cheeks. Once again the woman that the *Daily Express* called 'the Teflon tigress' had given me a non-instruction that could be adapted for every outcome. She was a politician who lived her life in preparation for the public inquiry. No doubt she would claim, whatever decisions I took, that she had encouraged a more intelligent course. What would she tell No 10? That she had instructed her ambassador to get a grip? That she was watching the situation carefully? That the world would quickly move on to the next celebrity wedding, royal tweet or act of terrorism?

In that moment, I remembered something a previous prime minister had said to me about an ambitious upstart foreign secretary – *I would swap all that intellect for an ounce of judgement.*

'Foreign secretary... Lynn... I need to do this. I can do this.' I was feeling for the first time in years a sense of purpose.

She was staring at her shoes. 'Edward, you're not looking for the truth. You're looking for escape.'

'This isn't some kind of Le Carré film, Lynn. This is people's lives. My family.'

'Unlike you, some of us never believed we were in a Le Carre world. That world wasn't open to us.'

I felt time slow. The most perilous choices always come when you have incomplete information and no time to reflect. Yet these were the moments on which you would be judged. And there was no neat, correct answer. I breathed deeper.

'Foreign secretary. A woman has been murdered. On UK territory. We owe it to her to find out what happened. I plan to do so—' I avoided her eye '—with or without my government.'

## 14

The senior team filed into my office. Brighter sunlight was now coming through the bay windows. I felt the dizziness from one too many coffees. We sat around the oval table, with its gold-plated legs.

Harry Parkinson looked like he hadn't been home, but then Parkinson always looked like he hadn't been home. He was, as usual, exuding nonchalant disrespect and disinterest. Was he really chewing gum? His ill-fitting suit was crumpled, his tie was slightly askew, and his grey shirt collar frayed. I had never owned a grey shirt. He had the detached look of a man desperately hoping not to be asked for a view.

Alem placed herself at one end of the oval table. She was wearing more make-up than usual. Her eyes were slightly puffy, but she sat in her chair, efficient and alert. Straining at the leash, I thought. She knows that this is her moment. How long before she tells London that I'm struggling? Maybe she already had.

Sophie sat next to Alem, glancing towards her every so often. She might one day tell her own embassy about this baptism of fire. Or maybe this was the moment where her career, her life, headed in another direction, the energy and enthusiasm gone. One evening of horror corroding her idealism, like metallic rust on an old battery.

I could not let that happen to Stephanie.

Emma was with her now and could help her start to process what she had seen. She could do that better than I ever could. The best way I could help my daughter was by finding whoever had killed Amina. By choosing to seek the truth rather than blindly tag along with a convenient consensus, I might also be able to hold us together as a family.

Maybe, when this was over, we could get up to the Welsh mountains. Let Stephanie be a girl again. Let Em be a wife again. If she would ever be ready to do so again. And I could take off the mask and be whatever I was again. An ex-excellency, a recovering ambassador. Pops.

Crawford, as always, remained standing until I had taken my seat. Whereas Parkinson looked like a man who had already had one too many adventures, Crawford was a man who had had one adventure too few.

'Morning all.' My tone was too jovial, a bit false. I course-corrected as I sat down and poured myself a glass of water. I was pleased to feel my hand steady.

'First, I want to thank you all for keeping the show on the road last night.'

Crawford and Alem nodded, Parkinson looked out of the window, Sophie stared at her papers.

There was no way to delay it further. Time was too short. The killer was still out there.

'Listen, I'm afraid I have news that won't help.'

I looked around the table. Parkinson had sat up, Crawford looked intrigued. Alem's eyes had narrowed.

'I fear that our government, and probably several others, are unwilling to find the truth about what happened here last night. They're looking for a convenient verdict so that they can get on with fighting these leaks. Amina Joshi's death is being treated as an inconvenience to be explained away. But I won't allow that.'

Silence. Sophie was pale. Was I letting my colleagues down at the crucial moment? Failing to do my duty?

But, in that moment, I knew my duty.

Alem's voice shook a little, but she steadied herself. 'We have a protocol to follow here, Edward. Amina's body is still upstairs. The UK police will be here soon, and they will do an initial forensics report before the French are back. That should reassure us that there is no cover-up. I checked with the Danish ambassador as you asked me. He had nothing more beyond intel that Pederson was brewing something, had linked up somehow with Amina Joshi. Our job now is to ensure our staff are in one piece and get some attention to those who saw the body. It would be quite normal in the circumstances for us to be traumatised and unable to think straight. That means me and Lenny, and, yes, you too, Edward.'

There would be no compassion in forcing me to take compassionate leave. I held back a flinch. 'We don't have time for that.'

Alem continued. 'And then we have to deal with the wider fallout. The overnight leaks are brutal. There are more on the way. And we have a growing number of people already blaming us. There should be no commentary from this building. We shut up until we know what to say.'

Parkinson was looking into the middle distance. He cleared his throat and addressed himself more to Alem than to me. 'We can't polish this turd. The French police say this is their investigation and that we – you – must do nothing more to disturb the scene. They've pretty much locked us in until we confirm that. They want us to waive diplomatic immunity for the whole embassy, including your family.'

I scowled at him. 'Amina's death happened on our turf. That makes it ours. She's become some sort of political football. But she is – was a real person. And we had promised to protect her.'

Parkinson snorted. 'When did it become our job to protect your family friends?'

Alem cut in before I could hit back. 'Edward, we're in uncharted waters. Deaths aren't meant to happen in embassies. The rules are designed for a different war. We have clear instructions from London to get this over with. Lump it back on the French before this all does even more damage to Britain's reputation. Or worse.' Her voice dropped slightly, and she avoided my eye. 'That's bigger than you.'

Parkinson saw his moment. 'I've had the Yanks on. They want to come and see the room. Get the grown-ups involved. They reckon there may be clues as to what leaks are coming out next. Clues that could save lives. They want to move fast to cauterise the problem and get some more dirt out on Amina Joshi. Whether she set all this up or was in with the wrong people, she had it coming. I always told you she was no angel. Anything we have. Time to create some fog around all this. I told them to come at twelve, once I'd checked with you.' He gestured towards me, but then let the arc of his arm take in Alem.

I looked at Parkinson. His puffy face had his usual air of disdain. I didn't believe for a second that he had agreed to ask his boss, if indeed he regarded me as his boss. No, the CIA would be on the way already. They might even be in the building by now. The usual tidemarks of perspiration were starting to spread from under his armpits like inkblots.

Or like bloodstains. Bloodstains on a floorboard. I jolted forward.

'No way.'

'What d'you mean?'

Parkinson was fully present now. He had an alertness to him that none of us had seen before. A cornered bear. Would he have been capable of killing Amina?

'Everything we do from now on will leak at some point. Turn the CIA back. Tell them to get out there and find the killer. I don't want anyone else anywhere near my – this – embassy, near my family.'

Parkinson glowered but said nothing. Crawford was smiling slightly to himself. Alem let out a frustrated sigh. Sophie was still transfixed by her screen.

But I felt back in control. 'We can't let the conspiracy theories kick too far in – politics abhors a vacuum. Penny will tell Stephanie and Emma to stay put upstairs. I need to speak to Aurelie at the Elysée. They need to start telling us what they know about the link between Amina and Pederson. I bow to no one in my distrust of the French, but we have to get back on the same side.'

I looked around the table. Max Crawford was nodding, but most of them were looking studiously at their notepads. I had lost Parkinson, if I ever had him. Alem was avoiding my eye. At the very moment I felt my conviction growing, I knew my authority was draining. I decided to steady the ship, get us back onto easier territory. I lowered my voice. 'Alem, we need to understand the link between what happened here and Magnus Pederson. Tell us more about the Dissenters. Keep it short.'

She opened a file. She had slept less than she was letting on. 'The original Dissenters were radical groups at the time of the English Civil War. They made a virtue of being ordinary people devoted to bringing down all forms of authority, property and law. They were about unrestrained liberty. This is the name now used by Pederson's internet anarchists. He's a devotee of Laurence Claxton, one of the original leaders of a group of Dissenters called the Ranters.'

Parkinson groaned audibly. Alem ignored him. 'Pederson wrote an article claiming that the church had created and then demonised the original Ranters in order to frighten people into not challenging the status quo. But then the Ranters turned on their backers. It became about bringing down the entire establishment. Pederson seems to have the same whacky mix of religion, zeal and grievance. But he's now able to weaponise the internet in their service. He's more dangerous than we all thought.'

'And so?' I was already worried that every minute lost could be the difference between grip and ineptitude, between truth and fog, between finding the killer and them striking again.

Parkinson was now up from the table and pacing irritably. 'Just another bunch of internet crackpots. Some offshoot of every other bonkers dark web project. But we can't underestimate them again. We thought they were destined to make as much of an impression on history as this Claxton guy. That it was all just cover for Pederson and his like to get paid and laid. Attention-grabbing pantomime. Nothing to see here. We were wrong. And it looks to me like Amina Joshi was helping them create this havoc. From under your roof. Don't you see how bad that looks, even before you decide to become an amateur Sherlock?'

'Steady, Harry.' Crawford had been silent throughout the meeting, but now leant across the table towards Parkinson. They held each other's gaze. Parkinson looked down at the table and shrugged.

My mobile phone went. Number withheld. Without thinking, I took the call.

Silence. But I had an acute awareness of a presence, an adversary, at the other end. More than an adversary, an enemy.

I found myself alert, every sense probing for danger, for answers.

'Who is this?' No answer.

I tried again. 'What do you want?'

The line was faint, but the words distinct. A high-pitched voice, the Danish vowels unmistakable. 'Be sure your sins will find you out.'

'Pederson?'

'Where were you when she needed you?'

'Amina? How?'

He laughed. 'Not Amina. You should have protected *her*.'

I felt the chill. 'Who? What do you mean? From what?'

'Be sure your sins will find you out.'

'Sins? What is it that you want?'

'Truth.'

More silence on the line, and then it was cut.

Alem looked at me quizzically. 'Pederson? What *does* he want?'

'I don't know. Revenge, I think.'

Penny opened the door from the outer office. She had never opened the door without knocking. I had never heard a tremor in her voice.

'Edward,' she stammered. 'Something terrible is happening outside.'

## 15

In Copenhagen, Pederson smiled to himself as he disconnected the call to Paris, removed the SIM card and snapped it between his bony fingers. Again, the pleasure in the moment before wielding the executioner's blade. Edward Barnes was now just a cameo in a much bigger story, but the pleasure in breaking him would make all the pain worthwhile.

Moments earlier, Pederson had pulled another cheap phone from the pile in front of him and punched in the number. The boy had answered immediately. Pederson could hear the demonstration outside the British embassy in the background. He had paused for a moment. The Roman emperor deciding a gladiator's fate.

'Your turn, Paulo.'

He had hoped to feel more from these moments of destiny. But it would do.

In the Rue du Faubourg St-Honoré, a man in his early twenties climbed on a makeshift stage. His eyes flamed with zeal and fear. His head was shaved, and his nose and lips were heavily pierced. He carried a heavy-looking rucksack, which he had placed carefully on the platform beside him. He wore tight jeans, heavy boots and a T-shirt with the picture of Joshi dying – the haunting, brutal, image that was now etched on every corner of the internet, and on placards, front pages and vulnerable minds. A digital death mask. Even through the haze of sedatives and terror, the man waited patiently for the cameras to finish setting up. Pederson had taught him to understand theatre.

'We have come here to remember a prophet.' Paulo's voice was low, each word intoned slowly, almost a chant. There were murmurs of approval.

Paulo's voice started to catch as he sped up. 'Amina was not an ordinary person. She knew that sacrifice was necessary for good to triumph over evil. To free us, she made the ultimate sacrifice. She did not do so lightly. She knew the risks she was running – and what her death would mean to those of us who loved her. But she persevered, so that we could enjoy a freedom that she could not. So that we could find our own courage, to take the actions within our power, to challenge inequality and authority.' He swallowed hard, his eyes scanning his companions. This was not meant to be easy. Focus on the words. Breathe.

The crowd was now silent. A dog barked. In the distance, there was the sound of a siren. The police looked on, bored and smoking, leaning on the metal fences they had erected.

His cheeks were flushed. 'Our parents have failed us. Let them now feel the pain they deserve. This place was Amina's Last Supper, where she shared her final words of peace. It was her Gethsemane, where she agonised over her death before she was betrayed. And this was her Calgary, where she died for us. This place of arrogant imperialism and vicious brutality will be the place from where we carry her message forward. Here she was murdered. But she will not have died in vain. We are all pilgrims to this place of loss.'

He let out a sob but steadied himself again. 'And here I end my pilgrimage.'

The crowd was becoming distracted. But a few protesters now exchanged looks and stiffened. Paulo trembled, trying to focus on Pederson's instructions to be strong, to be a man. He tried not to think about his mother. She would be proud, Pederson had told him. Would she?

A police radio crackled nearby.

And then Paulo lifted his rucksack and emptied it over his head. The viscous liquid soaked his torso and ran down his face. The crowd pulled back in shock. Only a few close companions drew closer, forming a ring around him and pulling out their camera phones.

In a Paris television studio, the producer screamed at her staff to cut away from the scene.

But there was no one to cut away from the internet. And the thousands who watched live would be joined by millions who watched later – again and again and again – as Paulo pulled a lighter from his pocket and set himself on fire. His face and shoulders were engulfed quickly in flame. For a moment he looked defiant, and then a sickening scream, choked after a few seconds. Several of those filming recoiled, lurched away. His hair and face burnt fast, the skin peeling away as the petrol ignited. But the charred body stayed upright for almost a minute at the centre of the blaze. Finally, it toppled slowly, like a headless statue. The flames lost their anger, leaving his lower torso and legs smouldering. One of the Dissenters was bent double, retching.

In the background, the Union flag fluttered red, white and blue in the wind.

In the warehouse in Copenhagen, Pederson turned away from the screen. He sighed deeply and rubbed his temples. The two women who had been tapping at keyboards stopped and looked up at him. He seemed suddenly deeply tired. But he drew himself back up and held out his arms wide.

'The bush burnt, and the Lord called out from it to Moses, "I have surely seen the affliction of my people and have heard their cry by reason of their taskmasters; for I know their sorrows. And I am come down to deliver them."'

83

How was Barnes reacting? When the initial shock faded, would he realise, yet, that this was a declaration of war? There were two kinds of execution. The swift, clinical death. Paulo and Amina had been lucky to get a death like that. And then there was the slow, painful, lingering death, in which everything you loved most was destroyed around you. That was what Edward Barnes deserved.

Pederson scowled and scratched deeply at the rash on the back of his neck. 'Okay, enough melodrama. Let's get back to work. Use the wide-angle photo, the one with the flag.'

Outside the embassy, the fire had burnt itself out. Part of a leg was left unburnt. The air was heavy with the smell of charred flesh. The rucksack stood to one side like a long-neglected gravestone in a country churchyard. The wind blew through the ash. There were more sirens in the distance. Those protesters still part of a makeshift ring around him let their arms fall and looked at each other, suddenly unsure what to do next.

And then the horror turned to rage. Someone had to be blamed. They joined others in the crowd, hurling stones and bits of debris over the embassy wall. Some had come to honour, some to bury, some to mourn, some to burn, some to break.

Now was the time to break.

## 16

We stared at the screen in silence. Crawford had moved to the window. His instincts were kicking in.

'This will get ugly. We don't have enough security on the gate. They could be in this room in minutes. They could come over the wall or around the back gate, behind the tennis court.'

I bit my lip. Angus Green had told me about the time the IRA daubed red paint across the gates. The staff had suddenly realised how exposed the building was. I had gone out to Tehran to help re-open the embassy after it had been trashed. People's jackets had still been on the backs of the chairs.

We had to protect the staff. I turned to Alem.

'Make sure Redwood is staying put in her room. Security inside and outside her door. Speak to Salins. Demand we get some more protection on the gate. But we hold our ground. I'm not handing the initiative to these fantasists. Or to the French.'

Alem tried Salins, but there was no reply. She frowned. 'Gone to ground. The French can see this one is a hand grenade. And someone has just pulled the pin.'

She moved closer, her voice dropping to a whisper. 'Edward, we're way out of our comfort zone. I'm calling the crisis management team in London. We need to get everyone out, including you.'

She glanced at Parkinson for reinforcement and then down at the ground. 'Especially you.'

'No.' I turned to her, fists clenched by my sides, feeling my anger grow. 'If we go, we tell everyone that we have given up. We leave the embassy and all it stands for at the risk of being overrun, vandalised. We are no safer out there. And we lose any chance of getting the truth about what happened to Amina.'

Sophie was staring at the screen, her eyes wide. 'The Dissenters' page has the footage of the burning body next to the picture of Amina Joshi. The photo of her used by *Time*, the wounded martyr on a crucifix. The headline is: *And here I end my pilgrimage*. His name was Paulo. He was the son of the Italian economics minister.'

I knew the minister. Decent, earnest, hard working. I'd always thought him somehow out of place. What would he now be going through? The story of Abraham and Isaac had kept me awake again the previous night. Yet this was the son betraying the father.

Meanwhile, the revolution now had its pin-up prophets. Whether or not Amina had chosen to be part of Pederson's insurrection, the insurrection had chosen her.

Crawford had been looking into the street, his shoulders tense. He now interjected, 'I'm asking your permission that my team carry our firearms.'

Alem was aghast. 'Surely it hasn't come to that? These are diplomatic premises. Can't we wait for help and let them decide what's best? Before your boys and their toys get carried away? What if a peaceful demonstrator is hurt? We become the target.'

Crawford spoke without the usual chummy deference. 'We're already the target. The firearms buy us time. We'll need it.'

At the gate we heard a window smash. There were stones coming over the wall, into the courtyard. So much for French protection. Years earlier, Margaret Thatcher had stood there and announced that she would not resign. 'I fight on, and I fight to win.' But she had already lost. The initiative was elsewhere. The decision had been taken away from her.

I felt the world start to spin. It was like the slow-motion fall of a prize fighter caught off guard, gasping for air and groping for support. I had to wonder: had Thatcher felt the same?

Sophie was scrolling through the contents of the embassy's social media accounts, her face screwed up in distaste. 'Already thousands more comments, praising Amina and accusing you and the British government of murder. Page after page of conspiracy. There are riots kicking off in Delhi, and violent protests outside the White House. The Dissenters are calling on people to attack British embassies. A fourteen-year-old set himself on fire in Stockholm, but the police managed to save him. He was also wearing Amina's face on his T-shirt.'

I was acutely aware that my every judgement would soon be examined by a hostile media armed with anger. And hostile parliamentary committees armed with hindsight. The murder of my wife's friend, suicide at my embassy gates, the humiliation of Ray Griffiths: what sins was I now being punished for? I looked around the team. When would they say I had lost control of the agenda? Lost control of myself?

I had moved too slowly in Afghanistan, as they awaited the clearance to mount the hostage rescue. I had wanted more time to balance the risks, more information. Her eyes would always haunt me. But it was the executioner who had seemed to stare even deeper into me as he made the cut.

'You have my permission, Crawford. But no shooting unless there is absolutely no choice.' He nodded. His eyes were alert, the laughter lines less wrinkled than usual. Alem threw up her arms. It was my turn to avoid her eye.

The British embassy is home to the only grass tennis court in Paris, the pride of the embassy social calendar and for years the best incentive to coax busy presidential advisers over for a drink and a gossip.

Kane, who had grown up on tennis courts, played the odd match against Parkinson on it. And it was from here that the inquiry later found that Harry Parkinson had texted him to say that I had rejected the CIA request for access.

Kane had messaged back, in terms the inquiry chair found 'inappropriately jaunty'. *One body is unfortunate, but two looks careless.* He had then texted Josh Packer, the president's chief of staff. *Access denied by his excellency. Man overboard?*

Harry Parkinson had always scoffed at the outrage in the chanceries of Europe when Amina Joshi had revealed the extent to which Washington was spying on them. The only thing that had surprised him was their surprise. In the intelligence world there were no permanent allies.

Packer picked up the message immediately and sauntered over to the direct line to 10 Downing Street. He'd pull his pinstriped prick of a counterpart out of whatever meeting he was having and get the Brits to remember who was in charge. 'Get me James Sheriff, I'll wait.'

## 17

I knew time was short. Once Crawford and his team were positioned near the entrance to the residence, I slipped through the gate at the far end of the garden that led to the back of the Elysée. Napoleon used to come through it to see one of his mistresses, a maid of his sister's.

I had been trained never to go into a meeting without a clear idea of what I wanted at the end. If you're not writing the menu, you're on it. I needed Aurelie Lafont to deploy security immediately. But I also had to ensure that they couldn't use the suicide of the boy outside as the pretext to get us out and take over the investigation. I wanted to know what their intelligence was saying about who had really murdered Amina Joshi, and what was really driving Magnus Pederson. And whether they knew yet who had placed the camera that had recorded it. It was still unclear to me why any government would have wanted to kill her, however much they disliked her. So why the cover-up? And why risk triggering the inevitable backlash? Unless they felt it was all directed my way?

Events were moving too fast. I had gone from an unknown diplomat to the centre of a global conspiracy in fewer than twelve hours. A slightly sleepy embassy had been transformed into a murder scene. A family trying to stay together was living through the moments that might finally break them. And Pederson was now directly threatening me. We weren't writing the menu, we were on it.

I knew the way to Aurelie's office all too well. Her PA got up too late to get between me and her door, and I pushed through. Aurelie was standing at the window, watching the demonstrations in the street below. If she was surprised to see me she didn't show it. She half-heartedly suggested a coffee, but I waved it away.

'I had always hoped that after the pandemic the fear of germs would be the ultimate deterrent for the mob. Sadly not. You've come about extra security? Don't panic. It is being deployed now at the front. The president thought it would be fun to watch *les rosbifs* panic, but I reminded him that France can't be seen to fail to protect visiting excellencies.'

We listened for a moment to the sound of sirens. Two armed people carriers were moving slowly through the crowd, forcing them to fall back. The French state was swinging back into action.

'Anything else?' She had retained the aloof detachment of her more traditional predecessor. I had once asked him if we could call each other by our first names. '*Pourquoi?*' he had countered, icily.

Diplomacy at this level was adversarial, full combat. The French had always been worthy adversaries. Would this be the slow lingering death, or the shot between the eyes? Aurelie smiled. She had green eyes with the most extraordinary eyelashes. 'You look tired, Edward.'

So, it was to be slow and lingering.

I didn't have time to play. 'I'm not bad, in the circumstances, especially if your people can keep the revolting Paris mob at bay. I've not yet been summoned home to explain how I let the world's most famous fugitive die on my watch. But I'm not going to let this go. Someone killed Amina Joshi. They're still out there. That makes them a threat to all of us. And there's clearly a connection between these Danish anarchists and the mess outside.'

Aurelie was wearing a sheer white blouse. With her back to the window there was a moment where it had gone almost translucent in the sunlight. I quickly looked back at her face. She was impassive.

Aurelie moved back into conspiratorial mode. She leant forward. Intimacy re-established. She gestured for us both to sit.

I looked at my watch. 'Aurelie, a crime has been committed in my house. On UK territory. I think that your people have already disturbed vital evidence. I need to know what you think happened.'

She uncrossed her legs and fixed me with an intimidating glare. How much younger was she? A decade? It was hard to say. I realised that I knew nothing about her outside the office. We could trade intimate stories, gossip and even mildly flirtatious banter. But life beyond politics was of course *la vie privée*. Separate, not to be touched, the French way. I could only enjoy the speculation. No doubt she would think even the speculation ridiculous.

'Crime?'

'Yes, crime. I don't believe Amina killed herself. Much as everyone seems to have wanted her to. She had been writing some kind of final post. But it wasn't finished. Someone got to her first. My problem is that every government disliked her, including yours. Why was she such a threat?'

She nodded vigorously. 'We despised her. And if she was indeed involved in these leaks, we had good reason. But surely you are not saying anyone hated her enough to murder her?'

'Look, I don't yet see what Amina was doing with Magnus Pederson. But everyone knows that the Dissenters are lining up the grenades, deciding which pin to pull first. Those phone transcripts are going to smash up your president's relationships with his counterparts. My lot are clearly terrified. The US are kicking off. I assume you are too. Amina was increasingly convinced she was some kind of prophet. So are that rabble outside. That threatened someone. What else did they have on the president?'

But she was not playing by my rules either. 'It seems you are enjoying your fifteen minutes of fame? I've never seen you this passionate.'

'Far from it, Aurelie. I'm as keen for this to be over as anyone.' I gestured towards the street. What did Pederson have on me? Had I failed to protect Emma? Steph? Why did he care?

Aurelie was silent. She pondered a moment. Would it be a graceful withdrawal? Or the point of no return? She crossed the Rubicon.

'Edward, I've always admired you. But you have never been cynical enough for this business.'

I felt a chill. I had received some savage beatings from Aurelie in the past. But this was different. There was no playfulness to the stiletto she was elegantly pressing into my forehead.

'So, enough, Mr Ambassador. It is time to try something else. I have just spoken to Salins. We have consulted our lawyers. After reflecting, we are now agreed that the suicide happened on sovereign British soil and is for the British government to handle from here. That's what you wanted, yes? You broke it, you own it. We will protect the embassy, as required. But inside it, you're on your own. *Bonne chance.*'

She was enjoying my shock. 'But Aurelie, your people have already been in. You need to tell me what you found.'

She smiled at the corners of her mouth. 'We found that this was suicide.'

'How will you explain that to the world outside? They don't trust us. It sounds like they're right.'

She curled her lip. 'Amina Joshi looked for attention. She had a martyr complex, saw herself as some kind of sacrificial lamb for a new world order.'

'And we let her killers get away with killing an innocent activist?'

Aurelie was steelier again now. 'She was a wolf in sheep's clothing. I wanted to tell you that – again – last night. You were wrong to take her in, wrong to trust her. You said yourself that there is some kind of suicide note. Everything she did was preparation for a glorious death, the ultimate act of freedom. Why do you think she took refuge in the first place? Are you too arrogant to see you have been played? She planned all this with Pederson, and whatever other surprises are coming at us. Salins will give your Poirots the evidence to conclude the inquest quickly. We will say that we fully support your conclusions, assuming you make the correct ones. We can then move on. You don't want your embassy to become a sort of shrine. Or—' She looked again at the street and spoke with menace. 'Some sort of target.'

I closed my eyes, trying to control myself. Slowly and with the rage mounting inside me, I stood. 'And what about the truth, Aurelie? You believed in that once. Doesn't that matter to you?'

Aurelie got up too, adjusting her hair in the mirror. 'Truth is an increasingly complicated concept, Edward. The more important thing is what you say to the public. And I hope that we are all agreed on what that will be.'

'Do you never worry that we have become the problem, Aurelie? America, France, Britain?'

'To some of us, you always were.'

She rose and walked towards her desk. I knew my way out.

## 18

Outside the embassy, French riot police and military had started to restore some order in the Rue du Faubourg St-Honoré and were clearing the streets. The Versaces and Guccis were being boarded up, Paris protecting privilege as ever. Protesters who had circled their man as he self-immolated were being taken away for questioning. Some sobbed. Others stared ahead, high with purpose.

I opted to stick to the back route again. The internet had ensured that my face was better known than it had been twenty-four hours ago. To most observers I was responsible. I removed my tie and ducked my head, staying close to the wall at the back of the residency. There was a handful of tourists in the street, apparently oblivious to what was happening on the parallel road.

The rock hit me on the back of the head with a dull thud and sent me forward onto my knees. I felt a dull, heavy pain. I reached back and felt the blood. I looked around, dazed and blinking.

Suddenly they were around me. Three of them. Faces contorted with rage. One had picked up the rock and was clutching it in his right hand while his left went to grip my lapels. His fingers smelt of weed and grime. I swung at him, but his companion blocked my arm and pushed me up against the wall.

They held back my head. They had obviously already realised that I was an embassy employee. Now they recognised the face they had seen all over the internet, the man blamed for Amina Joshi's murder. There was a look of triumph in the eyes of the man with the rock. He had lines cut into his eyebrow. I braced myself for the next blow. I thought of Stephanie.

And then the back gate opened behind me, and Max Crawford was there. He shot a pistol in the air. A flurry of fists. The man with the rock crumpled. The other two backed off, and then ran.

Crawford bundled me up, and half-carried, half-shoved me through the embassy back gate. I stood, trying to catch my breath as he grinned back at me. The gun was at his side. 'Get Lenny to get some dressing on that, Ambassador, it's just a gash. Why the hell were you outside?'

'I had to see the Elysée. The French are backing off, saying it's all our problem now. But I'm convinced they saw Amina Joshi as some kind of threat, beyond these leaks, and I don't trust them. Either way, they're leaving it to us. For better or for worse. And Pederson is still coming for us, for me.'

Crawford whistled softly. 'Be careful what you wish for, Ambassador.'

I grinned. I looked at the blood on my hand and felt again the wound on my head. My heart rate was steadying. 'This feels more like your world than mine.'

'War is long periods of tedium punctuated by short periods of adrenalin and violence. Diplomacy seems to be going the same way.' He smiled through gritted teeth. 'But we've secured the building.'

'Whatever happens, Max, please keep Steph safe.'

We went quickly back inside. After Lenny had dressed the wound, I climbed the stairs to the residence. I was anxious to check on Emma and Steph, and I wanted another look at Amina's room before the UK police crashed through it.

I stumbled through the door to our apartment. Max had a man outside Steph's room. Emma wasn't there, and I felt a surge of anger that she might be exposing herself to danger. But the mess was a comfort. In contrast to the deliberately intimidating grandeur of the embassy and formal areas of the residence, our private flat was small and slightly run-down. The kitchen was tiny – we only really used it for snacks or at the weekend. The living room had a small drinks trolley, a shabby sofa and an even shabbier armchair. Any formal guests would always be greeted in the shimmering *Salon Jaune* downstairs. Up here we could almost revel in the scruffiness of it. Emma in particular was adamant that it should stay this way. Her refuge. Mine, sometimes, too.

I scooped out some ice, poured a couple of fingers of whisky and moved towards the kitchen. I started to rummage through the bread bin. A couple of chunks of slightly dry baguette, but still edible. In the fridge there was some ham. I tore off a chunk of over-ripe Brie. A couple of cherry tomatoes. I piled the whole lot onto a plate and took it into the living room.

I looked out at the street. There was now a heavy French police presence. The demonstrations looked to have subsided. The devotees were lighting candles. Some were playing guitars. They seemed more peaceful for now. 'And here I end my pilgrimage.'

But my mind was not at peace. I had to straighten out some facts.

There was no doubt Amina Joshi had bled to death. The gash to her neck had been deep. If she somehow did it herself, she had even more courage than we had realised. Someone must have helped her. And the knife that killed her bore the embassy crest. Did that mean the killer had needed to arrive unarmed to avoid detection? Or was it someone who knew their way around the embassy? Either way, Steph, Em, my staff were all still at risk.

And Steph had said that Lenny had delivered some kind of recording equipment. Surely he could not possibly have been involved? If we found who had made the film, we would find whoever had killed Amina Joshi. That led us straight back to

Pederson, whose disciples had so swiftly and enthusiastically adopted her martyrdom.

Aurelie had not been surprised when I mentioned a suicide note. The French must either have had intelligence that she planned to kill herself, or they expected her to be killed. Everyone needed this to be a suicide, or for the Dissenters, a resurrection.

But I was convinced that it was a murder. And there were plenty of people with a motive. Whatever Amina had become involved with, I had enough respect for her – and for Emma's friendship with her – to want to avoid a cover-up. Besides, with the eyes of the world on us, a cover-up would never succeed: I would always be seen as guilty of obscuring the truth.

I took another swig of whisky and went down the corridor to Amina Joshi's room. I wanted another look at what she had been working on, before the forensics teams arrived. Perhaps it would be evidence she intended to kill herself. Or something that could tell us who had wanted her dead.

Steeling myself, I pushed the door open. Half a day after her death, the room now smelt of decay and dry blood. Her body lay in the same position, still covered by the white sheet. I tried to stop my stomach lurching and looked away.

I placed my handkerchief over my mouth and nose. Amina had used the space as some kind of recording studio, no doubt with the kit that Lenny had delivered. She was issuing regular videos, and another must have been planned. Had she herself been recording a suicide after all? A final act of eye-catching theatre of the kind that Aurelie had described, and Pederson had maybe demanded?

If she had not been recording, then the killer must have stood where I was. Had Amina known them? Did I? I closed my eyes and tried to visualise her last movements.

I was about to go back to the desk when it hit me. Senses alert and my heart beating, I looked back at the body. Her arm protruded from beneath the sheet. Beside it still lay the knife. The blood was drying on the blade. It was still pointing away from the body, next to Amina's right hand.

I retched again. There was now no embassy crest on the blade. Someone had changed the knife.

## 19

I headed back towards my office, anxious to find Max Crawford. The French police could have changed the knife last night. Or maybe the killer was still in the building.

Could it even be one of us? Harry Parkinson seemed the obvious choice, if the spooks were cleaning up for the Americans. But I could not imagine him having the physical courage to go through with it. Whoever it was, we needed to move fast to identify them. If they were actively concealing evidence, they might be a threat to anyone who had been in that room.

Only one person could be ruled out: Amina herself.

Penny was waiting for me in the office with two Northern Irish detectives. When Alem had passed on the instruction to what the Foreign Office persisted in calling 'non-essential' staff to leave, Penny had ignored it. She was essential and no one would have the courage to suggest otherwise. One of the detectives was looking at the floor. I felt the other examine me through narrow eyes.

'Edward. These gentlemen are ready to inspect and clear the room. Crawford is going to show them around.'

I don't know how long Crawford had been standing there, observing me. He nodded in solidarity as I noticed him. A good man to have in the same trench.

'We do need to get forensics in, Ambassador. You can trust these men. Head feeling better?'

I had forgotten about the blow. Penny looked at me, startled, noticing the wound. 'Are you all right?'

I composed myself, trying to imprint on my mind everything I had seen in the room, before it was too late. There was no time for explanations. 'Of course. Welcome to you both. We are anxious to understand what happened. Please let me have your thoughts as quickly as possible.'

Crawford took them off, the hint of a wink at me. Alem passed them at the door to my office. I had to buy time in order to find out what had happened to the knife that killed Joshi. But I also needed to regain control of the situation, prepare for whatever came next. We were letting Pederson play us all.

Alem was uncharacteristically flustered. 'Crawford told me about your head. What were you thinking?'

I waved the question aside. She paused. Did I detect a flicker of triumph?

'Edward, it's calmed down outside. There was no need for Crawford to get all macho. I just called the FCO again, to report that the UK detectives are in place. And I've updated Redwood. She's pretty angry that you're not leaving this to the French.'

'We don't have that option any more, if we ever had it. What does she *want*, though?'

Alem rolled her eyes. 'She's her usual cautious self. Doesn't want to get too far into the story until she can do so on her terms. Ideally never.'

'That's why we can't wait for her. But whatever I do, you need to cover your back. Take a note of your conversation with Redwood. We don't need both of us getting thrown under a bus. Get Sophie to call Jacques at *Le Soir*. Tell him that Lynn Redwood is expressing strong solidarity with the embassy, and with me. We'll get him more later if he plays it straight. Even better if he can get someone else's fingerprints on it.'

Alem looked uncertain. I gestured to her to get a move on. 'He leaks. You brief. I am committed to transparency. You'll get used to it.'

Alem had her hands on her hips. 'And then what?'

'I need to get Redwood back onside. I need her to keep London off my back and share whatever she knows about who might have wanted Amina dead.'

Alem raised her eyebrows. 'Negotiations, an old UN colleague once told me, are seven hundred days of failure and one day of success.'

'Maybe. But I don't have seven hundred days.'

Redwood was standing when I entered her room. She did not turn.

'You seem to have decided to keep me in the dark while you lose complete control of the situation,' she said, steely.

Fleming had in front of him a huge folder of papers, what looked like several phones and a look of exhaustion and adrenalin. I gave him a smile of solidarity. A wan, thin, bloodless smile back. He had the pale, androgynous aloofness that the French loved in Brits. There were bookshops full of their curious *bandes dessinées*, cartoon books to us but for adults, packed with English characters we no longer knew. Butlers and high teas. The best of enemies.

Would he sit here one day as ambassador, dealing with another set of screw-ups? Surely nothing like this.

Okay. Round One.

'So, Jack, do you need anything? Wi-Fi codes all working up there? Hungry? Thirsty? I'm sure you have a mountain of work to get through. I'll ask Lenny to get you properly set up.'

Redwood spun around immediately. What passed for a smile at the corner of her mouth where the lipstick was sharper. Had she applied some before I arrived? Maybe for me? Eyes piercing, she said, 'No need. Jack will stay with us.'

Round One lost. There was no way they would risk leaving me alone with her.

It wasn't that I had wanted or expected any discussion of the past, of our past. That was the least of my concerns in the circumstances. But I had hoped that we could find some form of connection again, a sense that we were in this together, some point of empathy. Redwood had signalled that this was not to be the case. The empathy had long gone.

I might be in a worse place than I had realised.

I joined her at the window and we looked out over the residence garden, past the art installation that my predecessor had installed, his last desperate effort to look modern.

Redwood turned to me, quietly seething. 'I shouldn't need to ask. But tell me everything.'

I was clipped, efficient, ambassadorial again. 'As I've said, Foreign Secretary, I don't think we're right to waive jurisdiction. But in any case, after the protester burnt himself outside, the Elysée have just told me they are leaving it to us after all. Our detectives are here, but their remit is only to do the forensics, arrange the autopsy and collect any evidence. No 10 are still saying it's for the French to investigate. That leaves no one to actually try and find the killer, let alone the truth.'

Redwood listened impassively. I inhaled hard. Summoned up my courage.

'Lynn, you know my view. I won't accept that it was a suicide. I don't believe the French on that. As I told you earlier, if no one else will, I'm going to find what happened. We owe it to Amina. But we also owe it to ourselves.'

Redwood paused. The piercing look with a slight flicker of insecurity, that nagging fear of being found out. And the fact I had used her first name again.

'I'm confident that the French will handle it. Why take these risks? These leaks give us more than enough to deal with.' Her eyes hooded. Her tone was withering.

I looked down the garden, towards the back gate. Now or never. Most people leave their song unsung.

'But Foreign Secretary, we both know this is bigger than just who killed Amina Joshi. There's more to all this than dodging blame. You thought that once.' I kept my eyes away from her. And from Fleming. I didn't need to see their reaction.

Too much. Redwood glowered at me over her angular glasses with mounting incredulity. She did disapproval better than anyone I had ever known. I felt like I was back at school, ten years old, trying to defend a lost homework assignment. Her heels were making small holes in the carpet.

I felt the distance increasing in the silences, the empty spaces between us.

'Edward, I dislike idealism, especially from my ambassadors. We need to get back to the basics here. To do our jobs. To focus on what matters to our security, and to manage the media fallout of this whole crisis. I need to be more confident that you're going to help us with that. You're making the wrong enemies.'

The look again. A moment of solidarity. 'Sometimes, you have to pick a side.'

We sat for a moment in awkward silence. Our eyes flitted towards the garden, anywhere but the present. We were two punched-out boxers, or two worn-out lovers. I wondered for a moment what our twenty-year-old selves would make of us. I had said too much already.

Jack Fleming was distracted by his secure Blackberry. It had, as always, been flashing and vibrating away as we spoke, its own ecosystem of frantic activity. He now sensed his moment.

'Boss, there are more kids trying to kill themselves. All in these Amina Joshi T-shirts. This is spreading, dangerously. And I've just had something in from No 10. From James Sheriff. They've been speaking to the White House. They want you back in London today.'

My two rules when I had been a private secretary. Never bluff, and always hold something back. The constant need to explain complex situations with little information. Fleming would go far.

Redwood groaned as she looked at me and then back to Fleming. At that moment, perhaps No 10 was the one thing she loathed even more than me. I felt a fleeting alliance of interests but then the steel returned. 'But what about my statement? Getting a grip, calming it all down? What about Barnes?'

Fleming had made sure that he had the answers before he had the questions. I wondered for a moment where he had been the previous night. Nothing and no one could be ruled out.

'We were moving too slowly for them.' A glance at me, of gentle accusation rather than complicity. 'Sorry, my phone is slow. I need to close some windows. You need to come back too, Edward. Urgent meetings with No 10 and Sir Angus.'

Fleming's tone was brusque, but he at least had the decency to look awkward. 'I don't get the sense it's a request. James Sheriff sounds adamant. You know what he's like.'

Redwood and I looked at each other. A flicker of sympathy, somewhere? A moment of shared fate. And then it was gone again. She had stamped it out. I was back in the headmistress's study. The best of enemies.

'Barnes. You're not a detective. You're not a philosopher or an activist. You are, at least for now, an ambassador. Get a grip.'

I left the room. What was it Fleming had said?

Too many windows open.

I needed to close some windows.

And Redwood, through the ice and the sparkling water and the regret. What was it?

Sometimes, you have to pick a side.

I had already picked mine.

## 20

I went back up to the flat, anxious to check on Emma and Steph. Pederson's threat was like a constant presence. Emma was dozing in a chair, and I thought about not rousing her. It had been years since I last watched her sleep.

But I didn't know when, or if, I would be back. I took a deep breath. I had no idea whether she would be relieved or angry that I was going to London. She turned towards me and opened an eye.

I stroked the hair from her cheek. 'You once told me that every wrinkle told a story. Life lines. I fear I might be creating a few more.'

She sat up, properly awake now, her head cocked to one side. More and more she looked at me in a way I could not read.

'You'll always be part of all of them, good or bad.'

'Em, I've been summoned back to London. They don't want to investigate Amina's murder. I can't allow that. We owe it to her. I owe it to you.'

She looked at me for several moments, her eyes narrowed. I wanted her to be proud. But instead there was a characteristic flash of disappointment and an uncharacteristic flash of anger.

'D'you not think this was a decision we should take together?'

I had never before felt her capable of violence. A tigress defending her family.

'Why d'you have to make this our problem? What about us?'

I hesitated. There was so much to say. 'But this is about us, whether we like it or not. Pederson seems to have some kind of personal issue with me. Whoever killed Amina is a threat to Steph too. She saw the room. She's on the camera. And so whoever wants this covered up might be a threat to her. And it's surely better for all of us that this is resolved. She needs to move on. We need to move on.'

She sighed deeply. 'D'you remember standing together at the school gates? Twenty years ago, is it? We didn't move for minutes after Steph had disappeared down the long corridor towards her classroom. I felt such a sense of hollowness, of a part of me having gone.'

I remembered it well. That strange mixture of pride and fear, of love and anxiety. The way Stephanie had looked in the car – cheeks slightly pinker than usual, slightly stiff in the tartan skirt and blue blouse, hair neatly tied back.

Em continued. 'Even then she was the most composed of us. Almost as if she understood that her job was to put us at ease, not the other way round. You kept fiddling nervously with the radio dial. Filling the space with your usual chatter. And all the while I was feeling the time slip through our fingers.'

The recollection was suddenly immediate. 'I remember the rush of the goodbye. And then silence, and we were alone. I remember you putting a hand on mine and moving me back to the car.'

I also remembered stealing one last look down the bustling corridor, full of life, colour, movement. And yet somehow empty. On the drive home we had pieced together fragments of conversation from the morning, reassuring ourselves that she would be fine, that she would cope wonderfully. Wondering how we would be fine, how we would cope.

And then the effort to summon the energy for the day, to keep on moving forward. A sense of every parting taking Steph further from me. And every parting taking me a step closer to the moment when I would leave her forever.

I breathed deeply. 'I remember waiting for her to come back down the corridor for a last hug. Hoping that she had forgotten something.' I smiled at Em. 'I would have waited there all day.'

Pederson's words were still gnawing at me. 'Em, did we protect Steph? Have I been there for her?'

Em was looking closely at me. 'Steph'll be fine. And you'll be fine. But this. All this.' The arc of her arm took in the door to the embassy, the body in the guestroom and decades of distance. 'We might not. You have to move on, leave it to them. Let them tidy it away. I'll always miss Amina, but maybe she sought this life, even this death, in some way. And maybe it's better for her and us that the world moves on.'

'I don't think it's that simple any more. Pederson has something on me. I don't know what. They can't protect me, us, from that.'

'How bad can it be?' She was elsewhere.

'Em, what's going on? What's worrying you?'

She fixed her eyes on a space above my head. 'Look, there are good days and bad days in a relationship. Good years and bad years. I was genuinely happy for you when you got Paris. But I used to see you more when you were back and forth to Afghanistan.' I looked to see if her mouth would twitch, if this was a half-joke. It didn't. It wasn't.

I'd made mistakes in Afghanistan. They were mine to carry. The stakes were high. We were operating under huge pressure. I'd always wondered if I would have called it right with her around. When I'd then gone to Copenhagen as ambassador, she had seen it as a joint project. She never said it, but she had found the work soulless and empty. What was it all for? Certainly nothing that could be measured.

'But we've always found a way to operate in the same space, to coexist?' I put my hands on her shoulders, but they were taut.

'Diplomats meet so many people. That's the job. We form relationships. But how many meaningful friendships can you really have as you pass through people's lives and move on? You've always been at the centre of my life.' Yet somehow each new relationship had left me less time for her. The relationship that should have mattered most.

She had hesitated before deciding to come to Paris. I guess now that we had both known it was make or break. And we had been pretty happy at moments, including in a strange way when Amina first turned up.

'Look, I know you loathe the whole Paris circuit. That's fine. And you know I think it's great you've found something at the bookshop.' More than the stubborn, practical devotion that I had tried to offer, and that she had stopped trying to reciprocate.

'Ed, surely even you've noticed that everything has changed?'

Maybe she wondered if I really minded. I needed to fight harder. I had never really fought for the things that mattered most to me.

But she was reading my mind. 'This isn't about Amina, really. I'm not asking you to change, Ed. I love your willingness to trust people, to believe the best of people, your certainty that the world will turn in your direction. But your wonderful Labrador enthusiasm isn't enough for this.'

Over the years, we had found a rhythm for rebuilding after rows. It was the lack of anger that should have shown me that this one would be different.

'I'd happily walk away from all the pomp and circumstance, Em. You know that? I'm ready to do that now, to help find what happened to Amina.'

I was at the school gate again, hoping the chapter hadn't ended. You don't know what you've got until you lose it.

She was silent for a moment and then spoke softly. 'I know that.'

Because that was how she had always felt about me.

And then she quietly rose and walked away.

## 21

The Paris air was heavier and beyond the Eiffel Tower the clouds were pregnant with rain. The city – dusty and soporific – needed it. As I dressed for the journey, I looked out over the dew glistening on the garden. There was mist behind the roof of Le Grand Palais.

This was a view to savour. But I knew it might be the last time for me. The embassy had been my fortress. No longer. But at least I had a chance to get London back onside, to make my case on why it mattered that Amina Joshi had been murdered. I could show them that this wasn't a solo mission, that it was in our national interest to get to the truth about who was responsible. A shabby cover-up was not going to hold. They had to see that it would play into the hands of those that wanted to exploit all this, especially Pederson.

And I had to buy time before Pederson moved again against me. I had to assume that any telephone calls were fair game, probably my emails too. Some student escapade? The pot? My fatal mistake in Afghanistan? Policies that would look bad with the benefit of hindsight? Maybe a staff complaint? I'd already seen what he had done to Ray and so many others. But somehow this felt more personal. And who apart from Amina had I failed to protect?

Alem saw us off. She would continue as *Chargé d'Affaires* while I was gone, and then who knew? I had tried to lighten the moment. 'The French still own the language of diplomacy, even as its power ebbs away.'

And as my power ebbed away, Alem had offered a half smile. I wished I had longer to talk to her about being in charge. *Walk down the middle of the corridor, don't let them see your shoulders slump, don't tell them they are great but that they can be great.* But her mind was elsewhere, and time was short.

Crawford had suggested I not go. Why the trip? Why now? Hold the ground. He sensed danger. He was right. 'Will you still be our ambassador when you get back?'

I tried to turn my grimace into a grin. 'Being an ambassador is like owning a boat: the first and last days are best.'

Lynn Redwood walked carefully down the embassy steps. A career built on not falling over. The gravel crackled under the wheels of the Jag.

Crawford insisted on coming with us, in case we ran into more demonstrators. He removed the British flag from the front of the Jag and tucked it into the glove compartment. He insisted we wore our seat belts, but he did not.

The drive to the Gare du Nord was not the best view of Paris. Traffic jams, grubbiness and the growing number of *sans domicile fixe* – the French didn't call them homeless, just without a fixed home. It made it somehow more romantic – vagabonds and hobos. Like diplomats, just with a little more alcohol and a little less entitlement.

Outside, several of the luxury shops were boarded up. The French guards were still out in force and several stood to attention as we passed. Otherwise the streets were quietening, the road blocked off to traffic, and no sign now of the protesters or Amina's wretched pilgrims.

I closed my eyes for a moment as we turned towards the Seine and raced through the early morning traffic. We had opted for no outriders – move low and fast, as Crawford said. As I sank further into my seat, I noticed that my fists were clenched, and tried to release some of the tension that was building up again. I had told Ray Griffiths that the first thing we learn is how to breathe. That's what we need to return to when facing crisis or pressure. I would seek him out as soon as we were safe. He needed to breathe, as Pederson destroyed his family. So did I, as I tried to stop him destroying mine.

Paris was lumbering and ponderous. What had yesterday evening felt playful and full of potential now felt closed and sinister. The city seemed to be carrying on its business, blissfully unaware of the death that had come to my house, and to my life. But then this was the city of the guillotine. Just one more severed head. The blood always washed away, into the darkness of the Seine and out of the city. Life went on.

Lynn Redwood's shoulders were high, tense. Her chin jutted towards the window as she looked at Paris flying by. She didn't want the conversations we needed. Not in the car, probably never. There was a small, black handbag on the seat between us. Thatcher had described her handbag as a weapon. Redwood's was more like a protective shield. From me and the world. I tried not to look at it.

'Edward, we have much more to discuss once we arrive. This situation is of real concern.' The steel again.

So much to discuss. An activist bleeding to death. The governments of the free world turning their backs. A body on fire at the embassy gate. All this on our turf. 'This situation'? What a euphemism for two corpses on my doorstep in twenty-four hours. And 'real concern'. Ghastly platitudes. What she really meant was that her job was threatened too. The only question for her was how she could use me to be her firewall.

'We do indeed, Foreign Secretary.'

Redwood looked again out of the window. The car had stopped by a light, and a cafe on the corner was packed with young couples, staring into each other's eyes over ten-euro menus and *pichets* of cheap red wine. I envied them. If anything, she looked as if she felt pity.

We pulled up outside Gare du Nord. As usual, it was a mess of taxis and luggage. Five minutes to spare. The platform smelt of urine, cigarettes, grease, steel and humanity.

As so often in airports and railway stations, I looked at the next three departures and wondered how easy it would be to run. Lille, Amsterdam, Nice. Places to hide, to write that book, to learn the piano again, to reconnect with everyone I'd stopped knowing. Including myself. To win back my family.

Redwood was wearing what looked like a long grey coat. I hoped it was fake. What was left of her base obviously liked the Cruella de Vil look. Once again, I wondered where that sunshine had gone, the playfulness, the sense of adventure I had once known.

We spoke little on the Eurostar back to London. Such distance now. Those windows closed. I had spent my life filling the space that others were happy to leave unfilled. Breaking the silence. But she and Jack Fleming plunged into their papers, and I plunged into my thoughts.

I needed to know who had changed the knife. The French had the most obvious opportunity, when I was looking for the killer. Salins had clearly wanted me out of the way. And his sidekick had been in the room while he and I were on the roof. Aurelie had done little to deny that they had wanted to silence Amina. Presumably the French thought that she and the Dissenters had something even more damaging on the president. With the amount of their security in place for the reception, they could have had someone kill her. And if they had, suicide was a more convenient explanation for them. It would explain why Salins was so exercised about the camera: the killer would surely be on the video. But was Amina Joshi really enough of a threat to Paris to take the risk of tampering with evidence to suppress a crime? I couldn't see it.

If not the French, the Americans. Perhaps working with someone on my team? Emma had said that Amina had feared that she had gone too far. If so, Harry Parkinson was the most likely accomplice. He played tennis with Kane. Amina Joshi's posts were increasingly targeted at the White House, including the one she had been drafting at the end. They were being circulated widely among opposition activists in the US. The Americans would have calculated that my embassy was friendly territory. Parkinson would have ensured that it was. He had always claimed that Amina was a much bigger threat than she seemed. But were these leaks big enough to risk a murder, with all it would provoke? I looked at Jack Fleming across the table, his face deathly pale. He avoided my eye.

Whatever London had in store for me, I had to get hold of UK intel on what we knew about the French and American contacts with Amina. I was increasingly convinced that she must have been involved in something more menacing than idealistic campaigning. I also needed to know if the Dissenters had placed the video equipment in Amina's room.

If Orla was right that they had been in touch with Amina, they might have set it up to help record her posts. But had she – or Pederson's followers – really planned to broadcast a suicide? Or was it because they knew she had been threatened by the Americans or French, and wanted to record any attempt on her life?

Either way, Pederson likely knew who had been in the room before she died. But he would surely broadcast the footage if it helped his cause. So why hadn't he? Somehow I had to get to him.

Before he got to me. The pot would be enough to get me dismissed. But it had to be more. It must be connected to Afghanistan. A call or an email, showing how I had failed. But when you made so many judgements, surely people understood that some would be wrong? On the evidence of the last day, the internet mobs were less forgiving.

I wrenched my mind back to the murder. It was all connected. I needed to discover whether Amina really had a reason to kill herself. Sure, she wanted more profile for her message. But at the cost of her own life? And could she really have acted alone? I was convinced not.

Again, I opened the note from her desk, holding it away from Redwood and Fleming so that they wouldn't read over my shoulder. The final quote was a clear warning that others would present a murder as suicide. Or was it simply a suicide that she and Pederson had wanted to convince the world was a murder? The change of the knife surely ruled that out.

When I looked up, Jack Fleming was staring at the back of the paper in my hand, eyes narrowed. I folded it again, remembering the number on the back. An Oxford number.

The coffees and croissants came and went as flat, empty French fields sped by.

I tried to catch Redwood's attention, gesturing out of the window. 'An overcrowded continent, really?' But she barely acknowledged it. She smelt death on me. I stretched my neck. I felt my instincts sharpen, through the tiredness. I had to be on my game today.

I had always thought that a tunnel beneath the ocean was the most terrifying and serene thing I could imagine. I felt the weight of the water above. An almost unimaginable feat of human ingenuity and arrogance. I shuddered as the walls outside the train windows went black, and I remained silent until we were once again back above ground.

As we emerged from the tunnel, Fleming jerked forward as his phone signal reconnected again.

'Boss, they're saying you'll be in the next batch of leaks. The spooks have managed to get someone close to Pederson, to try to get ahead of what's coming at us.'

She was alert again now, tensed. For the first time on the journey, she glanced at me with something that was not cold disdain. But then it was gone. She looked away from me and turned her head to the window. I looked for the words but nothing came.

I was alert to a fresh danger. 'What else is Pederson saying?' I forced myself not to ask if there was anything new on me.

Fleming was scrolling through the message. 'They're mainly looking for who he's coming after in the US and at home. He seems to be confident. Is claiming some kind of victory with the Amina crisis. "A blow against hypocrisy."'

Redwood sat in silence. When we arrived at St Pancras, the car took us through late-afternoon London. Westminster was jammed with the evening rush-hour chaos of red buses and taxis. Tourists spilled over onto the roads. There was a relentless sound of drills and car horns from Parliament Square. During the pandemic, the streets had been silent and empty for weeks. Now humanity had rushed back to fill the void.

The flashing lights were on, a message to the world outside of urgency and purpose. She was on a conference call with her media team, barely acknowledging me. We pulled into the back gate of No 10, facing St James's Park. Fleming was listening on one phone and scrolling on another. He suddenly sat back in his seat and looked quizzically at me. 'One more thing in this Pederson report.

I don't know what you've done to him in a past life, Edward, but apparently he really hates you. Might want to keep your head down after all.'

The car stopped. Lynn Redwood put her phone in her bag and turned briefly to me. Anything we had ever had between us was gone, but for a moment we were twenty again. There was a flash of vulnerability in her expression.

'Edward, I'm done with wrestling your ghost.'

She walked through the ambassadors' entrance of the Foreign Office. I watched her disappear, her back tense in self-defence.

She did not say goodbye. She did not look back.

## 22

I went up the steps separating the FCO and Downing Street, into the famous road itself. Coming from this side, no one ever noticed me. The cameras were trained in the opposite direction towards the big black gates, waiting to catch an unexpected visitor or the unconcealed page of a briefing note. So many careers and lives had been made and broken in these hundred yards. So much hubris and ambition. What did it all add up to in the end?

The famous black door swung open. There was never a need to knock – the policeman inside monitored the door on a security camera. The hallway had a black and white chessboard chequered floor. Churchill's scuffed old chair was on the right, much smaller than people expected. The security guard took my phone and placed it in a cubbyhole on the left, leaving me with a numbered ticket. I thought of Emma and Oxford. Fate, chance, a life shaped by a misplaced package and a cubbyhole. Her anger had been different today, somehow more raw and more final.

But I still felt that I could win back her trust by showing that I was different: by uncovering the truth about her friend's death, by showing that she and Steph mattered more to me than the job.

To the left, the corridor ran like an electrical current through the building to No 11 and the chancellor's offices, past the lift to the PM's apartment. The building was a rabbit warren of cramped offices and adrenalin.

I forced myself to focus on the situation. So many things to consider. So many moving parts. Amina taking refuge in my embassy. The burning boy. The way that the Pederson machine had focused on my role at the centre of a cover-up. And now Fleming was saying that our intel had Pederson's released files singling me out in some way. What did he have against me? And maybe more dangerously, what did he have *on* me?

A No 10 messenger in a cheap black suit swept me past the half-opened door to the Cabinet Room. I glanced in, taking in the familiar smooth, green baize like a billiard table. The bookshelves were packed with unread books, locked in cages. The prime minister's chair was pulled back from the table, the only chair with arm rests. There were small carafes of water and Glacier Mints in glass bowls. The last time I had been here an American general had taken a handful and eaten them like biscuits, the crunching sound filling the room. There had been no doubt who was in charge when it came to the Special Relationship.

We went silently past the door through to the PM's den and the small, cramped outer office where his private secretaries crouched unblinking in front of their screens. I saw James Sheriff leaning over a pile of red-jacketed folders, the intel. To the right and up the famous stairs, past the portraits of previous British leaders. The photographs were black and white until John Major. And then we turned left into the Thatcher Room. Her old study now overlooked a rather bedraggled set of kids' swings in the garden. The shelves and tables were dark and austere. A severe portrait of the Iron Lady hung over the long-unused fireplace.

I waited, looking out over Horse Guards Parade. A now locked Downing Street gate led out onto the gravel and into the tide of tourists and humanity. When I had last been here, Churchill's biographer had told me a story of a moment of rare desolation and despair during the War. It had been a cold, bleak wintry morning. Some workmen called out from the road to Churchill to give them the usual two-fingered victory salute. Churchill fumbled for his keys in his long overcoat. His private secretary, Jock Colville, prompted him to turn and respond to the call. The great man turned his rubbery face back towards him with tears rolling down his flushed cheeks. 'I can't do it, Jock. All is lost. They are lost.' And yet he had carried on.

I needed to carry on today. All was not yet lost.

James Sheriff was in his early thirties, and his job as the PM's foreign policy adviser had gone to his head. He was a man of feverish ambition, who enjoyed making and breaking careers. I had once cut him down to size in front of colleagues. I had long anticipated that revenge would be served cold.

Sheriff was never on time. Power was proximity, especially with a prime minister who distrusted the Foreign Office as a place of mandarins, boffins, and irrelevance. He had no time for warm relations and the platitudes that greased the wheels of statecraft.

I picked up a small display case. Inside, three moon particles, a gift from a previous American president. Simpler times. The Americans had square jaws and we had enemies you could find on a map or kill in a Bond film. I missed that sense of clarity, ambition and purpose. Kennedy had asked a man sweeping the steps of NASA, 'What are you doing?' Without hesitation, the reply came, 'I'm putting a man on the moon, sir.'

The door swung open and James Sheriff strode in. He looked shattered, his skin sallow and heavy. He was running on caffeine, adrenalin and influence. But every time I saw him his confidence seemed to have grown. And his gut, which was now barely contained above a straining belt. He smelt of late nights away from sunlight. We were twenty years apart, but I already felt my authority draining away. This was Sheriff's turf, and we both knew it.

'Welcome, welcome.' Bonhomie, for now. The overconfidence of Sheriff's expensively educated voice.

Thatcher's face stared down impassively. Sheriff gestured up at the portrait. 'One of the old boys told me she liked tall ambassadors, provided they had no beards. One even had to shave his off for her. The PM has a similar view of the FCO. He told a story last night about a policeman on Whitehall being asked, "Which side is the Foreign Office on?" "Not sure, sir, but I think they were on our side in the war." Ha! Very droll, PM.'

He grinned a little too long. There was a bead of sweat on his upper lip. It rested there for a moment before his tongue snaked up. Then he put a hand on my shoulder, and we were sitting next to each other in the deep, green armchairs, like two world leaders posing for a grip-and-grin photo. There was only the briefest of hesitations from my host, legs spread wide on the chair.

'Now, Edward, we haven't got long I'm afraid. It's the usual utter chaos. The closer I get to politicians, the less I understand them. Different breed.'

I had no time for the small talk. Everything had changed. But nothing seemed to have changed here. My mind was racing again. The blood on Amina Joshi's white shirt. Steph's horrified face. Em's fury. Redwood walking away. I tasted the acid in my mouth. I forced my thoughts back to the room.

'You go first, James. You're going to tell me to stop?'

He cocked his head. 'I've just got two quick things for you, Edward. One – whatever happens from here on, nothing personal. Yeah? I know the pressure you are under. The boss likes you more than most of them, for what that's worth. And as usual we've not exactly been generous with the reinforcements. More with less, the new motto, the last refuge of that miserable bean counter at the Treasury. Can you imagine Saint Maggie saying, "More with less"?'

These days Sheriff's questions were always rhetorical.

I interrupted. 'Why am I here, James?'

'I'm trying to explain. Look, Josh Packer and the Americans are going to bring down the heavens on this Danish anarchist, and whatever's left of his Dissenters after we've all kicked some doors in. Pity we haven't got another pandemic to force the protests all back indoors. All these copycat kids burning themselves outside our embassies gives us reason enough to round up the people winding this nonsense up. The White House are in full Vietnam mode. I've never seen their system like it. Everyone at Defence is trying to restrain the president. Meant to be the other way round, eh?'

Sheriff was relishing the drama of it all. It was just a game to these guys.

It was not a game to me. 'But, James, what have they got to hide? Surely the worst is already out there, whatever Pederson wants us to think?'

He glanced at the window and then down at his scuffed shoes. 'We don't think so. Our job, the PM says, is to get out of the way. This is not our fight. This Amina Joshi stuff means that we're in danger of getting between the dog and the lamppost. Leave it all to the French. Their country, their problem. We will waive all sovereignty. Don't want our hands in the blood, if that's not the wrong metaphor. Got it? Thank God Amina Joshi is no longer on your – I mean *our* – patch.'

'A woman was killed, Sherriff, have some decency.'

He didn't flinch. 'But imagine if she'd been sipping tea at your place now, as the grenades she and Pederson planted go off in all our faces? Terrifying. By the way, any undeclared skeletons in your closet?'

I thought of Redwood walking alone into the Foreign Office, waiting to hear what the internet had coming at her. Me too, now, apparently. Terrifying indeed. But that was why we had to get ahead of Pederson. A cover-up played into his hands.

I wasn't going to give Sherriff any more ammunition against me. I leant forward. 'I know it's our default to do whatever the White House asks. But we have responsibilities here that go beyond the Americans. Amina Joshi must have been on to something – or involved in something – bigger. I think she was too clever to be used as a useful idiot by these Dissenters. And whatever it was she was doing might explain her death. That can help us switch all this off.'

Sherriff was examining me closely. 'Edward, no more drama, understood? We all need to get out from under these leaks. Find a way to move on, fast.' His voice was firmer now.

'I hear you, James, but I don't think it's that simple. I know they want it to be a suicide. But I think the Dissenters know it wasn't and can prove it when they choose to. So what are the French and Americans *really* saying about who killed Amina Joshi?'

He shrugged. 'The intel is pretty straightforward. We have her last call with this Magnus Pederson freak, just before she died. Don't ask me how they got it. I've seen the transcript.'

'And?' Orla and the Danish ambassador had been right about the link between Amina Joshi and Magnus Pederson.

'Pederson told her to "finish the work we started". Lots of ranting about the biblical Samson. The analysts think Pederson saw himself as some kind of Samson. The hero brought to his knees by treachery. The man who had terrified his enemies, who had set foxes on fire and sent them running through the fields of his adversaries. The victim blinded. You know the stuff. And he was looking for the ultimate revenge – to bring down their impregnable fortresses upon their heads. That sort of junk. Nutjob. Are we still allowed to say that? He and Amina were working together. And her suicide was part of the performance, timed deliberately to embarrass us and to draw attention to the leaks.'

'But I still don't see how she could have carried it out alone.'

He looked pained. But to his evident relief a messenger stuck a head around the door with a gentle cough. 'James, Lady Winterton is here.'

Sheriff groaned theatrically. 'Oh, what did I do in a previous life? You'll love this, Edward. The PM wants me to offer her the Vatican ambassadorship. Seriously. Needs to get her out of London, and out of the party committee.'

'But James, we haven't discussed the next move. We need—'

He paused at the door. The fake bonhomie was gone. 'Closure.'

'—answers.'

And with that, he was gone. I was stood again in the sombre silence of the study, Thatcher looking down sternly.

The door opened. A messenger with two cups of tea and an apologetic but unsurprised look on his gaunt face. I took one and swigged. It was lukewarm, metallic, stewed, with a hint of coffee. I put it back down, half drunk, gave the messenger an insincere nod of thanks and followed him back down the staircase, not looking at the portraits of the former prime ministers.

The Americans – with our quiet backing – were going to escalate the fight with Pederson before he released more damaging material or inspired more kids to kill themselves. But everything I had learnt about Pederson suggested he would have anticipated this. And was ready for it.

Pederson and my world were heading towards further conflict. But Pederson and I were already at war.

## 23

The serenity and emptiness of St James's Park was somehow comforting.

I still had fifteen minutes before my appointment with Sir Angus Green, the FCO's permanent undersecretary and head of the Diplomatic Service. The meeting would be my best chance of getting the system into a better place. Focusing less on damage control and more on getting to the truth about what happened to Amina.

I sat on the nearest bench and looked up the park towards Buckingham Palace, solid and grey against the skyline. Around me the familiar landscape of ducks and tourists, the early evening air cooling.

All of this had been here long before Magnus Pederson and all of it would be here long after he was buried in the dustbin of history. But had people like me always underestimated revolution until it was too late?

Two teenagers passed my bench, deep in discussion. One wore the Amina Joshi T-shirt. Her eyes burnt with a determined zeal, but there was fear behind them. How old could she be? Fourteen? Fifteen? What was it that drew her to Amina? It was easy to rebel against something, but were these kids rebelling *for* anything? Part of me still felt close to their age, and yet they would see me as from another era. I wanted to follow her, to ask her, to shake her shoulders and tell her to go home to her parents.

It made me think again of Amina Joshi's note. How was her message such a threat? How was it enough to justify a murder? On an instinct I turned the page over and dialled the Oxford number. A male American voice answered. 'Oxford Data Centre, good afternoon.'

I rang off and searched for the centre online. Just a short landing page. A picture of the director, a Dr Peter Tatham. It had been taken on a sunny day in Oxford, a jumper slung carefully over his shoulders. Late forties. Handsome. But there was very little information on his work. Nothing published. What did it have to do with Amina Joshi?

A young woman approached from the direction of the Mall. She was pretty, mid-twenties, serious-looking, Asian origin. 'Anyone sittin' here?' She placed herself carefully down on the seat, not waiting for the answer. 'Edward Barnes, yeah?' she carried on – there was clearly no need for confirmation of that either.

But I have always been a stickler, at least when I'm in character. 'And you are?'

'Am based across the river, yeah?' The metaphor for MI6. But of course. What had kept them so long?

She was the new look for the service. Out with the sweaty seediness of Harry Parkinson and in with a generation altogether more diverse, more British, more ambitious. More effective, too, as far as I was concerned. Probably pretty impatient with the likes of me.

There was no point in asking her name again. I wasn't going to get it.

'Look, Sir Edward. Am not here to tell you again what you'll hear all day. But the French can deal with the Joshi case and the Americans can deal with Pederson. And it's better for all of us that way, yeah? All these people who attacked her when she was living are claiming her now she's dead. Let's not make ourselves a bigger target than we already are.'

I nodded. Maybe today was just theatre, so that they could later tell the inevitable inquiry they had tried to get me back on track. Fair enough. Get it done and get back to Paris. Keep Steph safe. Buy some time and space to work out what had really happened. Try to get ahead of whatever Pederson had on me. He was obsessed with the Old Testament, with hypocrisy. What was the sin that he thought would find me out?

'But you – we – must have a view on who killed Amina?'

'*If* she was killed. TBH, we don't know. We're certain that Amina Joshi was plannin' to kill herself, yeah? The calls show that. But someone else might have helped. We don't know who or how. Magnus Pederson had some kind of relationship with the Russians. Maybe she did too?'

I didn't take the bait. 'I know Amina was talking to a Peter Tatham in Oxford. Who's he?'

She glanced over my shoulder. When she looked back at me, her eyes were steely. 'Nuffin' to see there. He runs somethin' for us and the Americans called the Agonistes Programme. Data collection. Routine stuff. Amina Joshi was probably fishin' for more conspiracy to keep the eyeballs on her content. To stay edgy.'

Agonistes. Another Samson reference. James Sherriff, based on what he had read in the red folders, had said Pederson was obsessed. And now this. I mumbled the Milton poem 'Samson Agonistes'.

'*But what more oft in Nations grown corrupt,*
*And by their vices brought to servitude,*
*Than to love Bondage more than Liberty,*
*Bondage with ease than strenuous liberty.*'

Strenuous liberty. Alem had mentioned it as the creed of Claxton and the original Ranters. Liberty had to be fought for. Pederson would surely agree. Maybe Amina too.

She smiled sympathetically. They had emotional intelligence, the new lot. Way more dangerous. She was reading me, quietly and forensically. She seemed to hesitate for a moment. 'Just one more thing, Sir Edward.'

She spoke with a disarming mixture of respect and familiarity. 'You want answers about what happened to Amina Joshi? If anyone has them, Orla Fitzgerald does. She's mixed up in this somehow. We know she was in Oxford a few days ago but has fallen off the radar screen. If you find her, you'll let me know, yeah?'

A card with a number. No business name, of course. No name, of course. And she was gone, lost in a crowd of ice-cream-spilling, cagoule-wearing Chinese tourists. She would have noticed how I sparked at the mention of Orla. Had she meant to make it easier or harder for me to find the truth? What would she report back? *Barnes seems in good shape, considering, but needs close observation.*

She was probably not wrong about the last part.

I sighed and looked at my watch. Two minutes to get back through FCO security and to Sir Angus. I needed to get him onside, get authorisation to dig into the intel on Amina and Pederson, and then get back to Paris, fast.

An old friend at last. I was ready for one.

## 24

To a returning ambassador, the FCO HQ in King Charles Street is the mother ship. The corridors are designed to overwhelm the visitor. Observing the grandeur of the formal rooms, a parliamentary committee had recently called the Foreign Office 'all fur coat and no knickers'. But for anyone who actually worked in the cramped offices behind them, paint peeling and bins overflowing, it was all knickers and no fur coat.

Today, I didn't notice the portraits on the wall of pioneer diplomats in breeches and ornate hats, all bovine faces and swagger. I moved swiftly along the corridor towards the PUS's corner study, my shoes clack-clacking too noisily on the tile floor. They needed a new shine. Lenny would not approve. I needed to speak to him to find out what errands Amina had him running.

My route took me past the sprawling Digital Engagement Team. A roomful of diplomats hunched over laptops. Together and yet somehow alone. Diplomacy was once about human contact, those last three feet between two people. Not an Instagram account and the vast empty spaces of the internet. No doubt Kane would disagree. But once everything was automated, where did that leave us humans?

I passed the small but belligerent bust of Rab Butler. He was the building's favourite foreign secretary. The FCO liked ministers who knew what they didn't know and could issue a firm instruction anyway.

The red-carpeted grand staircase was on my left, leading to the foreign secretary's office. To her. She felt miles away. The paintings at the top of the stairs showed foreigners kneeling before Britannia, fearful and humbled.

Someone had once said the Foreign Office was divided into assassins, boffins and Boy Scouts. I have probably always been a Boy Scout, lacking in the end the killer instinct. Sir Angus was an assassin, but so carefully disguised as a boffin that he sometimes even fooled himself. He carried the weary disappointment of a man whose ambitions have all been fulfilled.

On the wall outside his office were black and white photos of grey former permanent secretaries. Every single one a white man in a white shirt in his late fifties. I remembered coming here on my first day as a new diplomat, nervous and overawed. On the whiteboard by his door was a list of the words and phrases never to be used in papers reaching Sir Angus – appropriate, utilise, necessary, currently, challenge, going forward. Most had been scribbled up in his own writing. I nodded approvingly, making sure that the outer office noticed.

Angus noticed too. 'What a joy to have a job that indulges one's pedantry. Edward, welcome, *bienvenue*.'

He swept the door closed before his private secretary could wedge a stubborn black brogue in. 'Bearing up?'

We had known each other back when we still had more hair and hope. 'Good, I guess. Sorry about all the blood.' Gallows humour: always the refuge of the British under attack.

What could be worse than watching a contemporary grow old? But what could be better?

Angus looked at me carefully, smiling with his mouth but not his eyes. 'Not quite what we all planned, is it?' It was safe to assume Alem had kept them all up to date. He was waiting for me to start.

'It's a relief to have someone to talk all this through with. I'm worried we're losing too much time. Our ministers don't get this, but we can't treat the situation as simply a damage-limitation exercise.'

He glanced at the door. It was not clear whether he wanted to close it on the world or get me on the other side again. Green's tieless predecessor had installed modern furnishings and bright lighting. Green had put back the large brown globe and the deep green sofas on his first day. His whole existence was a damage-limitation exercise. He waved at me to carry on.

'The staff are fine, but it's been a strain. Emma and Stephanie got swept up too. Steph was one of the first to see the body. Ghastly.'

I was speaking too quickly. Green looked slightly uncomfortable, gestured me to the sofa. No time for emotion. There was never time for emotion.

Change the subject. 'How's Lenny coping? He was always so loyal when I was there. And so admirably discreet. He managed to track down a Baudelaire first edition once when I was in the bad books with Georgina.' And much more, I stopped myself saying.

Angus avoided my eye. 'I'm still meaning to get rid of all these imperial paintings. Not very twenty-first century, even if we know they are always meant to be ironic.'

I groaned despite myself. 'Tell that to the demonstrators at Amritsar. Angus, do you ever stop to think we might be the problem?'

He looked sterner for a moment. 'Edward, our decline is obvious enough to everyone. But was the British Empire that much worse than the American one? President Hoon is dismantling everything I thought I had learnt about the place. I now understand why we spent so much time at Harrow studying the Weimar Republic. The economic consequences of the pandemic will be as great as after the crash of 1929. Look around us. People voting for policies they know will make them poorer; for liars to clean up politics; to take back control. Nations built on the promise of migrants voting for anti-immigration candidates. A global campaign against globalisation. Orwellian. I just can't get our political masters – or indeed mistress – to see that.' He rolled his eyes upwards, towards Lynn Redwood's office. A pause, to signify complicity. 'The flight from reason is somewhat contagious.'

I nodded. 'That's why what happened to Amina Joshi matters. Some of us remember how this ends. These institutions and relationships so carefully constructed over decades. And then swept aside with a swipe on a smartphone screen, like an unwanted date. "In order for things to stay the same, things will have to change." If we let this go, we're complicit in that.' Angus acknowledged the quote with a weary nod.

But I was determined not to let him divert me again. 'I know you don't want to hear this. The pressure is on all of us to move on. I've just seen young Sherriff across the road, oozing power and entitlement. Plus had a visitation in the park from the new face of Vauxhall Cross. But this case is more complicated than everyone wants it to be. I think Amina Joshi, probably with the odious Pederson, was on to something much bigger than these leaks. Pederson is the immediate threat. But there are others out there.'

Angus looked unconvinced as he peered back donnishly over his glasses, forehead furrowed. We could just as easily have ended up in an Oxford Senior Common Room. We probably would pretty soon. But again, a frown and the slight wince of discomfort. Was he unwell?

'Case, you call it.' He let the word hang in the air. 'Caaaase.' I tried not to give the half-grin that would concede the point.

Angus waited a moment, then tried another tack. 'Edward, I worry that you're letting your relationship with Amina Joshi get in the way here. The Dissenters want a martyr. Amina wanted to be that sacrificial ram. Then that unsettling burning bush moment outside your residence gate. These other youngsters following suit. Ghastly. It's the drama that allows them to pump out their leaks, lies and invention. We only win by denying them some of the oxygen. If it transpired that she *was* killed, it will be our enemies who celebrate. They're already protesting outside at least five of our embassies. We may lose fine people.' A pause. 'You of all people should remember how that feels. More kids will be radicalised. What good does that do?'

I felt my cheeks redden slightly as I leant forward on the sofa. 'I disagree. They want to rip all this down, just like the original Dissenters. But this time they can weaponise the internet. They'll shout conspiracy, or whatever. Our best response is to be straight with people. To be honest. Humble. And then to attack the Dissenters from something at least approaching the moral high ground. From the territory they're trying to take from us. That they may somehow have *already* taken from us all in the eyes of the kids I see everywhere wearing her T-shirt. If I learnt anything from my mistake in Afghanistan, it was *not* to wait too long.'

Angus looked grim. 'Maybe. But diplomacy is already hard enough, Edward. Why pick another fight? Everywhere I now go I see this navel-gazing national mindset. This moaning about the state of our national mental health. I got a note today on our FCO history. They'd simply written "a period of steady decline since 1946". Diplomacy is about making it through the century, not just the next media cycle. The younger lot have lost that sense of Britain as pioneers, the appetite for even the slightest risk.'

I tried to recall the last risk Angus had taken. Or me, before this week.

He cast his eyes again towards the floor above. 'God knows our foreign secretary hasn't helped. She doesn't wear her heart on her sleeve. And that's not because she has no sleeve.'

I felt suddenly sorry for Angus. For him too this was a moment of unburdening. He paused to ensure his joke had landed. We were back on level terms again. The FCO does not do actual argument: we are too conditioned to see the other person's viewpoint.

'Angus, I met a couple in Northern Ireland who were holding a banner calling for an end to the conflict. I asked them, "What brought you here?" She spoke first. Clipped, but with emotion. "My father was killed in the last bombing. He was one of those who didn't get out." I thanked her for being there and turned to the man. "And you, sir, did you also lose a relative?" A pause. He was awkward for a moment, and then looked me in the eye. "No, I was the bomber." Isn't that what this is really about? That effort to coexist vs the extremes of Hoon, Pederson or Lynn Redwood and her friends in the media?' I realised even as I spoke that he had diverted me again. 'Maybe our – your and my – world is in decline, our way of doing things with restraint and decency. Maybe the lack of money means we're more Prosecco and Pringles than champagne and canapés. God knows you and I are in decline, Angus, look at us. But that's no reason not to fight for the truth. Whoever killed Amina Joshi is still out there. Pederson knows that too.'

Angus looked unconvinced. In front of him on the table was a report on technology and diplomacy, produced by one of his more breathless ambassadors – he saw me glance at it and arched his eyebrows in mock horror. He had always been a humane sceptic. I listened to the sonorous ticking of his clock and wondered how much longer he'd sit it out before taking an ermine robe and a quieter life.

'Sometimes, Edward,' he said, 'I wonder why I ever wanted this job. We used to say the past is another country. I now sometimes feel the present is another country. Maybe you're right. I've learnt in this office that all our senior colleagues think they have one more job in them than they really do. Maybe I'm no different. Maybe I should have jacked it in after Paris, or after Georgina passed away.'

He sighed deeply. A helium balloon sinking to earth. His wife had died during the pandemic, one more statistic quietly set aside as his government praised their 'world class response'.

He looked like a man preparing for his own execution. Crumpled and deflated.

It was to be an execution of sorts. Suddenly Angus sat up straight and looked me directly in the eyes. The permanent undersecretary was back. 'Edward, I can't sugar-coat this, and I won't. No 10 and Redwood have serious concerns about your handling of this crisis. We're putting you on indefinite leave – unless you can convince me that you can get back on-piste.'

He stared at a space above my shoulder. Had Angus been relishing it? Surely not. Trying to find the right euphemism?

'Angus, you know me as well as anyone. You know I can't do that. This comes from the Americans?'

He nodded grimly. But there was a hint of something else. Respect? Compassion? 'I feared you would say that. James Sheriff will go out as an interim ambassador. I'm guessing he made no hint of it just now? These guys love waving the sword of Damocles over people, but they leave it to the likes of me to actually let it fall.'

I clenched my fists at my sides, trying to retain my dignity. 'And the decision is final, I suppose?'

'I'm afraid so. I tried, Edward, I really did. I spoke again to Lynn Redwood just now. She could have bought you more time. But she was adamant you have to go. I don't know what microaggression you've dropped to upset her, but she's no fan of yours. I tried the Palace. But Pederson is blackmailing them too, apparently. Some classic story about a spare heir and a sex cartel; diplomacy is only the second oldest profession, remember.'

The assassination was complete. Clinical and efficient. Another body. Another sacrificial ram. And it had been Redwood who had wielded the knife.

Green rose wearily to his feet, dusting imaginary crumbs from the sharp crease in his suit trousers. The meeting was clearly over. 'I'm sorry, Ed, I really am. The chaps outside will take your diplomatic passport. No drama. They are informing your team… the team… in Paris now. James Sheriff will be on the train tomorrow if all goes to plan. I'm sure that smart deputy of yours can ensure no one else gets killed in the meantime.'

I rose too but stepped between him and the door. 'Do me one last favour, Angus. Are you aware of a Peter Tatham at Oxford? Is he connected to all this?'

Angus glanced at the black and white photo of his wife, and then back at me. His eyes were hooded but alert. He nodded his head almost imperceptibly, held my eyes for a moment. It was enough.

I walked to the door in a blur, chest thumping, the room spinning slightly. Thirty years of public service. *Service*. And this was it.

'Edward? One final thought. As a friend. Pederson is coming after you personally. Why is that? Now's a good moment to look through whatever ghosts you have locked away.'

'Is that a threat?'

'Friendly advice, Edward.'

'And you'll have my back if it's on our hostage failure in Afghanistan? You always told me that anyone could have called it the way I did. We got more of those right than wrong.'

He was examining a painting intently as if struck by an obscure detail.

I paused at the door. 'But, Angus… as a friend then? Why am I really being kicked overboard? What did I do wrong here?'

Sir Angus Green put a hand on my shoulder and gently but firmly guided me through the door. The Private Office were all staring at their screens now, suddenly absorbed. I was toxic.

Angus couldn't look me in the eye. '*Pas trop de zèle*, old boy. *Surtout, pas trop de zèle.*'

BREAKING. Breaking. Breaking.

## 25

I had boxed as a young diplomat in Nairobi. The moment you take a punch, time slows, your limbs feel heavy, and you can hear the blood pounding in your ears. An instinct for survival takes over. You feel the acute fragility of the place where confidence and fear wrestle. I have never felt more alive.

Diplomats feel we have failed when the fights break out. We are more velvet glove than iron fist. But we share much with boxers. Resilience, a bit of carefully choreographed pomp and pageantry, the subtle dance it takes to get your way. The long periods of patience. I'd had the Mike Tyson quote on the embassy wall in Paris. 'Everyone has a plan until they get punched in the face.'

Someone was now taking that poster down. I'd been punched in the face.

I staggered out of the Foreign Office courtyard and onto King Charles Street. My heart was racing. I looked around, lost. For a moment I stood in the road, facing the Treasury. I remembered arriving with twenty other new entrants three decades ago, over-scrubbed and eager, all of us hoping not to be found out.

Later, rolling Stephanie's pram out of the gate after collecting her from the nursery. The pride in fatherhood, but also in belonging. This was my club and my raison d'être. In a moment I had lost my cause and my community. And they had found it too easy to let it happen. What pieces of silver had been paid, and to whom? By whom?

I turned first to the left, towards Whitehall and parliament. I needed a drink, to sit down. Then I turned back – Whitehall was too full of colleagues. Should I now call them *former* colleagues? I felt exposed and vulnerable. I had often wondered what it would feel like when I retired. A relief? Liberated?

Instead, I turned right, retracing my steps towards St James's Park. Past the entrance to the Churchill bunker. Past the memorial to the Brits killed in a bomb in Bali. British grit, British sacrifice. Always the same myths and the same stories.

The clouds were darkening, and a gritty wind had picked up as night fell. I found an empty bench towards the Mall. It was less exposed to passing diplomats heading home. I closed my eyes. Would Emma and Stephanie be turfed out of the residence straight away, without ceremony? Penny would find Sherriff a huge irritation having house trained me, but she was a pro. Alem would be fine. Parkinson would be smug. Would this be one order too many for Crawford?

Slowly I worked through my options. I couldn't go back to Paris. I could check into a hotel in London, somewhere out of the way. But for what? To protest? No point. Angus would never have signed this off unless he felt he had no choice. *Sans domicile fixe.* Homeless. Better in French.

No, I had to get out of town. To get my bearings. To put my family back together again. To get ahead of whatever Pederson planned to release on me or those close to me. To seek the truth.

I felt again an adrenalin I had not experienced since the ring in Nairobi. I knew where I had to go next.

I called Emma. No answer. She must be at the shop. I tried Stephanie. She picked up straight away. Her voice was upbeat, trying too hard to be positive.

'How's London, Pops? We miss you already.'

Would she one day resent me for having dragged her to Paris? Pederson's disciples saw this battle as generational. How else had I failed her?

'Listen, it's a long story. But they won't let me come back to Paris. I don't know what happens next. We need to hold together... the three of us.'

Silence. I could hear the catch in her voice. 'Oh Pops. I'm so sorry. This isn't your fault. None of this.'

Her sadness knocked me off guard. 'Don't be ridiculous. If anyone is to blame, it's me. But this all spun out of our control too quickly. I'm just sorry that you're swept up in it all. I need to get the truth about Amina. For Mum, you. For me too, I guess.'

Stephanie was weeping gently on the other end of the line. I felt hopeless, distant. Maybe I should have told Emma first, and then got her to tell Steph. But this was my mess, my responsibility. 'I'm sorry, love.'

And then, suddenly, the other Stephanie: composed and rational. Once again, like a parent. Did that make me the child?

'Whatever happens this week won't define you – unless you let it. These guys don't get to write your epitaph.'

Was this the mark I would leave? One more diplomat sent to lie abroad for their country. A father? Maybe. A husband? Barely. A cameo in the Magnus Pederson or Amina Joshi saga? Or something else?

'At least I know who my enemies are now, Steph. But also what I really believe in. I feel a sense of purpose about this case I haven't felt in years. The truth matters.'

She was silent for a few moments at the other end of the line.

'Steph, one more thing. It will sound silly. But did you ever know this Magnus Pederson when we were in Copenhagen? Or in Paris?'

Her voice was calm. 'Don't waste time on him.'

I hesitated. 'Whatever comes at us next, we'll be okay. I hope you'll still be proud of me.'

'Mum always says you travel lightly. I'm not sure if I still agree.' Then, deadly serious. 'Pops, look after yourself.' She said it like it was an instruction not a sign-off. And then she was gone.

I heard the usual clicks on the line and wondered how many intelligence agencies were now carrying the transcript to their chiefs. The French, of course. Probably the Russians. No doubt the Americans. The Brits too, now? How much of my life is transcribed somewhere on a file I will never see? How many of my conversations might my curious descendants, eavesdropping on me long after I am gone, read one day? A curious, unwanted digital epitaph.

Was all this worth fighting for? I was feeling something that I had not felt for a long time. Passion? Zeal? I was fighting for the truth. And maybe that truth could help me save my family, show Emma that I had not lost a sense of purpose beneath the platitudes of decades of diplomacy. Maybe even show myself that the fire of passionate youth had not completely burnt out in me.

And the place to start that battle was with unravelling the truth behind Amina Joshi's murder. Just because this was a crime that no one wanted solved did not mean it was a crime that could not be solved. The best way to take on those taking apart my world of coexistence and curiosity was to take on their worldview.

Pederson and his Dissenters, who plotted their way into my home and left it shattered like broken glass around them.

Hoon telling people she could give them everything, promising bread and circuses, and preparing the scapegoats for when it inevitably all went wrong.

Redwood and my former bosses, running from the sound of gunfire, neglecting the sense of justice and fairness that our predecessors had fought for.

And I might not be a warrior. But in that moment, I felt as strongly about my values as they did about theirs.

Was I being watched? Would my pretty new friend from across the river be writing it up later? 'Barnes sat quietly for several moments, and seemed to compose himself, before standing and walking in the direction of Pall Mall.'

Let them all watch me now. Liberated. Alive.

I took a deep breath. It was time to get moving.

The wall of my father's study. The smell of tea, old newspaper and a damp cricket jumper shoved in an old cupboard. Of time stolen. His voice cracking as he quoted Goethe.

> *What you can do, or dream you can, begin it,*
> *Boldness has genius, power, and magic in it,*
> *Only engage, and then the mind grows heated—*
> *Begin it, and the work will be completed!*

## 26

When I woke, Oxford was serene and confident in the early summer sunshine. Crisp sunlight bathed the Bodleian and the Radcliffe Camera. It was the kind of day they put on the prospectuses. The jumble of spires and colleges coexisting with a bustling city. Town and gown had always had an uneasy relationship here.

Coming from London, you never get the view of the city that you expect. You drive through a gap in the chalky hills and then along a heavily canopied road, and then suddenly you are on the outskirts. I had dropped the hire car in a park-and-ride just off the mercifully quiet M40 and taken the double decker bus into town. I had called ahead to reserve the guest room at the college, a familiar refuge.

It had been, my old tutor had always said, an utterly unexpected First. None expected it less than me. I had driven straight to our place in Snowdonia to celebrate, jumping naked under the waterfall. I was returning now to find Tatham. And maybe myself.

The students were on their summer break, but the city was, as usual, packed with tourists, seeing it through their camera lenses. The bustle of an academic market town. Introverted academics scuttled by as they had done for centuries, avoiding eye contact as they wrestled with burning questions over the land rights of Ukrainian peasants in the early 1340s. Suddenly I saw them in a different way. Like they were institutionalised. It felt good to be free.

The college notice boards were filled with normality – concerts, sports fixtures, and guidance on everything from lost property to lost sexuality. I didn't recognise the porter, which was a blessing. The pigeonholes were unchanged. There was no plaque for Emma and me, and a story told at a hundred dinner parties. We could finish each other's versions. Had we done that for the last time? I felt her absence.

My key was ready, and I filled out the forms. I asked the porter to check the location of the Oxford Data Centre for me and headed back into the main quad. On my left was the circular staircase to the main hall. Ahead of me stood the chapel, dark and forbidding as ever. The sunlight reflected off the stonework of the buildings around the quadrangle. There was barely a cloud in the clear blue sky. The grass was cut short and gave off the smell of cricket pitches and youth. My youth.

Often it made me feel old to come back. Today I felt renewed. My old friend Winter, now a struggling don, always said that the reunions changed over the years. In their twenties, there was competition and bragging. This job, that car. In the thirties exhaustion had set in, as families and commutes took their toll. Back to bragging in the forties, as the corporates and lawyers hit partner level, and hit on new partners. By the fifties a more sedate descent into drunkenness, the awareness of time passing, more nostalgia. And then from sixty on, a pride in still being there, and the evening spent listing the various athletes and rowers who had already died.

I let myself into the stairwell and up to the guest room. I knew it well, having visited many times as an Honorary Fellow, staggering up these stairs with a bellyful of port and brandy. The room was filled with traditional but slightly incongruous furniture. A desk. A tea table. A large dresser. An ancient television that looked like no one had tried turning it on in years. It was all somehow comforting in its creaky familiarity.

I tried Emma again and this time she responded.

'Em, I'm back in Oxford. I miss you. I'm sorry we haven't had more time to talk all this through properly.'

She was silent at the other end of the line.

I continued anyway. 'Look, we have to be on the same side here. I saw Angus. He's put me on leave. There was pressure. From No 10, the Americans, it doesn't really matter. But they want me out of the way. It's for the best, actually. I need the freedom to find out what really happened to Amina. Unless we do that, our family could still be at risk from whoever wants to cover all this up. But we need to hold together if we are going to work it out.'

Em cut in. 'Don't we need to hold together for our own sake? Why are you so obsessed with Amina? If you really want what's best for us, can't you let this drop?'

I waited in silence, feeling her calming herself.

When she spoke, the serenity had returned. 'We'll manage. I've always hated the residence, and I always warned you not to rely so much on the FCO. Steph and I can move in with friends from the shop until we have a plan.'

I pictured the bookseller. His attentiveness to her. The sense of an untroubled mind.

'Em, this could get worse. It seems personal for Magnus Pederson. He has something on me. Maybe Afghanistan. Maybe the odd spliff. Maybe a staff thing. I don't know.'

'Or maybe it's not always about you?'

'Em. All of this. The life. The job. What I'm trying to do now. It's always been for you and Steph. I've wanted to give us a life that's different. Let's do this together.'

The seconds before she answered were a lifetime. 'I need some time to think too. Get some rest, Ed. Be careful.'

She had always seen my work as something that took me away from her. Maybe it would do that no longer. Maybe that was what she would come to see she wanted.

I went to the bathroom and splashed cold water on my face. I tried Orla's phone again. She could help me understand what was going on between Amina and Pederson. No answer.

A sound from the bedroom made me freeze. I edged back into the room. A floorboard creaked and I flinched. There was someone outside. The faintest of shadows flickered under the door. I froze, waiting.

Hearing nothing more, I moved as swiftly and quietly to the door as I could. I stood for a moment with my fingers on the door handle, trying to hear any movement from the other side. I took a deep, silent breath and threw it open.

The corridor was empty, but there was an envelope on the carpeted floor. I thrust it into my pocket and ran down the hall towards the stairway, descending two stairs at a time and ran out into the quad, looking for any sign of who had left it. But all was still.

I ripped open the envelope.

The language was more coherent than I expected, but still staccato and with that grandiose sense of destiny. It could only be Pederson.

> Ambassador Barnes. By now even you must under-
> stand that someone in your embassy murdered
> Amina Joshi. But worse than that, your govern-
> ment has done nothing, while Hoon and her people
> murder what is left of the freedom you are meant to
> defend. Are you really too blind to see the hypocrisy?
> I hear you seek the truth. But it is the truth that will
> find you. I've told you before: your sins will find you
> out. Keep an eye on the news.

I went back to my room and sat for a while. The sky outside had darkened, and I watched the rain start to fall on the window. This was the best university in the world. And yet the loneliest. The room smelt of damp towels and stale tobacco.

I checked the media coverage again. Nothing new on me, yet. Maybe Pederson had some personal connection to the hostage we failed to rescue? But surely people would see how hard these calls were? Did every mistake have to have a scapegoat?

On every channel, there was increasing amounts of 'informed speculation' that Amina's death had been a suicide. Official sources close to the French police. A UK member of the Foreign Affairs Committee was quoted. A Republican senator. The steady drumbeat of the establishment falling into line.

But the cover-up only held if Pederson held onto the video of who had been in the room at the time of her death. Why wasn't he releasing the evidence? Maybe it suited him to let a thousand conspiracy theories fester instead. Or perhaps his threat was about doing precisely that. Who was on that film? Was there evidence against Parkinson? Or had someone else been involved?

Lenny had been in the corridor at the time but was surely not capable of murder.

I had always prepared for worst-case scenarios. If not Afghanistan, what could Pederson have uncovered on me – on my family – that could be genuinely damaging? Three decades in diplomacy had left me hiding everything, yet hiding nothing.

Maybe he knew about my old relationship with Lynn Redwood – this could also be the looming leak against her. Maybe he had something on Em? The bookseller? Otherwise, we had little to hide as a family. Perhaps leaking the occasional joint would be the least of my worries.

It was only later that I realised I should have taken Pederson and his threats far more seriously than that.

## 27

The Oxford Data Centre was easy to find with the porter's instructions. A nondescript detached house on Woodstock Road, ten minutes from the centre of the city. One more faculty building. A small sign on the doorpost. No sense of cutting-edge technology. It might have been an English language school or centre for Byzantine studies.

Across the road was a small Italian cafe with tired ciabattas in the window. I ordered a sandwich and a coffee and sat at the table with the best view of the Data Centre.

For the first hour, there was nothing. A thickset man with short, cropped hair arrived in a car and entered the building. Half an hour later, another arrived on a bike. He had tanned muscular arms beneath a light blue shirt, with three buttons undone and sleeves rolled up to the elbow. Black wavy hair, rich person's hair, swept back. He wore colourful threaded cotton and leather bracelets on each wrist. His eyebrows were thick and dark. A slightly regal, deliberately unkempt air, like a prince on a gap year. He took the bike down the side of the building and disappeared.

I wanted to get inside the building, get a better sense of what the Data Centre claimed it did. I paid for my coffee and crossed the road.

I pressed the bell and the door buzzed open. Inside the decor was more spartan than I had expected. More like a tech start-up than an Oxbridge academic base. There were expensive chairs in a waiting area. A smartly dressed man sat behind the desk, the first man I had seen entering.

He rose as I entered. 'Can I help you?' An American accent. Chicago? He was chewing gum. He watched me as I clocked the weapon at his belt, smiling as my eyes met his.

'I'm here to meet Dr Tatham.'

The receptionist narrowed his eyes. 'He's not here, I'm afraid, sir. You'll have to leave a message. And all press enquiries have to come through the university.'

I glanced at the leaflets on the reception desk, trying to get more of a sense of the story this place wanted to tell the world about itself.

He looked back at me impassively. 'Who shall I say was here? And would you like to leave a number?'

I reached into my pocket for a business card and then thought better of it. 'Please just tell him it is about the Agonistes Programme. I'll be back.' I backed quickly away from the door. I had decided to wait in the cafe until Tatham emerged.

I ordered another coffee and resumed my place by the window. Another hour passed.

But as I gestured for the bill, I saw another figure walk briskly up the road and turn in to the drive. She was dressed more smartly than usual, in a pair of sensible trousers and a white blouse. Her blonde hair tied back. Efficient and businesslike. She walked up to the red front door. It opened before she pressed the buzzer.

Orla Fitzgerald had always been taught to follow the money. Every hack needs a Watergate.

When she emerged an hour later, I could see that her antennae were up, eyes narrowed. He had sparked her curiosity. I envied him.

I threw some coins on the table and left the cafe. She turned left towards Oxford, walking with purpose. I followed, slotting in behind a group of Spanish tourists. But they were moving too slowly, and as we passed the Parks, I overtook them. There was now no one between us, and she was thirty yards or so ahead. She halted to cross the road and I froze. If she turned now, she would see me. But she looked straight ahead and continued walking. Deep in thought, she narrowly missed colliding with a cyclist. As she neared the King's Arms pub she slowed and then ducked inside. I waited a moment and then walked past the pub and turned left, entering it by the side entrance. The smell of stale beer and chip grease was comforting.

Orla was at the bar. I crossed the pub and stood next to her. She was rummaging in her bag for her purse.

'What's the correct protocol for greeting an Irishwoman from a French newspaper in Oxford? One kiss or three?'

A variation on our private joke, one we'd shared since we had both been posted in Lebanon. Her for *The Times*, me for the embassy. She had once chirped back 'as many as you can get away with' to a similar question. But today she looked up, startled. Her eyes darted past me to left and right. When she finally spoke, her voice was flustered. 'What the hell are you doing here?'

'I was going to ask you the same question.'

Close up, she looked shattered. Her eyes burnt as always, but from under dark lids. She had a hunted look.

She paused, still deciding if she trusted me. 'I'm seeking refuge. And I guess I'm following a lead.'

I was still deciding how much to trust her. 'I know the feeling.'

She tried half-heartedly to find an excuse to leave, but there was relief and curiosity as we made our way to a corner table. I brought over two pints of Brakspear, an old favourite. A packet of salt and vinegar crisps – so hard to find among the ridiculous new flavours. Orla hunched, looking tired. But she felt like normality somehow, even out of context. The world kept turning. Forty-eight hours ago, I had been standing up to speak at the reception, catching her eye in that moment of control. Two days was a long time in diplomacy.

But I was relieved to have someone to talk to. I had to trade something to get something. I told her quickly about the FCO the previous day, Angus and his genteel assassination, having made her promise not to publish any of it. I felt a growing sense of complicity. Eventually, as the second pint broke down her reserve, I saw Orla soften slightly.

'Are you mansplaining all this, Ed?' she said with a slight wink.

I grinned. 'No, I'm just a man trying to explain what's happening. Is that allowed?'

'You're different without the ambassadorial baggage, Ed. It suits you.'

I found myself taking in what she was wearing. Blonde hair just below her shoulder, and now mysteriously fixed, tied back studiously but mischievously from her forehead. She had a freshness returning to her that I envied. An energy that I coveted. We are all at our best halfway through the second pint, while the self-doubt is fading and before the remorse kicks in.

I felt grateful for the camaraderie in her calling me Ed.

Her cheeks were now flushed from the beer. She had something of her mischievous twinkle back. What was she hiding? What did Crawford always say? Proceed until apprehended.

I grinned. The beer was at last taking the tension out of my shoulders, giving me a sense of courage, bravado. There were reckless moments when I felt ready to throw everything at her. And then she seemed too vital, too independent and too hard to catch, out of my reach.

'I need to ask you some questions, Orla. Let me buy you some fish and chips.'

She blinked, but somewhere her eyes sparkled back at me. A French accent. For once the Ferrero Rocher line didn't infuriate me.

'Why, Mr Ambassador, you are really spoiling me.'

## 28

We were hungrier than we realised. After the food had arrived, I looked at Orla, the skin taut but soft on her neck as she leant forward to eat her chips.

'Orla, you still haven't told me why you're here.'

She shrugged. 'Following a lead.'

'And that leads you to Peter Tatham.'

She recoiled slightly and glanced for a moment at the window. But when she looked back at me it was once again with poise. 'A bunch of pointy heads in a dingy lab? What's that got to do with Amina Joshi? Trust me, she would have no time for him.'

'I don't know him yet. But you clearly do?' I needed her camaraderie. But I also needed her skills as an investigative journalist.

She squinted at me, her head on one side. The curiosity of a fellow rebel.

After a few moments of thought she insisted that we turn off our phones and take out the batteries, using a safety pin to prise them open. I played along with the pantomime. Just as I had when I last saw Orla in the embassy garden. Back when Amina was still alive. The anticipation of Lenny's gin. Back when life was still normal.

I thought of the spook in St James's Park, asking after her. What was it that she knew?

'I'm just following a lead I picked up in Paris. Amina was deep into all of it.'

I picked up the hesitation. 'Who from, Orla? Who told you about Agonistes? Was it Amina? Pederson? How well do you really know him?'

She hesitated, a look of fear in her eyes. 'It doesn't matter, Ed.' She looked at her feet. 'All that matters is that I got that interview with Tatham today.'

'What's he like? Handsome guy.' Half statement, half answer. I was more curious about her reaction than I should have been.

But Orla curled her nose. 'Maybe. He would be more attractive if he liked himself less. He's the sort of guy who prides himself on lots of one-night stands. But those guys never ask why we don't come back for a second. A public-school voice, but the posher vowels slightly moderated. A man used to fitting in. An adaptable accent. Bags of charm. He had one of those chins with a permanent five o'clock shadow. But everything about him was thought through. He reminded me of those people you meet at a party whose eyes constantly dart around for someone more powerful.'

I had encountered plenty of those, probably been one of them. 'What was it like in there?'

She didn't miss a beat. 'Deep brown leather chairs. Large bay windows looking out onto Woodstock Road. I remember being struck that the desk was empty. There was nothing on the shelves. The art on the walls was modern. It looked expensive.'

'And did you get what you wanted?'

She looked exasperated. 'Not really. He was on a script. He told me they "do sentiment". Analyse it. There's masses of data produced every day. More photos taken this year than the rest of history. The internet taking over people's lives – not just some of the time but all of the time. Cataloguing every move you make, every question you ask and every conversation you have. The next generation are broadcasting constantly. He said that the vast majority of that information has been wasted. The only people who've recognised the true value of it are tech companies and the Kremlin.'

I wasn't sure which was worse. But Tatham wouldn't be the first to try to exploit online data. Several of the world's biggest companies made a living from it. Had that been enough to get Pederson's attention? Amina's?

'And so?'

'There was a slightly messianic certainty to him. He claimed that they were going to mine all that sentiment for the good of humanity. Ask the right questions. He reckoned they could start to understand the shifts in public opinion, the needs of the population. For the first time, not just be able to read people's thoughts, but to anticipate their needs. He said, "We will understand what they want before they do."'

I could see of course how Whitehall would love it. And not just the spooks. But I was troubled. 'Who gives the permission to have their sentiment mined? What about the people who don't want to join in?'

Orla nodded vigorously. 'Exactly. And how do you ensure that government is acting in the right interests? I asked him that. But he just went on about how it was all so liberating. He quoted Milton – it is "strenuous liberty". That's why they named it after Samson Agonistes. Liberty doesn't stand still. In the internet age we need a new way to guarantee it. That's what he thinks he's building: the ultimate crowd-sourced freedom. Says they have "assumed consent".'

I leant across the table. 'And what will humans do, when governments can anticipate their every need before they can?'

Orla grimaced. She pulled out a notepad. 'He said, "Humans are works in progress. They're restless. The Stone Age didn't end because they ran out of stones." He said that people would be free to study, create and innovate. The robots will do the rest. I noticed he always used "them" for humans. Not "we".'

'And who's funding all this strenuous liberty, Orla?'

'Fair question. That's when he stopped the meeting. Just said that it was valuable data. He stood up and shook my hand like he had finished interviewing me for an undergraduate place. But as I left, I asked him, aren't you playing God? It was the moment he stopped trying to look down my top. His voice was chilling.'

'What did he say?' I thought of the photo of Angus's wife. One more statistic.

'He said, "We're not playing."'

Her eyes narrowed. We were silent for a few moments. Orla stared straight ahead. She was angrier than I had realised. Was this because of what she had heard? Or because of what she had not heard? This did not feel like a sensational story. And Tatham had been so nonchalant about sharing the detail with a journalist he had never met. Was this just a desire to show off to an attractive woman? Putting her off the scent? Or was it that it didn't matter?

I tried to cheer her up. 'It sounds like you were incredible in there, Orla. On your game. The hunter and the prey.'

She stopped and turned to me, eyes flashing.

'For God's sake, Ed. He's not the prey, he's the hunter.'

As we finished our drinks, she narrowed her eyes at me. A slight tilt of the head. 'Ed, you're looking to feel young again. That's fine. But I'm not the person to help you with that.'

Enough, I said to myself. Enough. We walked to the door and out into the cool summer air of another Oxford evening.

After we parted, something made me turn to watch Orla walk up the high street. Probably the beer. Maybe nostalgia for the younger man who would have tried to convince her to stay. I shook my head. The streetlights marked her passage out of my night as she passed them, one by one.

I couldn't lose any more time. Tatham was more than a data geek. Amina had been on to something. Whatever Tatham was doing might be the reason she was dead. Working that out might help me protect my family from whoever killed Amina. Working it out might also help me understand how to stop Pederson coming after me.

Two roads diverged. When she was out of sight, I turned back towards Tatham's Data Centre.

## 29

The building was completely dark, except for one security light over the front door. From the cafe earlier I had clocked the three cameras on the front of the building. They were like the cameras we had on many of our embassies: for display. That normally meant the real cameras were better hidden. Scanning the walls, I went around the side, looking for an open window. I knew that Tatham had cycled earlier, so there might be a shed.

I found it against the back wall of the garden. There were fresh tracks on the muddy grass outside. The door was unlocked. Inside it smelt of earth and damp. An old wardrobe was against the back wall and a workbench with scattered, dusty tools. Otherwise, the space was empty except for Tatham's bike on a metal stand. A small window. I used the light on my phone to scan the shelves. Some empty seed boxes. A flower pot. Parkinson had once told us that even spies kept their passwords in their desk drawer. I ran my hands under the table. A small hook, but no key.

Alert for sounds, I circled the back of the building, looking for any possible opening. No visible cameras. But the windows were tightly sealed, and the door locked, with an alarm to one side. I cursed myself for the wasted trip. It was the beer and bravado, plus my sense that Orla was holding so much back.

As I entered the back porch, I heard footsteps coming towards the door from inside the house. There was no time to run. I slipped back into the cycle shed, and into the corner by the wardrobe, pressing my limbs against the wall to make myself as small as possible. In the stillness, I was conscious of the trails of a spider web on my neck. What the hell was I doing here?

Through the window of the shed I watched as the back door opened and a man walked out. In the light of the back porch, I could see his brown brogues: confident, strong shoes. A man who knew his place and didn't need to ask for attention. Peter Tatham stood for a moment in the porch, breathing in the night air. I clenched silently. He let the door close behind him with a click.

I held my breath, but the shoes didn't move. He was taking a call. I picked up a rusting hammer from the workbench, wondering if I would remember how to defend myself.

As he spoke, he walked towards the cycle shed, swung the door open. 'Yeah, nothing like a good conspiracy to get the dogs-on-string brigade frothing. Draining the wrong swamp.'

His phone wedged between shoulder and ear, he tried to shake the bike free from its stand. It jammed for a moment, and I thought he would look up and straight at me in the darkness. I tried to suppress my breathing, cursing myself silently for coming.

But something on the call distracted him. He listened for a while and then interjected, less nonchalant now, 'That's what AJ said. When the public sees that they'll be crazy not to join in.'

AJ had to be Amina Joshi. He didn't speak of her like an adversary. Was she also somehow involved with him?

He now had the bike free. In the darkness I tried to sink back further into the wall, one fist clenched at my side, the other holding the hammer tight. The back of my neck was damp with sweat.

A pause again. 'Yeah, but we're able to hoover up the most agile brains of the next generation here, before they get lost in government or some corporate beehive. We're building the plane as we fly it. Outside US jurisdiction. And we have morality on our side – they can't do this themselves.'

I had a memory of something my old history tutor had once told me after berating me for suggesting blithely that there was a right and a wrong side of history. 'The shits always win in the end. All we can do is make it harder for them to enjoy it.' Dr Peter Tatham was enjoying it all a bit too much.

He listened for a while longer and then rang off. But he didn't move. We stood opposite each other in the blackness. Surely he could sense my presence? Time slowed. I could smell peat and mould. I wondered whether to confront him, ask him straight out about Agonistes. Get away from this unfamiliar world of action and back to my comfort zone of talk and interrogation.

But how could I explain being here? He was opening and closing a drawer in the work bench. Then he stood straight again for a moment. Through the gloom I tried to see if he had picked up a weapon.

He kicked the door back open and I pressed back against the wall, trying to avoid the light from the porch. He was looking at his phone, swiping with his thumb as he reversed his bike. Another pause in the doorway. I held my breath, gripping the hammer. Then the phone vibrated, and he was absorbed again in whatever message had just arrived. And then he was gone.

Through the window, I watched as he disappeared into the night. Oxford was once again as silent as the grave.

I waited ten minutes, feeling my heart rate slow. I felt again beneath the table for the hook. The key was not there. I opened the drawer of the work bench. An old copy of *Time* magazine. Beneath it a ring with two keys.

I returned to the back porch and tried the lock with the larger key. The door opened.

Maybe it wasn't only data scientists who assumed consent.

I flinched, waiting for an alarm. Nothing. I eased the door open and entered a tiled corridor. There was a utility room on the left and a small kitchen on the right. And then a wooden door which must lead to the main corridor. I slowly opened the wooden door. Part of me expected the thickset American to be on the other side. But there was only silence. A single clock ticking.

At the end of the corridor was Tatham's study, with its windows looking out onto the road. I listened for a moment but there was no sound. I didn't have long.

I checked myself. I'd never broken into a building before. But I had no choice. I needed to know what Amina was after. Pederson too. And now Orla. The top drawer held nothing but old pens and paper clips. I looked around the room. Virtually empty, as Orla had said. Maybe they didn't need to worry about security cameras on the back door – there was nothing in here to protect. Tatham and his people were not the sort to create physical evidence: everything must be online, behind layers of encryption. No wonder they could allow the place to look like a graduate accommodation block.

In the second drawer there was an A4 page with initials and phone numbers.

I took a photo on my phone of the contact list. But this felt like a wasted trip. Whatever Tatham was hiding, it wasn't here.

There was a sound of car tyres on the gravel outside. The lights dimmed as it pulled into the drive. Had he seen me in the shed and called the American? For a moment I wondered if they had caught my shadow through the bay window. It was time to get out. As quickly as I could, I slipped out of the study and back down the corridor. I returned the back door key to the shed and waited at the side of the house, trying hard to steady my breathing.

The car revved its engine. The tyres spun. And it was gone.

When I got back to the college, disappointed and drained, Orla was standing outside. Her hair was matted and her eyes dark. She fell into my arms.

When she stopped sobbing, she showed me her phone. She told me she was used to intimidating messages from anonymous accounts with numbers instead of names. Normally, she dismissed it all. Just dark minds in a dark corner of the internet. A growing reality for any woman online. She tried to hide her sense of intimidation. 'It's mainly troll factories. Automated accounts. I'm used to it.'

'So what's different now?'

'You tell yourself it's only machines. But the scary thing is that you know there is someone telling them what to do.'

'Who do you think is doing this, and why? Pederson? Tatham?'

She didn't reply. She was far away again. But she flicked back to the home screen. It was the now famous photo of Amina Joshi, throat slit. But her face had been replaced by Orla's.

## 30

We crossed the border into Wales at midday. I hadn't wanted to stop driving until we were well away from Oxford. Orla was slumped next to me in the passenger seat. She was very pale, much smaller somehow. Her spark had gone. I wanted to wrap her more tightly in the blanket.

It was a greyer, brisker Oxford morning after the sunshine of the previous day. I had slept more soundly than at any time since Amina's death. The beer and chips had helped. But now I cursed myself for losing vital hours.

There were no new threats, but her photo stream had been replaced by shots of her in the King's Arms pub the day before. It was impossible to delete the home screen photo of her face imposed on Amina's. The same chilling threat.

Surely Pederson.

And if he was capable of doing this to Orla, then surely he would do it to us, too, if we were in his way. And not just me. My family. Steph.

I had insisted we head to the cottage in Snowdonia. We would be safer there. We needed to be away from technology, away from the twenty-first century, away from the reach of the Dissenters. A place of refuge and simplicity.

We spoke little in the car. She slept. When we spoke, she was again dismissive of the Tatham story. 'I'm just not sure I have enough to make it exciting. They're boys with toys, getting

carried away. This is not the first slightly megalomaniac applic-
ation of technology in history. And humans have proved pretty
impervious to having their lives controlled, even by an allegedly
benign force.'

I disagreed silently. I did not want to alarm her further.

'Orla, you have to tell me. Did Amina and Tatham know each
other?'

She shook her head. 'I don't think so. Why would they?'

Another half an hour of motorway went by outside. She dozed.
I thought about the scribbles on the pad in Tatham's drawer. Of
Tatham talking about working outside US jurisdiction.

When she woke, I shared my ideas. 'What if they have new
ways to collect sentiment, for example direct from the micro-
phones on smartphones. We know that intel agencies can do that.
If this is an isolated programme then no big deal. But what if
other institutions are doing similar things? Who's managing all
those results? The US government – the Hoon administration
for God's sake? I don't trust them. That they're doing the dirty
work outside the US only makes me more worried. No one can
regulate or control it. That's the story. And we know that all
UN programmes remotely connected to online rights have been
slashed since Hoon pulled the funding.'

Orla stared silently out of the window. She had turned her
phone off again and put it in the glove compartment.

Only when we had climbed the winding road up through
Capel Curig did I pull the car over. This had been a family
tradition ever since I had first come here with my parents. I
stepped out onto the flinty path and breathed deep. The crispness
of the thin air and the vastness of the view hit me – as always – in
the chest. Slate, thin air and vast nature. The mountains rising up
like grey-green tidal waves and the translucent shimmer of Llyn
Gwynant in the valley below. Lungs filling again with life. Orla
stayed in the car. She was shivering slightly.

I called Emma and left a message. 'Keep Steph close. Don't trust anyone.' At some point the previous day, part of me had decided not to ask more about the bookseller. He was not the cause of all this. I was. I tried to put it from my mind. In any case, how would I explain that I was taking this fragile beauty with me, to our place?

We stopped in Beddgelert and I picked up two bags of shopping. Whisky, some red wine, spaghetti, the basics. Filling the space as ever, trying to distract her, I told Orla of the legend of how the town got its name. Max Crawford had told it to me. He loved the story, told it often.

So I told her about the loyal hound, Gelert, wrongly accused of slaughtering Prince Llewellyn's beloved son and killed in a fit of anger by his master. Then later the discovery of the child, alive and unharmed, with the body of a dead wolf alongside. Honour and loyalty had been rewarded by death.

I had always wondered how it felt for Prince Llewellyn, broken by remorse, losing his trust in those who were most loyal to him. Did he think of the loyalty every time he held his child? Did he curse himself for having failed to understand it?

At a hiking shop, I bought some boots, a fleece and a couple of changes of clothes for Orla. As always when I got this close to the cottage I was impatient, anxious to get there and shut the world out. Orla again stayed in the car. Her eyes darted. She was suddenly suspicious of everyone. It was no use explaining how remote we were. For her the Dissenters were now everywhere. Even here.

Finally, we had crossed the cattle grids and were climbing the road up from Nantgwynant. It was wide enough only for one car, and we had to pull into a siding when we met a tractor coming the other way. Orla pulled herself down in her seat, paranoid. I parked the car by the stile at the top of the hill and consolidated our provisions. I could come back for the rest once I had settled Orla.

We started down the path, which was still wet from the dew. Underfoot, the flinty rocks were slippery. Sheep turds, black slugs, moisture in the air. We passed over the rickety wooden bridge and across the fields.

The cottage was white fronted. I had re-plastered it the previous summer. It had originally belonged to the shepherds who worked the surrounding fields. The front windows had bright blue frames, which Emma and Steph had painted one holiday. We would be here again, together, after all this. It was raised on a mound from the surrounding marshes, with a stone wall surrounding it and a large wooden gate to keep nature out. There was a slate roofed barn attached to the main building, where I chopped and kept the firewood. At the end of a small path between the two was a small outdoor toilet – just a wooden bench over a bucket of bright blue disinfectant. A loo with a view, Steph called it.

I found the rusted iron key in its usual hiding place and let Orla in. I settled her by the fireplace, changed into a pair of old cords and a battered checked shirt, made tea, and started to busy myself with the old routines. Connecting the gas cylinder, switching on the mains, wiping down the surfaces, checking for woodworm, fetching two buckets of mountain water from the stream, bringing in kindling and firewood from the barn. I felt serenity through familiarity. Habitat. This was a place that had watched me grow and would now help us both to recover.

Orla quickly fell into a deep sleep, her knees cradled against her chest, curled tight. I did the usual checks of the plantation and marshland behind the cottage. No dead sheep near the water supply.

This was where I felt most alive. I stood on the terrace looking out across the fields. To the right, Snowdon loomed dark and large. There were patches of sunlight on its outer peaks, but ominous darker clouds moving towards it. To the left were the ranges reaching up to Cnicht, its distant peak almost lavender. I would get up it tomorrow, maybe, once we had settled. That was the place to get my blood pumping, clear my cluttered mind, think. To work out what had happened to Amina Joshi and how to start to get my life back on an even keel again.

I remembered a moment here with Stephanie. I had woken her in the night to show her this patchwork of the universe, to talk to her about how much we all had to learn. A younger man. More naïve, more hopeful. I had recited Em's favourite poem. 'Tread softly, for you tread on my dreams.'

Orla didn't wake until early evening, curled on the moth-eaten old sofa by the fire. She had smiled weakly up at me and, for the first time since we had left Oxford, started to relax. But there was a new fear to her, ever present. I had made us both big bowls of steaming spaghetti Bolognese, with handfuls of Cheddar cheese. Two large glasses of good Rioja, robust enough to leave red trails on the glass. We rested the bowls on our knees. I could see her strength coming back. In the light of the fire, she reminded me of Steph, sitting there in woolly socks, the same determination.

Later, I swam once again beneath the waterfall. Balancing precariously on the rocks. The place hidden by trees, cocooned. The bite of the cold sent a charge through me. I put my head under the white water as it rushed over the rocks above. I felt a calm amid the noise and churn of the river. I let the water bite, feeling my legs and then my upper body becoming comfortably numb. My mind felt clearer. Amina had been in contact with Tatham, looking to smoke out whatever he was doing. She would have hated the potential for governments to use data surveillance to such an extent. But then why had he spoken of her with complicity?

I brought back more buckets of water from the stream, heated them in the gas burner in the old cow byre and carried in a heavy tin bath. Brushing aside the cobwebs and dust, I poured in the steaming water, added a generous squirt of bubbles. I checked the temperature with my elbow to make sure it was not scalding and put extra logs on the fire. It was time for some truth from Orla.

She was still stretched out on the sofa. A moment of awkwardness. I offered an excuse to bustle off on more errands. But Orla was suddenly timid. The sky was darkening outside. We might get hit by a storm later. She didn't want to be left alone for even a moment.

With no drama she slipped out of her clothes as though I wasn't there. She threw the jeans, the fleece, a blouse onto the sofa and reached behind her back to unclasp her bra. Such a simple and oft-repeated action, yet every time was the first time. I turned away, mumbling about the view up to Snowdon, the darker clouds. I heard her remove her underwear, fixing my eyes on the horizon beyond the window and trying to ignore the flicker of a reflection.

Behind me she gasped a little at the heat of the water, and then sank slowly into the tin bath. An overflow of water and bubbles onto the stone floor made me turn.

I glanced at her and then away, fumbling for a towel as I dried the floor next to the bath, trying to avoid looking again in her direction. The bath was not large enough to lie down flat in. She was propped back in it, her shoulders and the top of her breasts out of the water, without any trace of self-consciousness. Her knees bent. A soft pinkness as the warmth spread through her body.

'Shall I give you some privacy?'

Firmer this time, fear in her eyes. 'Stay.'

Her eyes were half closed. Her cheeks had their colour back now and her eyes were less haunted. The wine and the heat from the fire were loosening her limbs. She had tied her blonde hair back in a knot. She was languid.

'Temperature okay?' My voice was hoarse. No reply. I pulled myself together and went out to the terrace.

## 31

When I came back in with more logs for the fire, Orla had put on my checked lumberjack shirt and a thick pair of hiking socks. The bones of the cottage started to thaw. She lay with her head on the old cushions, her hair tousled.

When we finally spoke her voice seemed deeper, steadier, more assured again. It was now dark outside.

'So… Ed… What the hell do we do now?'

What now indeed? Someone had told me we were always only three bad decisions away from ruin – had we just avoided one such decision? My mind back again in Paris. Amina's lifeless body. A burning man on the Rue du Faubourg St-Honoré. Stephanie sobbing.

For Orla, the moment had also passed all too quickly, and her eyes were again more anxious. She sat up and took another large gulp of wine.

'Ed, I can't stay here. They will come. I know what they're capable of.'

I stood, my frustration rising. 'Who, Orla? I can protect you here. We're ten minutes' walk from the road. Anyone crossing the field would need a torch, which we would see long before they got close. We're far from the world, far from the internet. Even the mobile signals don't work here, so no one can trace those. Trust me.'

I felt her look through me, look through the lie. She shook her head. She looked broken again. 'I don't need your protection, Ed. I'm not your daughter. And they will come.'

'Who?'

She didn't mean Tatham. It was time to finally get some truth about Magnus Pederson from Orla Fitzgerald.

I remembered her occasional visits to the residence. The long sessions locked away with Amina. 'Orla, you knew Pederson during your time in Paris, right?'

She looked for a long time into the fire. Then that hunted look again. She nodded.

'So how are you a threat to him? You could leave the story now. Cameo over. They have every journalist in the world writing their copy for them. They have their notoriety. Amina even has her martyrdom. No doubt Pederson will soon get his too. What else can they possibly have over you?'

She looked belligerent for a moment. 'Who says I want to leave the story, Ed?' And then a sigh. 'Sure, I did get to know Magnus. He was too interesting a source to dismiss. He has huge charisma. But fascinated by the idea of sacrifice. Obsessed by the Old Testament, the son of a priest. He's scarred.'

'Is that why he wanted to convince Amina to kill herself?'

'Maybe for shock value. But I don't think he ever thought she would actually do it. Maybe because he hates to feel women have anything over him. Me included. He never wants to love again.'

'Why? What happened to him?'

She curled her legs under her on the sofa, took another sip of the wine. 'He once told me his childhood was surrounded by books, laughter, debate, curiosity. No particular pressure to succeed, just a natural expectation that it would simply happen.'

'So what changed him?'

'Somewhere in that emotional wasteland between the football sticker album and beer, he discovered girls. Don't you all?' I looked down at the table. 'Or rather, one girl. He never told me her name. But she moved on. The older boys had bigger cars, deeper pockets, better banter. Pederson was relegated to the status of an envious observer. And then to an accomplice, the alibi she needed to slip out of the house.'

'But he wouldn't be the first lovesick teenager in history.'

'No. But he thought she would tire of the guys with their joyriding, their cigarettes and their wandering hands. Maybe she would come to see that one person would always be there for her. He waited. And watched. Until one night a couple of years ago it all broke. She had told her parents that she was with friends. He waited as always to walk her home.'

'So if this is some kind of turning point, what happened, Orla?'

'She never came. Instead, she staggered to the police station. She had been raped. She didn't want her parents to know, so it was Magnus who was there.'

For a moment, Orla looked as if she too had the innocence and hope knocked out of her. I winced. 'Go on.'

'Magnus never spoke to me about how it had changed him. But I think that was the moment everything broke. It was his way of displacing the blame. He carried this cold, hard anger at an unjust world that destroyed anything good, that wouldn't change unless those who controlled it were also broken. He became a man driven by revenge. And he moved from a desire to protect one woman to a need to protect himself from all of them.'

'And all that was why he wanted the drama of Amina's suicide?'

'Not all. Amina had developed even more of a martyr complex than before. But I never really understood the dynamic between them. I often asked her about it. They were from different worlds. She felt the stakes were becoming too high. I imagine him telling her that it was better to die on her terms than face an inglorious death on your government's terms, bundled into a car in a back alley, among the wheelie bins and the dog turds of Paris. The original Dissenters had seen suicide as the ultimate freedom. Nothing left to lose. How better to demonstrate liberty than to choose her own fate? But she wasn't really into all that stuff, not like him.'

I was about to defend my government, and then remembered I no longer served it. I slumped slightly, feeling like a statue without a plinth. I took another swig of the wine.

'Did you not worry you were too close to Pederson, Orla?'

She was defiant. 'I'm a journalist, not a diplomat. Getting close to people is how I do my job.'

I looked out at the mountains, black and heavy with damp and time. The Dissenters had moved swiftly to capitalise on Amina's death. The protests that had broken out had been coordinated. So was Orla supporting the suicide theory?

It certainly matched the explanation that my government anticipated and hoped for, as did the French. If Pederson had persuaded Amina to kill herself there would be no one else on the video. It was better for him to leave the sense there might have been, to increase the damage to all of us. It was a convenient truth, more than it was a convenient untruth. But she was holding something back.

'Go on, Orla.' She took a moment to compose herself. She seemed suddenly more vulnerable. 'I know why you're hiding. But you haven't told me who gave you the Tatham lead that brought you to Oxford.'

She flinched and then composed herself. Her eyes narrowed. 'You don't trust me?'

'Someone I love told me recently that trust wasn't enough any more.'

She was studying me carefully, the psychologist turned journalist. 'It was the last batch of leaks. Hints of a covert US data

174

programme. I felt that the Dissenters had something big prepared. I sat there in Paris with my team, like every other journalist in the world, trying to find the nuggets. And then I remembered Magnus obsessing about Oxford. He could get into huge troughs of paranoia and delusion. You never knew how to separate those from his more rational moments, when he was utterly cynical, utterly clinical.'

She knew him better than she had let on. It was 'Magnus' when her guard was down. I nodded at her to continue.

'I had thought the Agonistes stuff was one of his biblical side-tracks. The wounded hero attacked from all sides. It was classic Magnus. Always putting himself at the centre of the story. Always convinced the world was against him, just because he was against the world. The leaks were not enough for him. He would have wanted more. He never intended this to be an exercise in gossip, in entertainment alone. He wanted to change society forever. And in Tatham he thought he had found his nemesis.'

Classic Pederson indeed. And classic Orla: blinded by a Pulitzer. But still not enough reason for Pederson to threaten her in this way. She was still holding that back.

Outside, the Welsh night was drawing in around us. The mountains were blending with the darkness. Just a small light from another cottage across the valley.

## 32

Trying to show Orla why I needed to talk, I showed her the note Pederson had written to me. 'And what about this? What's his thinking? The threat. I get why he's angry with all of us, but what does he actually want? And why me?'

She glanced at the note and rolled her eyes. 'Classic paranoia and conspiracy. He doesn't trust anyone. And he wants the rest of us to stop trusting each other too. So the more he exposes hypocrisy, the more people are forced to think for themselves. If he sets us all against each other we become more vigilant. At least that's what he might claim. The original Dissenters were about radical liberty, complete freedom. He thinks all this somehow gets us closer to that.'

I looked again at his note. It had got under my skin, just as he intended. 'But ultimately we all have secrets, even – especially – Pederson. And his objective is actually very different to Amina's. She wanted more global governance, not less. They were on different sides.'

Orla thought for a moment. 'Maybe, but he always saw her as a means to an end. Maybe she saw the same in him? What they shared was a belief that undermining national governments was the first step.'

I thought back to the call Tatham had made outside the Data Centre. Clearly, he'd been talking to the Americans. I wondered again how much I could risk sharing with Orla if she had been this close to Pederson. 'And that's I think why Tatham is such a threat to him, and vice versa. Tatham wants to use tech to make governments stronger. Magnus wants to use it to weaken and destroy them. Same weapon, different target. But why do you think Amina was mixed up in that?'

'You won't understand, but Magnus was incredibly hard to resist. And so was she. She was much more ruthless than she let on. And he was much more idealistic. So I guess there was some common ground. The deal – his deal – was always that he would leak the data required to kick off an uprising. But they must have decided that it needed her suicide to ignite the actual rebellion on the streets. I was supposed to write the first draft of history, start the canonisation. Only she never made the recording we expected. If she had, the protests would have been raging in a far more destructive way by now.'

I was increasingly frustrated at how dispassionate she seemed about the consequences of all this. 'For the parents of these kids setting themselves on fire, they're raging. This isn't a game, Orla. What was really going on between you and Pederson?' The way she spoke about him I wondered whether the question was really 'what *is* going on?'

She was suddenly deflated. I wasn't sure whether to walk away or embrace her. Instead I watched her chest rise and fall as she suppressed a sob. I scolded myself for not moving faster. Get a grip. I put my ambassador's face back on. She needed to feel secure.

'I'm sorry, Edward, I really am. I don't know who to trust any more. I never thought they would actually go through with it all.'

There was still an innocence beneath the worldliness. You could take the girl out of the convent but not the convent out of the girl.

She drew the blanket closer around her. 'I went to find Magnus's parents in Copenhagen. They were lovely. They had always hoped it was all a passing fad. The long black coats and torn black jeans. The cigarettes and loneliness. The rapid decline after he moved to Paris. The constant scrubbing of his hands as he fought off an image of her fingernails caked in dirt. He never spoke of the girl again. But maybe he transferred some of that feeling to me.'

Orla looked up at me. A tear on her cheek, which she brushed away with the sleeve of my shirt. Another gulp of wine.

'And now he thinks you let him down, Orla? What did you do? Or was it something you *didn't* do?'

The tears had gone now. She suddenly looked resolute, fierce. 'I was there earlier that night. They know I was one of the few people who were in contact with Amina. And then the suicide clearly didn't happen as planned. Amina was meant to deliver a monologue before doing it. Her usual stuff. She fluffed the moment, denied them the theatre.'

'They think you talked her out of it?'

I felt suddenly cold and wary. Something still didn't make sense. Could Orla have been present when Amina died at the embassy, despite her claims of distance? Sometimes a journalist's great story needed some help. But hadn't she been there that night in the garden? The emerald dress, the provocation.

But then I recoiled as another thought hit me: Lenny. I felt a rush of anguish and rage. How could I have been so stupid? I felt guilt wash over me, and hatred for Pederson. I clenched my fists.

My questioning became efficient. Brisk. I needed answers. 'Tell me the truth, Orla. Show me that respect at least. Was Lenny passing messages from Pederson to Amina? Was he helping somehow?'

Orla held my gaze. There was sadness in her eyes, but also a coldness. A detachment. At that moment I believed her capable of anything. Deception. Murder. Anything but the truth.

Outside we heard a sheep bleat as if startled. Orla looked at me in horror. I shook my head. 'Ignore it. It happens all the time.'

178

But I went out onto the terrace, to reassure her and to clear my head. The night was completely clear now. No clouds. Crisp. Not much wind. Maybe the chances of a storm had passed. Already the stars were out.

The silence of the mountains. They would be here long after we were all gone. What mark would we humans really leave?

I needed to sleep. I needed to talk to Steph, make sure that she wasn't getting any of the threats that Orla had received. I needed to call Emma. First thing tomorrow. We were tired and world-weary enough to cope with the fact I had brought Orla here. Em would understand, just as I had maybe always understood what the bookshop on the Left Bank had really meant. We would muddle through, as always. Reset.

I went back in. First, I needed more truth from Orla.

But she was walking from side to side in front of the fire, shaking her head, eyes darting to the windows. 'Ed, there's a torch. Up there near the road, where the car is. Oh God, I told you they would come.'

I tried to reassure her, but she was adamant. She flinched, her face pale with dread. 'Lock the doors. And the gates at the back. What have you got here that we can defend ourselves with?'

I went out into the barn and picked up one of the axes. The handle was worn from years of log cutting. But I had sharpened the blade on my last visit, and it still had a film of black grease around the cutting edge.

There was no light up near the bridge, and no sound. It must have been a car turning in the narrow road, probably lost. I wondered again about this woman I had brought to the mountains. The flash in her eyes. Those sudden looks of hatred towards me. She surely had an alibi for Amina, as good as anyone's. As good as mine.

Even if she had somehow helped Amina to kill himself – was capable of such an action – she had no motive to harm me, surely?

An image of Orla holding the axe, standing over my lifeless corpse flashed through my mind. I told myself not to be so stupid.

But my heart was pounding despite myself. Something about her fear was infectious. From the terrace I strained my eyes to see into the night. Still. A slight wind now, the breeze coming through the woods behind the cottage. No sound but the crunch of bracken beneath my boots.

A shiver ran through me. The night smelt of woodsmoke, soil and stone.

## 33

We locked the bolts on the front and back doors to the cottage. Orla was purposeful now, every sense straining for any sound or lights outside. A light rain started to tap against the window.

The beam of the torch was now closer to us. I tasted the red wine on the roof of my mouth and the food turning to acid in my stomach.

'Who's coming, Orla?'

She stood by the main window. The torch in the field outside had stopped blinking. We strained our ears.

'Amina had told me she planned to kill herself. Magnus had been getting messages in to her, you're right, pushing her towards a big gesture. I was meant to see her that evening, to take down her testimony, make it part of the story.'

'Why the hell didn't you try to stop her, Orla?'

'I didn't think she would listen. But in the end, she did. When I saw you at the reception I knew that they would start to release the leaks. But I thought I'd talked her out of the suicide. What would it add? Why play his game?'

'And that's why Magnus is coming for you?'

'Yes, I must be on the recording. He must blame me for it not working out like he hoped. He's cleaning up.'

I needed to call Steph and Em. Had they seen Amina that afternoon too? There must be a risk to anyone Pederson believed to have put Amina off, even if she had in the end gone through with a suicide. I was still not convinced she had.

Outside, a sheep bleated and ran. I turned off the light so we wouldn't be illuminated. I had placed the axe on the table. I did not know if I could use it.

Time slowed. I looked through the darkness for Orla and saw her crouched below the main window. I tried to quieten my breathing. There was a sound from the kitchen. A latch falling? A floorboard. The wind rattled the window. I glanced at Orla, her eyes alert with fear. Alert for any sound on the other side of the door, I gripped the handle of the axe with one hand and slowly pulled back the bolt. I felt the presence of someone on the other side. Taking a deep breath, I threw the door open.

In the darkness I could just make out the shape of the man. He was leaning heavily on a worktop.

Holding the axe in front of me, I switched on the light with my elbow.

Max Crawford raised his head. He was covered in mud. A cut above one eye.

'What the hell, Max?'

Behind me Orla had picked up the tongs from the fire and was holding them in front of her. She looked at Crawford with rage and fear.

Max calmly raised his hands. They were also filthy. One was smeared with blood, which he wiped on his trouser leg.

'Ambassador, Miss Fitzgerald. Don't worry. You're safe now.'

I lowered the axe. Orla kept the tongs in her hand.

Max repeated himself, looking at Orla now. 'I said, you're safe.' Reluctantly she lowered her arm. She sank back into a chair.

'What's happened, Max?'

He looked grim. 'You had a visitor. I've dealt with it.'

'Where?'

'The field. Outside. Do you have any whisky?'

Shaking, I went to the cupboard and poured him two fingers. I glanced at Orla and poured us both two as well.

Max knocked his drink back.

'But Max, how did you know we were here? Why did you come?'

He stretched his neck painfully. 'First things first, I'll need your help, Ambassador. We need to bury a body.'

'No way, we go to the police now.'

Max shook his head. Orla stood up. 'He's right, Ed. If you get the police involved now, you can forget finding out what's going on here. We'll be tied in knots. And meanwhile Pederson will be out there, coming after whoever's next on his list.'

I could not risk that person being Steph.

There is not much I can recall of what followed. We walked out to the field. Max lifted the body over his shoulder, up to the marshy bog behind the house. This was where I usually buried the contents of the privy bucket. 'Turd Cemetery', my brother had called it as a child. There were strict rules for each 'burial' itemised in the logbook by our father. Find a place with not too many rocks. At least two spade-lengths deep. Replace the peat carefully. Should be impossible to discover the next day, even by the person doing the burial. Return for a strong drink.

The burial had taken longer and the hole I had dug was deeper. But he would never be found under the wet brown peat. The rain and remoteness would see to that. I tried not to look at him. I scrubbed and scrubbed my hands under the waterfall.

We returned to the cottage, and I poured another four fingers of whisky, my hands still trembling.

'Right, Max, I need answers. Why did you come? And how did you know Pederson would send someone for Orla?'

Max looked into the fire for a while. He had cleaned most of the blood and mud from his face but there was a thin line of dry blood above one eye.

'Ambassador, whoever that was wasn't sent by Pederson. Much more skilled.'

'Then who?'

'Whatever you two were doing in Oxford, you've got the attention of people you don't want to know. Trust me.'

Orla interjected. 'But how do *you* know that? And why should *I* trust you?'

'From where I'm standing, you don't have much choice.'

I couldn't lose time with them arguing, and we had to get away from this place. 'Orla, could this be Tatham's American backers? Did you have more on the Agonistes Programme than you told me? Maybe I was too complacent about them tracking our phones to here.'

Orla was chewing a thumbnail. 'Whether they were the Dissenters or Tatham, you're right. We can't stay here.'

We bleached the room. I pulled on fresh trousers and a shirt and we left the cottage. Normally the final morning before leaving I would soak it all up, squeeze the juice out of every second, taking last longing gulps of the view. Today, as the first light of morning broke through, I almost ran to my car, stumbling across the damp field, the whisky in my throat.

I felt nothing except fear, dread, guilt. And the vast silence of the mountains.

I had to get away from here. Death had followed me into my home, into my family, and now even to the place I considered a refuge. Mountains that had before left me breathless now left me nauseous. Crawford had suggested Hereford, the SAS base. Orla had shrugged, reluctantly. For me it did not matter. Anywhere but this place of dampness, now fetid memories, and death.

Orla climbed into my passenger seat and Crawford followed in his Land Rover. As the car reached the turning back onto the main road and into range of phone reception, I felt mine buzzing in my pocket. The signal and the noise. I thought that I should call Steph. I pulled the car over. Maybe connectivity would bring some kind of escape from the body under the peat and moss.

There were text messages from Stephanie. I felt a wave of relief that she was fine.

> Just checking in, Dad. All okay?

> Hope you're recovering in your mountains. Will join you soon.

> Not too much whisky! Careful under the waterfall.
> Get some walking in but don't overdo it.

> Not to worry about anything. I'm patching things up with Mum. We'll be fine.

I called her three times but there was no reply. I messaged her to stay put at the apartment. And messaged Penny to find her for me, urgently.

A voice message from Emma. 'Ed, I'm staying on in Paris. I don't know how long. Amina... Look, this has all been much harder for me than I can explain. We have to focus on Steph. You need to find whatever it is that's calling you. And it's not me, Ed, I can see that. I've got a room with the guy who owns the shop. It's nothing significant. He's been a good friend to me. I know you'll understand. Edward, everything has changed. Don't call for a while. Let's give ourselves some time.'

She hadn't called me Edward for decades.

I rubbed my temples. More than two decades, and was this how it would start to end? But somehow, I felt no rage. I had nothing left to give. Had this week made me more immune to my emotions? Or was it decades of insincerity? She was right

– something had died, even before death arrived unasked into our home. Sudoku and solidarity were no substitute. I had met the bookseller once. He was scruffy, French, decent, on the heavy side, a gourmand. Unthreatening. But with what I could now sense as an air of awkward apology to him.

The lies we tell ourselves are the worst ones.

The rain was now coming down harder on the grey slate roofs. There was a bleakness to this hopeless landscape. I slumped for a moment over the wheel, forgetting Orla's presence in the car. A marriage ending in a whimper and a voice message. A corpse on a mountainside. A life fading away from me. The only homes I had really ever known – the cottage and the Foreign Office – were now closed to me. Truly, *sans domicile fixe*.

## 34

I barrelled the car through the dawn light, away from the mountains, and back across the English border. By the time we reached Hereford the shops were opening. It was a high street like every other. In medieval times, pilgrims had come here to the shrine of Saint Thomas, leaving models of the legs they wanted cured, or the ships they wanted to return.

As I turned into the cathedral car park, I knew that I had already lost any last innocence in the mountains of Snowdonia and any last idealism in the corridors of Whitehall. All that was left of my own pilgrimage was to protect my daughter and continue to search for the truth about Amina Joshi.

The battered green Land Rover flashed its lights at me, wipers going hard. I could make out Crawford's angular profile. and dutifully followed his car out of the town and through the winding roads towards the SAS base. He had promised refuge and some space to think. I needed the camaraderie, but also access to whatever information he had.

Orla had been silent most of the journey, sleeping fitfully. As we approached the base she urged me again not to trust Crawford. 'Who sent him? How did he know we were there?'

They checked the cars and waved us through the gate. No one asked who I was. The building was a mixture of dark oak-panelled club rooms and over-lit spaces that reminded me of school. There was a memorial to fallen special forces soldiers, and an exhibition honouring Fijian Talaiasi Labalaba and the nine men who had held the fort of Mirbat in the 'secret war' in Oman in the seventies. The place had been furnished by men who preferred to be outdoors.

Crawford seemed unfazed by my forced sabbatical. He continued to call me ambassador, despite my half effort to stop him. Was it sympathy alone? He poured us strong tea and a half tumbler each of whisky. At some point, several plates of toast arrived. I felt suddenly ferociously hungry.

A man in uniform brought me another round of toast and tea. I felt the warmth start to return to my bones. He was in his early fifties, trim, straight-backed. In another era he would have had a moustache.

I craved the refuge of small talk. 'Based here long?'

'Since Iraq. Picked up an injury too many.' The accent was identifiably Scottish but worn down by decades of soldiering.

'Did you serve with General Crawford?' Orla rolled her eyes but was listening intently.

He grinned. 'With Max? Aye, we all served with Max at some point. I was with him in 2003.'

The height of the insurgency in the Sunni Triangle. The longest summer. On both sides, few I knew who had been there could remember much before the sand, wind and blood. Sixteen Brits had been lost to car bombs in a fortnight. There were too many coffins arriving back at Brize Norton. Too many questions in parliament. Too many parents staring without words at the photos of their hopeful, unbroken sons.

The man continued. 'I was the only guy with Max when he took a helicopter into the middle of the camps of one of the main warlords. I remember the intense heat. Dust everywhere. As we walked towards the militia guards, I wondered if we would even hear the first shot. Would it be a slow death, gradually rotting out there amid the desolation? Or slowly decapitated on film? We'd been told to stare back at the camera if that happened, a final act of resistance.'

Crawford came back into the room. He had changed and cleaned up. He looked at us both, grinned quizzically.

'Recovering, Ambassador?'

I nodded. And then gestured at the soldier to continue. He glanced at Crawford, who shrugged at him to carry on. Maybe he could see I needed the diversion.

'The militia leader – Abu Omar they called him – couldn't believe Max had just turned up like that. Strolling into the militia's camp. He offered us a coffee in his tent.'

He laughed, but then was serious again. 'It was dead quiet as they were preparing the coffee on the fire. I remember the tent door kept flapping. And we were just sat there. Guns everywhere and us just sipping away.'

Crawford was looking out of the window now. He made no attempt to stop the story. The man had clearly told it before.

'So Max drinks his coffee really slowly and thanks the guy who made it. It was that hard, bitter stuff they like. And then he looks at the warlord and goes, "I appreciate your hospitality, Abu Omar, and so I will show you the same respect." And I'm looking at the guy closest to us with his AK, and I'm thinking there's not that much respect around, Max.

'Max leans forward. And he is speaking really slowly now. He goes, "I'll be back here, Abu Omar, on this exact spot, in one month. And by then my men will control this piece of land. We'll be preparing to give it back to the Iraqi government." Abu Omar looked right pissed off. The Iraqis hated each other even more than they hated us. Their war would continue long after we buggered off.'

I nodded at him to continue. The Brits had never had the patience for the Middle East. Intervene and it bites you back. Fail to intervene and it bites you back.

'Max slows right down. And he goes, "I'll invite you then to join me for a cup of coffee, should you wish. It would be a pleasure to drink it with you." He put his hands out like this was an invitation to the pub. Abu Omar's smiling, but you can tell he hasn't got a clue what's coming. And then Max starts talking in almost a whisper, so the guy has to lean forward to hear. The militia guys are all straining too, but he doesn't want them to hear. And he goes, "But if you make the wrong choice today, Abu Omar, I shall drink that cup of coffee anyway. I will sit here and drink it beside your smouldering corpse."'

The soldier grinned mischievously. I looked across to Crawford, who was also smiling. He shrugged at me. 'Abu Omar, top man. Worthy adversary. I didn't hate him, but I would have killed him when the time came. Thankfully, after that, it didn't.'

'And what did you do?'

Crawford winked at the soldier, who continued. 'There was a long silence. Abu Omar's body clenched like a fist. I counted the seconds, savouring each one, thinking of the pool in France. Of my boys. Grown up now. Able to cope alone. I had a letter for them set to one side, in case I didn't make it back. Nothing very poetic. Simple words about courage, curiosity and working out who to trust. The things I had learnt, bit by bit, battle by battle. I had always said that a man was fortunate if he could choose the moment of his own death. This was too soon, but it was at least on my terms.

'Finally, Abu Omar told his men to lower their weapons, his palms towards the ground. And he gave me a huge smile. I remember how creased his face was from the sun. He was still deciding what to do. Deciding our fate. To condemn. Or to free. Enjoying the power, even at the moment he was losing it.

'I was crapping it by this point. Could feel the sweat cold at the base of my back. But when he spoke it was as though he had never thought about doing anything else. He just goes, "Let's talk," and more coffee comes. And Max pretty much did the deal there and then.'

Crawford and the soldier were smiling. Just one story among many. I laughed with them, but it caught in the throat as reality crowded back in. A body was below the peat. The shudder rocked me.

Orla cut in, ever the journalist. 'Just one question, Crawford. Does any of this keep you awake at night?'

Crawford paused. He looked grave for a moment. And then the face cleared. One eyebrow cocked. The hint of mischief. 'Not really. I keep people awake at night.'

'And who are you fighting for now?'

Crawford paused and looked across at me. 'I've always fought for the guy next to me.'

I held his eye. 'I really need your help, Max.'

## 35

Crawford nodded at the soldier to leave us. Max looked pretty drained. He didn't need to tell me how terrible I looked.

Orla had tied her hair back, and suddenly seemed pensive. She spoke first. 'They'll come after us again. And after anyone else in their way. But who are they?'

I nodded. 'We're not safe, even with Max. And I'm not going to bury anyone else. The only way to reduce the threat to us, and to Steph, is to find who killed Amina Joshi.'

Max stood. 'If you want to get back to your family, back to the job, can you not accept it as suicide, like everyone else?'

'Too late for that. The knife was swapped. She never finished the note. She wasn't strong enough to slit her own throat. Orla, you said Lenny was running errands for Pederson, but surely not murder? Is he now a danger to Steph?'

Orla shook her head dismissively and gestured towards Max. 'What about your spooks?'

Crawford looked past me. 'Personally, I think the Dissenters can get us too, whatever happened to Amina Joshi in Paris. Harry Parkinson and the spooks have been trying to understand how the camera was installed. Maybe that was where Lenny fitted in?'

Orla stood. 'Not just the camera. If the US and your lot were so worried about the potential data leaks, maybe you had a motive to take out Amina?'

Crawford sighed. 'Harry Parkinson prefers the shadows, for sure. But not murder. He was interested in what the Russians were doing in Paris, and worried Amina Joshi might be part of that. Why wouldn't he be?'

'And were the Russians in contact with Amina?'

'I don't know. The station were monitoring a Russian cultural attaché called Churkin. The kind that didn't do a lot of cultural promotion. No contact with Joshi. But he had been meeting Pederson regularly in the run-up to her death.'

Orla sniffed. 'Magnus was probably playing them too. Is that so suspicious?'

Max deadpanned back, 'In our world, it makes sense to always be suspicious.'

Orla shot back at him, 'In my world too. What did the Russians have to gain?'

'From the leaks? More than anyone. They undermined the Americans, the French, us. Ever since they lost the Cold War, they've been looking to weaponise the internet.'

Crawford had his back to me now, looking out of the window at the rain driving against the glass. 'Different weapons, Ambassador. But I think our real enemy here has never changed. The Russians. The problem is you're running out of people who can help you prove that.'

'I think there's still one who can. And he also has the video showing whoever was with Amina. So how do we get to Pederson?'

Orla was logging on to her laptop. She had her sense of purpose back now. 'Ed, of course I'm scared of what Pederson may try to do next. But surely the immediate threat is from whoever came after us to Wales?' She gestured towards Crawford. 'And that means more answers from him.'

Max shrugged. 'Who's to say that wasn't Pederson's guy on the mountain? We can't know.'

Orla stood and turned towards him. 'Because you killed him! Why not keep him alive?'

Max's eyes narrowed uncharacteristically. 'If I hadn't come it would have been your body under that bog. So let's ease up on the moral purity?'

I calmed them down. Orla was too willing to deflect attention away from Pederson. Max was too willing to deflect it away from the alternatives.

'Max, if it wasn't the Dissenters coming for Orla, then who was it?'

Crawford shifted uncomfortably in his seat. 'In this place, we want to believe the best of America, our "Shining City on a Hill". The first enlightened superpower. Yes, they blunder a bit. But we believed JFK about America paying any price for the survival and the success of liberty. We know what that meant in blood and dollars.'

Orla rolled her eyes. 'So the Americans came for us? Or they sent you to find us and bring us in?'

Max shook his ahead. 'Like I said, I fight for the guy next to me. What were you really doing in Oxford?'

I moved in again to calm them. 'We know Pederson is a threat to Orla. Whether that was his guy or not, we need to be ready for that. I'm convinced that Pederson is a threat to Steph too.'

Max turned to me, fired up. 'And it's clear from the intel that he has something against you personally.' He paused. 'That's what we need to worry about. That's why I came to the mountains.'

Orla rolled her eyes. 'We're focusing on the wrong story. Magnus Pederson has half the world after him. Tatham has the answers.'

I stood. 'This isn't just a story to me, Orla. We just buried a guy on the mountain. My daughter's not safe. I'm losing my job, my family, everything I've worked for, everything that matters to me.'

Max cut in, placatory. 'Okay, let's do it her way. What do you have so far on Tatham?'

I calmed myself. 'We know they're collecting data for the Americans as part of the Agonistes Programme. But Pederson must have more than that. You were clear, Orla: that's what was firing up his discussions with Amina. Max, what else do we really know about Agonistes?'

Crawford shrugged. 'Not much has reached us here.'

I held his eye for a few moments, searching for what he really knew. But he stared back, unblinking. Whatever it was, he wasn't going to share it in front of Orla.

Orla was opening and closing documents on her laptop, the investigative journalist again, trying to make connections. 'What if Agonistes was just one programme among many?'

I looked around the room, trying to connect the dots. On one wall was a cabinet with instructions and kit to use in the event of a biological weapons attack. Inside were N95 masks, disposable thermometers, protective goggles. This was pretty standard stuff since the pandemic.

'What kind of data was thrown up by the pandemic?'

Orla cocked her head. 'It was a gold rush. Everyone sacrificed what they could to stay safe. Governments needed to map who was most vulnerable to infection. Why?'

'Amina Joshi and Pederson wanted different things. And neither had an ego that could accommodate a partner. But there must have been a big enough threat to make them work together.'

Max nodded. 'In war, we sometimes have to make tactical, temporary alliances.'

Great people finish your sentences; the best ones start them. I leant forward, energised again. It was becoming clearer to me where I needed to be next.

'In diplomacy too. I need to get on a plane.'

Crawford grinned. 'Copenhagen?'

I drained my coffee, feeling my strength return. 'Yes. But that means we all have to trust each other, just a bit more. Max, can you get Orla back to Paris?'

Max glanced across at Orla. She winced. 'I don't need protection from either of you.'

'I'm not offering you my protection, Orla. I'm asking for yours. You need to help Steph understand the danger she could still be in. She won't take that from Max. Or me. And Emma… look, I just need your help.'

Orla shrugged. 'Okay. But on one condition. Whatever you get from Magnus, we then go after Tatham together. I'll work on the pandemic link.'

'Max, what do we have on how I can find Pederson?'

The Scottish soldier came back in, handed Max a note, avoiding my eye.

Max looked at the ground. 'Sorry, Ambassador. Message just in. You're no longer "we".'

It hurt more than I hoped he saw.

He reflected for a moment. And then handed me an envelope. 'But like I always say: proceed until apprehended.'

## 36

Copenhagen was drizzly and overcast, the sky darkening as I walked towards the warehouse. A slight wind, and storm clouds coming in from the Baltic Sea. I was knife cold, and I could feel the damp soaking through my impractical brogues. But for the first time since Amina's murder my head felt clear. I was where I was meant to be. I would not leave until I had some answers. And until I had the space to fight for my family, and for my old life.

There is no such thing as the end of history.

I had known that I would have to go to Copenhagen long before Crawford's intel on Pederson's relationship with Moscow. Long before losing any last trust in the Americans. Even before his threats had escalated. I had known when I saw the fear in Orla's eyes, and then imagined it in Steph's.

Crawford had seen me off, looking less bullish than usual. He had wanted me to stay longer at the base in Hereford, take time to think through the next move. A role reversal for the ambassador and the man of action. He had then offered to come with me, but I wanted to do it my way. Orla had been businesslike, setting everything up to go back to Paris.

I had spoken to Steph, told her not to leave the embassy until Orla got to her. Penny had agreed to ensure that decent security stayed outside the apartment. Steph had been silent when I warned her again that she might be at risk from Magnus Pederson. But she had begged me not to go to Copenhagen.

As I left, the last thing Crawford said to me was, 'Move fast, stay low.' I had smiled at the solidarity. The reception in Paris seemed years and continents away.

I booked a last-minute flight for the following morning and checked into an airport hotel so that I could get rid of the car. I wanted to be away from Wales, from Hereford, from the sense that events were moving too fast. I needed to take back control.

Digital technology gives us a sense of agency: the ability to book a flight, order anything we need. And yet it takes away something too. The modern world was not doing me any favours at that moment. The original Dissenters could never have dreamt of what could now be done in their name.

I travelled light. I always did. I did not plan to stay long in Copenhagen. Crawford had arranged for a car to collect me at the airport and take me to the address where the intelligence said that Magnus was holed up. I had to get there before whoever else wanted to find him.

The driver said little on the journey. His hair was matted, and he had a scar on his neck. He had a faint Russian accent. I thought of messaging Crawford to check that he was the guy he had sent. But I didn't want to look needy any more.

Twenty minutes from the airport, he pulled over and turned down a dusty road through a field of sugar beet. I tested the doorhandle, but it was locked from the outside. Once we were three minutes from the main road, he stopped the car, looked at me for a while and started to open the glove compartment. I pressed back against the seat, cursing myself silently for not having told anyone else I was coming, for not having left behind the evidence I had accumulated. I tried to think of Steph but instead of her face, I could only see Orla as she had been in Wales, that terror in her eyes.

He would not kill me in the car. My best chance of escape would be as he tried to get me outside. His shoulders were sinewy through the T-shirt. Clearly ex-military. I could at least leave evidence – keeping my eyes on him, I pulled hairs from my scalp and dropped them on the floor of the car.

I felt strangely calm. My capacity for shock had been run down in Paris and the mountains.

He straightened up and I prepared myself.

But he turned to me with a grin. 'Mr Edward.' He handed me a package, bound with tape. 'A gift. From the general.'

Inside was a revolver. A Glock 43. I felt its weight in my hand, unfamiliar after many years. My last weapons permit had been in Afghanistan. I opened the cartridge, reaching back in my mind for my hostile environment training. Six bullets. Good old Crawford. Loyal as ever. I exhaled too hard. The driver chuckled to himself.

I held the gun for the rest of the journey, my mind now alert, feeling its weight. The driver pulled up at the edge of an industrial estate near the docks where the bright red, blue and yellow containers came and went every day, loading and unloading their cargo into slate-grey warehouses. A human ant hill, yet strangely empty. Empty car parks. Empty garages. There was a bleakness to it all.

'All okay?' he asked. I nodded, grimly. He gestured towards a large steel warehouse, with the look of an aircraft hangar. The place looked like it had been built for people who loathed beauty and creativity. 'Max told me to wait here. It only works if Pederson knows you are truly alone.'

I left him and walked up and down the road. There was no sign of any life. The breeze had picked up and blew clouds of dust into my face. I waited across the road from the warehouse, watching for activity, feeling the Glock in my jacket pocket and smelling the fish and petrol on the air.

For the first two hours, there was nothing. I started to get hungry and restless. I was about to head off to get a sandwich when a woman in a long black coat came towards me up the street. I ducked into a doorway but she was focused on her phone. She had short spiky hair, badly dyed blonde. She walked past the front of the warehouse, ignoring the main door, and then – with a brief look up and down the street – down a side passage. I counted ten seconds and crossed the road and followed her. My footsteps on the gravel were like a screwdriver on a glass vase.

At the end of the passage, she turned right. I waited a moment and moved to see where she went next. She typed a code into a keypad by the back door. Five or six digits? And then she entered.

I waited. I couldn't see any cameras along the back wall of the warehouse. After five minutes I went to the keypad. It was letters not numbers.

I wondered how many mistakes it would allow before they were alerted. Three, maximum? I breathed deeply, trying to read the mind of my enemy.

Orla had spoken of his Samson fixation. I tapped the letters – S.A.M.S.O.N. But the door stayed locked. I chewed my thumbnail. Something else biblical? He was more Old Testament than New. Not big on love and forgiveness. Isaac? The son whose life mattered less to his father than a loyalty test from God. Again, nothing.

This was too far to come without seeing Pederson. I thought about trying 'Amina'. But Pederson would not have preserved her in this way, whatever pedestal she had fallen from. He had moved on, and – if she had not killed herself – she had let him down.

And then the door swung open. Pederson was playing with me.

The first four hangars were empty. Crates and dust. In one, hooks that must have suspended sacks of flour or grain. There was a slight odour of animals. I felt again for the weapon in my jacket pocket. I was uncertain whether I would have the confidence to use it. Unsure whether I would need to.

There were rubbish sacks outside the fifth hangar, full of shredded paper. I opened one but could only decipher numbers. I crouched outside the door for a while, trying to sense how many people were inside. But there was no sound. I felt the sweat around my neck.

A sliver of light under the door. I listened for several minutes. Still no voices. But daubed on the wall above the entrance were the words from an old Apple ad:

> *Here's to the crazy ones... the ones who see things*
> *differently – because the ones who are crazy enough to*
> *think that they can change the world are the ones who do.*

I swung the door slowly open.

Inside, though, there was nothing. Some old boxes and crates. The thin layer of dust suggested it had not been used much for a while. A stale smell of damp and grime. Had they packed up and moved on? I scanned the warehouse. In one corner was an open door. I crossed the warehouse and looked down into the gloom. It led down to some kind of basement. It was not lit.

I checked my phone signal, having promised Crawford I would put the location tracking on. I took out the weapon and started to descend the stairs, trying to keep my steps light. There was a steel door at the bottom of the staircase. In the dark I felt for a handle but there was nothing. I leant against the frame, but it did not move.

Standing in the dark, I wondered whether to knock. And then the door above me slowly shut, the hinge rusty and heavy. The noise echoed down the steps behind me. I was trapped.

I placed the weapon back in my jacket and waited. A single light bulb came on. The bright light made me recoil. The door opened from the inside.

The basement was cramped and dark. There was a small shaft of natural light from the street above, but it had the feel of a bomb shelter. The air was warmer and heavier.

Magnus Pederson was behind his laptop. He was unwashed and scowling. I recognised him immediately from Orla's description. But his hair was longer and greasier. How long had he been cooped up here?

A girl with short blonde hair and a white T-shirt with the sleeves cut off was at the large industrial table next to him, scanning through documents, staring at a screen. It was the girl I had watched arrive. They could have been a pair of tramps. The Bonnie and Clyde of web anarchists.

My footsteps echoing through the basement, I walked slowly towards them and into the centre of the web. I had known all the way here that this was probably a trap. It had all been too easy. But I had to be here. And I still believed then that I had nothing left to lose.

Pederson looked up. His face contorted to a sneer, but there was also a glimmer of recognition and satisfaction. We faced each other in silence. Paris, London, Oxford, Wales, Copenhagen. For a moment, I wondered if he felt a sense of anti-climax.

'I was so glad to see you book the flight. I thought you would come sooner once you got my note. We have so much to discuss.' Pederson's voice was deep, more commanding than the nasal snivel I had expected. It dripped with disdain and lack of curiosity.

The disdain was real. The lack of curiosity was not. He had been relishing this moment. In my way, so had I.

## 37

Pederson folded his arms as he looked me up and down. I had told myself only to ask questions. But now the days of frustration were welling up in me.

'Of course you knew I would come. You know everything. So you must also know I'm here because you came for Orla.'

Pederson smiled thinly. 'Orla? We haven't spoken since before Amina died. I gave her what she needed to write her stories. I'm just frustrated that she hasn't done more of that.'

'And what's that?'

He rolled his eyes. 'What do you really believe in, Mr Ambassador?' He said the title with the same tone I had used when addressing Lynn Redwood as 'foreign secretary', shifting power away from the person with the title. 'Democracy? The UN? British values? Maybe moderation. Tolerance? Tell me, I've been dying to know.'

I breathed out deeply. I realised that my fists were balled at my side. I needed to compose myself, to de-escalate. *Remember why you've come. Don't get side-tracked. Don't take the bait.*

Actually, thanks to him, I did believe in something. I believed in my family. And I believed that if you scrape away all the detritus of conflict and filth, you still find a human instinct to collaborate, to cooperate. That there is an inherent solidarity to us.

You can't put any of that on a T-shirt or a poster or build a movement with it. You can't chant it at a demonstration or turn it into a hashtag. But this week had shown me that it was enough for me. And this man wanted to tear it down.

'Why does it matter so much to you what I believe?' I stepped towards him. 'You're not really offering people anything new, just a rejection of the status quo.'

Magnus Pederson had cocked his head to one side and was watching me intently. He seemed to be waiting. Orla had talked of his need for a nemesis. Perhaps we shared that need. A silence, but then the dismissive shrug.

He was an insecure man disguised as a prophet.

'What choice do we have? A slow corrosion of our species as we give in to their algorithms? Or a proper reset. Your institutions and values can't defend us. The twenty-first century is a terrible time to be a control freak, Barnes.'

I felt my certainty grow. This was the argument I had been having, with Lynn Redwood, with Angus Green, with Peter Kane, with myself. Now my real adversary was finally in front of me. But why me, among all the other faceless bureaucrats?

He was standing now. His left hand scratched at his right forearm. I noticed the scars, long and deep, purple against the thick dark hair.

Pederson snarled, 'Amina was right about one thing. Nation states are done, Barnes. You surely know that – you represent one. Or is it *represented*, now? Don't you feel power slipping through your fingers? You are not necessarily guilty, but you are deeply responsible. Who is really more dangerous? Me? Hoon? Or Peter Tatham? Ask yourself that, honestly.'

I tried to keep my voice calm. He needed to rile me. 'Yes, diplomacy fails, politics fails, again and again. But that doesn't mean we need less of it.' I looked around the room. The door had shut behind me. For the first time, I wished I had taken Crawford's offer to come with me. I couldn't see how this ended.

'Oh Barnes, it's too late for your moral mediocrity.' Pederson was laughing now. 'Technology is moving too fast for you. Look at what the printing press did to society. The internet will make that look like a minor twist in history. I'm just a symptom. So are Tatham and his data scientists, selling the American government data on who to target. Think what can be done by Elizabeth Hoon with all that data: the end of freedom. But whether he wins this round or I do, you are all losing ground by the day. And you are just spectators, Barnes.' He spat out the words with increasing virulence. Maybe he had also waited too long for this argument. 'You tolerate the intolerable.'

The girl had stopped listening and had gone back to her screen. But Pederson didn't need an audience. His eyes darted as he spoke, constantly searching for enemies seen and unseen.

'And Amina's death is tolerable. Collateral damage? What about all these kids whose minds you're twisting? They had families, futures. You poison them with talk of suicide and sacrifice. How is that tolerable?'

'Suicide has always been the ultimate weapon in a war of ideologies. Amina thought she could get people to listen, but she was always going to fail. That's why I needed her to commit suicide.'

'But it didn't go to plan, did it?'

'We could have really ignited something. But she botched it. Failed to handle the theatre.'

We were now standing just a few feet apart, squared up. I could almost reach out and hit him. The girl continued to scroll through her screen, ignoring us.

'So how did she die?'

'We'll get to that, Barnes, don't worry.'

We stared at each other in silence for a moment.

'Tell me about Tatham and the Americans.'

I wanted to buy time while I worked out where this ended. I instinctively rested my hand on the outside of my jacket, feeling the outline of the gun.

Pederson sneered. 'You are a Tetris mind in a Minecraft world. Everyone can see that but you. You are a part of an organogram, a plaque on a door, a gong. What gives you legitimacy any more than me? An appointment letter from a monarch? Distrust gives humanity the violent jolt it needs to reset itself, to find its moral compass again.'

'Was Tatham the reason Amina died?'

Pederson laughed, his yellow teeth showing.

I could feel my anger rising. I thought of the footage. Hundreds of teenagers trying to set themselves on fire. *And here I make my sacrifice.* 'You're so certain of yourself that you deny others the currency of uncertainty. You're telling them there's only one way to think. And that's a denial of *their* freedom.'

His face was reddening now, his self-assurance gone. 'You know your problem? You still think people want to be free. You people have given up our collective liberty for safety: your safety. You created terrorist threats that allow you to monitor us and access our data. You stole the internet and made it a place of oppression.'

I squared my shoulders. 'And what have you sacrificed, Pederson?'

'I'm ready to give up everything for liberty.'

'You're fighting against the future, Pederson, not against me. Think you're some kind of prophet? So did the original Dissenters. And history won't pause for a moment by your corpse, any more than it does by theirs.' I thought for a moment of Crawford and Abu Omar.

'Enough, Pederson, I came here for some answers.'

He yawned, a smile playing on his lips. The frenzy had passed, and he was back in control. Every pore seemed to ooze apathy and scepticism. I was disarmed again. Everyone has a plan until they get punched in the face.

He sat back down and stretched his gangly legs out on the table. 'Truth? I've warned you again and again. Be careful what you wish for, Ambassador.'

## 38

Magnus Pederson was relishing the moment. He was almost licking his lips with anticipation. A sense of certainty. I stood, glaring back at him. Every path, every conversation, had led here. And I needed to stay, despite every instinct telling me to turn around now and walk away.

'You say that you're all about truth and transparency, Pederson. Give me some.'

Pederson stared back at me. 'Be my guest. Where do you want to start?'

'Why are you threatening Orla?'

He laughed. 'I have no idea where she is. But she's nothing to me now. She let us down twice: once when she refused to help us bug your embassy, and again when she convinced Amina not to kill herself. She even tried to get me to keep you out of all this. We could have made her the greatest journalist alive.'

I wrenched my mind away from the body on the mountain. The smell of moss and blood.

Pederson hadn't noticed me flinch. 'Meanwhile, Tatham and his scientists are continuing their crimes. What we have released online so far is nothing compared to what we are putting out in the coming hours. Your world will come crashing down around you. And the Agonistes Programme will die a public and agonising death, like every act of tyranny before it. Mobs will be storming that building in Oxford. They will put the heads of Tatham and his scientists on the spikes where they belong.'

'Why coax me here?'

He snarled back, 'Coax? You're terrified about what I have on you. Like everyone. With good reason in your case. And you are curious about me.'

'I'm not terrified about what you have on me.' He could see I was lying. 'Is it the recreational drugs? A student fling with Lynn Redwood? Maybe my mistake in Afghanistan. Do your worst. I'm flawed. I own my mistakes.'

He smiled broadly. 'I'm not sure with everything else we have out there that your pot-smoking really counts as scandal. And I hadn't realised you were part of Redwood's misadventures.' He turned his head, wearily, the neck cracking. 'And no, I didn't hope you would come because I wanted a debate about who ends up on the right side of history. You choose your history and I'll choose mine. You choose your truth and I'll choose mine.'

'So why me?'

'We'll get to that. Maybe I wanted to see how you coped with truth. Maybe now you're here, I need you as protection, too. Think of yourself as a human shield. Leverage. The Americans are inside our organisation. They must already know what is in the next leak. And, assuming they're tracking your location, they know by now exactly where we are. They probably gave you the intel. Good. Our destruction will be another perfect work of art. But you'll buy us time, Barnes. They might not come charging in all guns blazing now you are here. And if they do, your sacrifice will be one more way to get the world to listen. It may be the best thing you ever do for freedom.'

I felt numb. Why had Crawford let me find this place? What did the Americans have to gain from letting me find it? Who now had I been wrong to trust?

Pederson swung his legs off the table. 'You are probably a good man, Barnes. But you are an idiot. Now at least you can be a useful one. You gave Amina refuge, and now we will give you a form of refuge. From a world that you no longer understand. I hope for your sake we prove to be better at providing safety for you than you did for her. But somehow I doubt it. And maybe your brief time with us will help you decide whose side you're *actually* on.'

I scowled. 'And Amina? A woman died in my embassy. Just because everyone seems to have wanted that doesn't make it acceptable to me. I know Lenny was helping you run messages to her. And you must know who killed her. You have the video.'

He laughed and stood up. 'Who really cares what happened to Amina Joshi? She chose her path and her friends. I was one of them for a time. The Russians wanted her dead, too, but they probably couldn't get into your residence without leaving too many footprints. The Americans wanted her silenced, but surely even Hoon wouldn't sanction an attack on a British embassy. And we wanted a sacrifice that could launch the revolution. Yes, your butler was a great help. I understand he was a great help to you too. Those purchases that ambassadors don't tend to make? Anyway, he got the camera in, helped to prepare everything. One more person you were wrong to trust.'

I felt the anger rising. 'Lenny was one more useful idiot to you. One more chance for you to play God.' I strode towards Pederson. The blood was pumping in my temples.

'Pederson, what's on that film? Why keep it hidden till now?'

'The only question for us is whether it helps or not to release it. I'm still in two minds. The conspiracy theories help us, especially once your governments claim it is suicide. We think she was suicided. You want to watch a film with me? We gave it to the Russians already. I'm keen you watch. Or you can ask your military adviser what happened.'

I had prepared myself for Lenny. But not Crawford. I felt my stomach lurch. And yet it suddenly made sense. He had fought alongside the Americans for decades. If they had ordered him to help carry out the crime, he would surely have done so without flinching. He was one of the first in the room. In Hereford, he had also put me off the idea that anyone inside the embassy had helped. He had made it too easy for me to get here.

But now it was my turn to flinch, and Pederson was enjoying watching it. Was Crawford the real threat to Steph?

The betrayal surged through me. Crawford had been my most loyal adviser. All this blood. It was time. I confronted Pederson. 'All this because you couldn't protect a girl who didn't even want you around? Orla told me the story.'

I had found the weak spot. He was angry too now. 'How dare you lecture me, old man. Least of all about protecting her.' He struggled to compose himself. 'You want to know what is on my video?'

He gestured to me to sit and opened his laptop. I braced myself. A few keystrokes, and there was Amina Joshi's face. She was wearing the white blouse in which I had found her. The picture quality was good. She was sitting, in her room at the residence, staring back at the camera, composing herself. She swallowed hard. I felt suddenly cold, but unable to tear myself away. It was like watching the Afghan video again, knowing what was coming.

Pederson was watching me as I watched the screen. 'Lenny wasn't enough, Barnes. The answer is closer to home. Let's watch the video together, if you can. You can have your truth. And then I'll tell you why I wanted to see you so badly.'

On the screen, Amina smoothed down her blouse. She looked outwardly calm, but a vein in her temple pulsed. She glanced at someone off camera and nodded. What had Crawford done?

Pederson paused the video. He was smiling at me, relishing his moment. 'You have to remember that Amina Joshi was above all an artist. And we wanted to set up her death like the perfect piece of art. What can be more beautiful than suicide? The ultimate freedom of choice. Penance for the bad decisions she had taken. She hoped it would inspire the millions who will come after us. Every teenager in her T-shirt is an act of terror to their parents and community. Time bombs. The only question is who in your embassy was ready to help.'

I shrugged. 'Play the bloody tape, Pederson.' I was determined not to give him any more satisfaction. I leant forward, waiting to see who else would be on the screen.

He paused, alert. The slightest of noises, over by the door of the basement. A brief look of terror flashed across his face. The nonchalant, greasy internet rebel was gone and instead he was cat-like, poised, eyes darting around the building, his instincts sharp.

For a moment he had forgotten I was there. But then, satisfied there had been nothing by the door, he turned back to face me with a snarl. He gestured to the assistant to start the tape. 'Leave the gun in your pocket, Barnes; you wouldn't have the guts. Let's watch our film.'

It was at that moment that the room suddenly went dark. I crouched in fear, alert for any sound, heart pounding. Was this one more act of theatre from Pederson and his box-office anarchists? Was my humiliation to be beamed to a watching internet? I could hear Pederson's breath, heavier now. I was almost relieved to realise that he was as terrified as me.

And then the basement was full of sound. Bullet pops, loud and close, two seconds apart. I spun, trying to hide, trying to escape the noise. And then silence.

I lay face down on the ground. I tried to hold onto an image. Any image. Steph as a child, crying in my arms, snuggled on my shoulder. A waterfall in Snowdonia. A sunset in the Rift Valley.

My eyes became accustomed to the darkness. Two figures were lying next to me. Rag dolls on the stone floor. Limbs spread, awkwardly. I blinked a few more times. It was Pederson and the woman. The laptop lay between them, the screen smashed.

There were footsteps behind me. Would I hear the bullet before it hit me? If this was the Americans, I was here because it was helpful for me to be collateral damage. I had a feeling of relief amid the fear. No more searching.

The blood pumped in my temples. The image seared back into my consciousness – the ram, bleeding, breathing, staring. I tried hard to stay conscious.

Too much blood.

As the edges blurred and everything started to go black, the last thing I heard was a familiar voice. Max Crawford. I screamed at him, furious at his betrayal.

'Like I always say, Ambassador. Proceed until apprehended.'

## 39

I came round in a Copenhagen hospital. My head ached, there was a bandage on my cheek, and one of my knuckles was grazed. I felt trapped by the smell of disinfectant and laundry. For several hours I drifted in and out of consciousness.

They told me a missile had hit the warehouse, killing everyone in the basement. But that I had already been taken outside, and a car had dropped me at the door of the casualty wing. I had been hit by debris from the building but my life had been saved. They had treated me for concussion and shock. Had I imagined the shots? The moment of betrayal? Max Crawford's voice?

As I came round again the American strike on the city was all over the television. Throughout the hospital, doctors and patients were gathered around monitors, transfixed. President Hoon was behind a Rose Garden podium, smiling resolutely. There were shots of what was left of the warehouse. The docks and the sirens. The aerial shot of the building before and after the blast. Shock and awe for a reality-TV presidency.

I was hollowed out, incapable any more of shock or awe myself.

I tried to piece it together. Pederson was clearly dead, the target of the US attack. I was certain, even through the fog, that Crawford had been there in the warehouse. He must have killed Pederson, to prevent the Dane showing me that Crawford had killed Amina Joshi. 'Closer to home.'

And he had then changed the knife. He had then turned up in the mountains to find out what we had on Tatham and the Americans, killing Pederson's assassin (or perhaps just placing a body) to ensure my trust. Following orders throughout. From the UK government? Or direct from the Americans? It looked as if he had died in the strike. Perhaps having worked so hard to tidy up for the Americans, it had become necessary for them to tidy him up.

I felt my anger rise again. But whatever his betrayal, Crawford – or someone – seemed to have got me out of the building after I had passed out. Could he also therefore have got out himself? And was he still alive? If so, might he be the real danger to Steph? But why go to all that trouble to get me to go to Copenhagen, and then pull me out of the wreckage?

I was also troubled by Pederson's final words. He had seemed genuinely uninterested in Orla. After working so hard to use them to get my attention he had seemed unexcited by the potential leaks he could use against me. He had relished telling me that Amina Joshi had been helped by someone at the embassy, and that Crawford knew more than he was telling me. But he had also said that the Russians had the film.

But how I could prove any of it? Without Crawford, I would no longer have access to backdoor UK intel or analysis. And I could not trust what he had given me in Hereford.

On the screen in my hospital room, CNN were interviewing Josh Packer, the president's chief of staff. I turned the volume up.

'You know, the president has the toughest job on the planet. She is bulletproof. When the world looks to America for leadership, by God she provides it. These are not normal circumstances. And it's her job to keep the lights on in the Shining City on a Hill. Sometimes that means she has to act against threats to our way of life. Hardworking families up and down the country were fearing for their kids. Our troops were being placed in danger. These terrorists were clearly such a threat.'

The CNN reporter, teeth white, shoulders broad, looked breathless. These stories came along once in a lifetime. 'Mr Packer, sir, can you tell us how and when the decision was taken?'

'Clearly we are dealing with very highly classified issues. But I can confirm that the Chiefs were informed. I can also confirm that the Chair of the Joint Chiefs has resigned with immediate effect. That is a matter for him.'

'But who exactly was in the warehouse?'

'We knew that the leader of this group and one of his associates were in the building. And one other individual, whose identity is not clear, but who had fired rubber bullets prior to the strike. That individual had already removed a further person, who we believed to have been injured, before returning to the scene. He is a British citizen, and we are in touch with the relevant authorities to establish his whereabouts. The president is clear that America deserves respect. Now if you will excuse me...'

The footage switched back to the reporter. 'But sir, one final question, is there a name for this operation?'

Packer paused. His lip curled slightly. 'Sure: Drain the Swamp.'

We had known that President Hoon was erratic. But a strike against a civilian target in Copenhagen? Data leaks and suicides were not enough to explain the rationale behind such an action. And protecting details of Tatham's sentiment mining was not a big enough incentive for someone to have tried to kill Orla. There had to be something else.

Coverage switched to more burning bodies. Kids with wild eyes killing themselves in T-shirts with Amina's face on the front. *And here I make my sacrifice.* Terrified parents, panicked leaders. Every hour lost was costing someone something or someone they loved.

I looked at the camera roll on my phone for the photo of the contact list I had found in Tatham's desk. Orla and Pederson both knew there was something they hadn't found. Both felt Amina Joshi might be hiding something from them about her contact with Tatham and the Agonistes Programme. This was the only opening I had.

I called Winter, my Oxford friend. He answered with initial irritation. 'What is it?'

'Guy. It's Ed Barnes. I need your quick advice on something.'

'Ed! Apologies. I was immersed. You've been a busy chap, I gather.'

'Long story. Look. I don't have much time. Do you know any of the epidemiologists at the university?'

He paused for a moment.

'Just one. Dr Suzanne Morley. She's been at the college for a few years. Not a great team player. Science-type. Introvert.'

I looked at the list. There was an SM.

'Anything else?'

'I can't imagine she's great at parties. The small talk alone...'

Now it was my turn to be irked.

'Anything else *relevant*?'

'Not really. From what I gather, her research focuses on how different people have underlying immunity – or not – to various diseases. She had a moment in the sun during the last pandemic. Enjoyed it a bit too much. Got a little... hoity-toity. We all thought so anyway.'

I thanked Winter and hung up. Dons and spies. Never far apart.

A root round the internet for anything on Morley showed that her focus was on using data to improve health outcomes. 'In less than twenty years, there'll be no need for the smartphone. It will all be integrated with the body. We'll monitor health conditions and make changes to their diet. We'll extend their lives. The next great leap towards immortality.' When she had been asked how people would consent, she had said – enraging the twitterati – that 'it would take a pandemic to shift people's ability to trust a system they need.'

She had been de-platformed from one academic conference for comments on variations in immunity, comparing diet, ethnicity and social background. Morley had noted that conservatives had been less likely to die in the last pandemic. She put it down to less travel, less interaction with different social groups, more remote communities. She speculated that the most probable types of pandemics in the future would be more likely to kill older, mainly white and Western men with high-sugar diets. Different social groups had different underlying vulnerabilities. So the choice of where to focus research and funding was hugely political.

The TV screen showed a still photo of Pederson's body. His head was disfigured. But the insolent curl of the lip was replaced by something else, maybe even the slightest hint of a smile?

Like leading the Americans to him had indeed been the best thing I had ever done for liberty. Like he thought he had won.

## 40

Trying to get the image of Pederson's corpse out of my head, I tried to work out my next move.

I called Steph, who confirmed she was safe with Orla at the apartment. Penny had sorted the extra security.

'Dad, have you spoken to Mum?'

'Sort of. You?'

'I'm too angry with her.'

I struggled to reply. 'Don't be, Steph.'

Silence. 'Did you find what you were looking for in Copenhagen?'

I was reluctant to say much on the phone. 'Not really. But I'm learning not to trust anyone.'

'It was a mistake for you to go.' Her voice was hesitant. 'What did he say, Dad?' She had clearly feared Pederson too.

'Just tell Orla she was right about Max Crawford. Whatever happens, don't let him near the apartment. And stay put. We can't assume we're safe just because Pederson's gone.'

I needed to keep moving. I was still in the fight. I had no desire to be part of whatever aftermath there would be in Copenhagen. Every time I paused, I was haunted by images of Amina, of the body on the mountain, and what might happen to Steph. I did not want the Americans or anyone else to find me, and I had to assume Crawford had told them I was there. I was no longer sure who I could trust.

At the centre of the mystery remained the camera footage. I assumed it would show Crawford. But was that enough to explain why Pederson was so angry towards me personally? He clearly had more to tell me than Crawford's role, and his next leak was meant to blow the lid on whatever Tatham and the Americans were doing with all that data. Assuming everything in Copenhagen had been destroyed, that left only the Russians with the information I needed. There was only one person I knew who could get me a meeting with them.

I messaged Orla. She confirmed Steph was calm and safe. She knew not to ask about Copenhagen on an open line.

> Orla, I can't say more here, but I think your instincts were better than mine on our friend from Hereford. Either way I need to get to the Russians, to Churkin: the spy that Max said was Pederson's handler. Are you still in touch with Nasib in Lebanon? See if he can get me a meeting with the Russians. At the right level. Tell him to say it is about what happened in Paris. And that I won't be empty-handed.

Lebanon. For decades it had been the place to trade secrets. But if I could sit down with the Russians, what would they ask of me in return?

Orla messaged back immediately.

> Only if I can come, too.

Nasib was everyone's favourite ex-warlord, the great survivor. Orla needed her story. I needed an ally. If I got what I wanted, she could write it up, expose Crawford and the Americans. If I failed, she could at least tell Emma and Steph why I had tried.

I sat back on the pillow. The smell of antiseptic was making me nauseous. Surely it would not be long before they found me here. I would be asked the questions I was not ready to answer. Why were you in Copenhagen? Why did you obstruct the investigation in the embassy? Who were you protecting? Who is the body on your mountain?

I texted back.

Let's see if the arak is still good at our usual place.

It was not difficult to find a space on the flight, and I had hit the gin hard in the British Airways lounge. After the sleepless nights following Snowdonia I had then slept most of the flight, a restless, alcohol-soaked sleep. I dreamt I was under the soil in Wales, fighting to escape. That I was kneeling in the sand in Afghanistan, facing a camera, watching a hooded man approach with a blunt knife. When I woke my face was drenched in sweat. I felt disorientated. Remorseful.

As we circled Beirut, I was handed a landing card. Name, address, purpose of visit, profession? I paused. What was I now? Ex-excellency? Recovering ambassador? Failed husband? Liability? Detective? Absent father? Accomplice? Accessory? Useful idiot? Truth seeker?

I opted for 'diplomat', but with no capital 'D'.

Below me lay the ramshackle southern suburbs of Beirut. This was Hizballah's base, and the chaos was just a veneer. On our right as we turned to land was the Mediterranean, with yachts and fishing boats dotted towards the horizon. In the distance stood the skyscrapers and marinas of the new Beirut. Alongside the pockmarked Holiday Inn, a ghoulish remnant of the civil war.

And something else was down there. Was it adventure I was looking for? Or just distraction? And what else might I find? Closure? Liberation? Death?

I moved as quickly as I could through the lounging security guards and duty-free shops of the airport and out into the raw air of the Middle East – it smelt of jacaranda and carcass, life and death. I took a taxi, rattling and defying death between the potholes, straight to the slightly faded grandeur of the Phoenicia Hotel. The building had been the most exotic place in town during Beirut's glory days. But then it became the battleground of civil war militias. Arafat had been photographed at the piano, a Kalashnikov at his side. It had been a time of blood and treachery. No one was safe from the hiss of the sniper bullet. At one point, one militia had even raised funds by offering American big game hunters the chance to come and shoot at humans from the top floors of the hotel.

Now the hotel lobby was full of European and Middle Eastern businessmen. The bustle of the East meeting the West. The Lebanese were history's greatest traders. Millennia of business had given them the eye for the deal.

I checked into a room looking out over the brash new marina and pressed a lukewarm iron over my crumpled white shirt and mustard trousers. I took a long shower and ran a hand through my wet hair. Then a shave, the disposable razor scraping along my tired jaw. I headed across the road, past the statue of one more assassinated prime minister, to the St Georges Hotel. This had always been the watering ground for spies and supermodels – Kim Philby's last drinking spot before he had fled Beirut for Moscow. It was a place of jaded glamour and effortless sensuality.

It was the perfect location to wait for Orla Fitzgerald and whatever crazy escapade we had ahead. The air was closer than Paris or Copenhagen.

And on the breeze, I felt that Lebanese electricity that came from never knowing if today would be your last.

## 41

Orla looked less tired than she had in Hereford. Her sense of purpose was back.

I pressed her on Steph. She kept repeating that she was fine. Safe. Calm. All was under control. But they were still both holding something back from me.

I ordered a round of arak.

Where to begin as the ice and the aniseed hit our throats?

'Welcome to Lebanon: your files have been corrupted.' She grinned across the table at me. We appraised each other, clocked the extra lines. She squinted at the scar on my cheek. It had been a long time since anyone told me I looked well.

'Surviving, Ed?'

The simplest of questions but the hardest to answer.

'It's good to see you, Orla.'

I watched her reading my face and wondered what she found there. In the circumstances, yes, I was – just about – surviving. For a man who had lost his job and wife and seen too many dead bodies close up in seventy-two hours. For a man with no one left to trust. I felt again the lurch of sickness that I had been working so hard to suppress.

'How does it feel to be here without the embassy paraphernalia?'

'I'm still an embassy, I guess. The first embassies were people not buildings. I'm just not sure whose embassy I am any more.'

'And Magnus Pederson? Whose embassy is he?'

'No one's. Not any more.'

Orla could see that I didn't trust her with more. She changed tack. 'So I was right about Crawford then? He turned up to see what we had on Tatham.'

'I'm afraid I've lost faith in everyone around me. At moments, even in myself.'

'And yet you're still going?'

'I guess so. At times, I've felt a loss of control, the sense of events being dictated to me. But also some kind of strange purpose amid the upheaval.'

'Welcome to my world.' Orla smiled back. 'This place is as insane as ever. The Lebanese are somehow holding it together. Against all expectations, especially their own. Never think you understand it, never think you can fix it, never think you can leave it unscathed.' I nodded with a grin. Lebanon was famous for the warmth of its welcome. And its capacity to devour its guests.

Orla poured another two araks. 'I just walked up the Corniche. Even after twenty years, the contrasts shock me. Bullets and Botox. Warlords and wasta. Dictators and divas. Hijabs and hot pants. Machiavellis and mafia. This place is *Game of Thrones* with RPGs. When you think the politics has hit rock bottom, you hear a faint knocking sound below. And the Lebanese still just party and pray over the cracks like this is somehow normal. I guess for them it is.'

'For a few centuries at least.' Was she losing her zest for all this, ready to jack it in? This was not a woman who had ever wanted to colour inside the lines. She had run from those lines all her life. But then that smile, the laughter around her eyes.

'I wouldn't swap it for anywhere.'

I smiled back at her. The memories of my time as a young diplomat in this bewitching and bewildering country were friendly ghosts. The most religiously diverse country in the world yet a bruised society struggling to cope with its history. The Lebanese were mountain people: resilient, tough survivors who put family and clan first. And sea people: adventurers, dreamers and traders.

Maybe that was why I loved them so much.

I hadn't felt this free in years. I was liberated somehow of responsibility, maybe even of a code. The arak was doing its job.

I gestured out at the Mediterranean. The boats were coming into the harbour as they had done for millennia. A warm breeze carried the smell of salt and fish.

'You remember why we're called Europe, Orla? A Greek god kidnapped a Phoenician princess – Euroba. In those days we Europeans were the ones doing the hostage-taking. Another of our exports.'

I paused. I had told the story many times. 'This place has seen civilisations rise and fall. It will be here long after Elizabeth Hoon has buried the American dream. Long after whatever comes next in China. Long after all these deranged kids stop setting themselves on fire. Long after you and I are gone. This is the place to come when you need to forget. But also when you need answers.'

Answers and then – perhaps – to be able to forget.

Orla nodded. 'I need to know why Amina Joshi was really such a threat to them all. And how it all links with Agonistes.'

'So what did Nasib say, Orla?'

'I dug around my sources to gauge his mood. Not coming down much from the citadel these days. Fed up with the modern world. But his usual quixotic self. My colleagues say he still likes a good session up there now and then. Gets all the old stories out, embellishes them and puts them back.'

She cocked her head. 'But he was clearly intrigued to get your message. Said he'd try to make it happen. Now, we both know

Nasib well enough to tell that this isn't just courtesy, however politely he frames it all. Or even just curiosity at your sudden, er, notoriety. He'll have something to trade too.'

I nodded. Nasib could switch from disarming affability to heavily armed menace without missing a beat.

'But what are you trading, Ed?'

'I think the Russians have some of the answers I need. Amina Joshi didn't kill herself: she had planned to, wound up by Magnus Pederson. But she was talked out of it by you and backed off. The Dissenters were angry that she'd decided not to be their martyr. But the Americans, Tatham, whoever, also needed her to die. The Russians can help us with that.'

'Surely it's the Americans, Ed? Occam's razor. Hear hoofbeats? Don't expect zebras.'

'Except... the Americans knew the Dissenters wanted to create a martyr, and they wanted to avoid that. The one person who *would* benefit – Magnus Pederson – had failed to convince her to go ahead, and he was still seething about that when he died. He told me someone in my embassy was there, at the end. That's why I think I've been betrayed by Crawford. And I reckon he was there again in Copenhagen, to stop me finding that out. There's a film of her final moments. And the Russians have it. I guess they must also have whatever Pederson had on the data programme. That's why I'm here. Get that, and we can move on. You can write the story, reveal what Max did. And I can get home.'

She looked at me with sympathy. She knew I couldn't say where home was.

Orla focused us again on the next step. 'Nasib always used to say that the Brits are his oldest friends. But the comrades are his most reliable.' Orla was relishing the drama. Always one more adventure. Keep colouring outside the lines.

Neither of us were surprised when the message came. Nasib had enough guys at the airport to know when I arrived. And enough people at the hotel to know where we were drinking.

But it was old school. An envelope, with a handwritten note inside. The penmanship of a French Jesuit school. Slightly shakier now, with the time and the bombs and the booze and the guilt.

> *Edward*, mon cher. *So delighted that you have arrived safely. I would be honoured to invite you to the citadel tomorrow. I have someone here who is very keen to meet you.*

I grinned at Orla and gestured for more arak.

## 42

We snaked up the road and into the mountains, the Mediterranean shimmering in the rear-view mirror. A deep valley gaped to our right. We passed small villages with picturesque churches or mosques. Once cedars would have covered every inch of this climb, but several empires had seen to those. Now the hills were gashed by concrete quarries. This was a landscape carved by time and war, scarred by history. The losers and persecuted of the twentieth century had sought refuge in these mountains, not anticipating the need to coexist with numerous cults even more besieged than their own.

Orla drove like a woman who had spent her life in the Middle East. She attacked the corners, overtook on blind bends, shouted at the other drivers, kept one eye constantly on her phone and hit the horn as if it were a punch bag.

Even before the drive, I had already woken feeling faintly nauseous. The aniseed from the arak felt bitter in my mouth. I was tired by the constant effort to crowd out thoughts of the body under the moss and the nagging pain of Emma's absence.

I thought of the raw fear of that warehouse in Copenhagen. The raw disgust at Crawford's betrayal. It was clearer than ever to me that he must have been working with the Americans to cover up the murder of Amina Joshi and then to silence Pederson and the Dissenters. His death in Copenhagen was either 'friendly fire' or they were killing two birds with one stone. I still couldn't see that the leaks alone, or Amina's relationship with Pederson, was enough to justify the Americans taking that risk. But if they had a programme connecting political sentiment and vulnerability to pandemics? It was the best theory I had.

Even in the midst of this betrayal, I looked forward to seeing Nasib. He was something somehow more reliable after the betrayals of this week, despite featuring high on most of the region's more menacing hitlists. I had known him twenty years earlier, and we had kept in sporadic contact. Nasib would forward articles and cartoons with his trademark caustic commentary. One moment he could be acerbic, the next hilarious, the next self-deprecating.

Nasib called himself the Last of the Mohicans. I called him a Renaissance warlord. He had inherited the leadership of his sect in his mid-twenties, after his father was assassinated. Historically, the Nasib family had rarely made it to retirement age. I recalled Nasib twenty years earlier in a black leather jacket, with a cigarette dangling elegantly from his lips. He was a reluctant fighter. A playboy. A James Dean militia leader. But also a philosopher prince, just as comfortable navigating the perfumed literary salons of Paris as the deadly sniper allies of civil war Beirut. When he had recaptured the family citadel after a bloody battle with one of the mobster clans that had thrived during the war, Nasib had solemnly reburied the remains of his ancestors. And then set up the biggest speakers he could find on the terrace and blasted Hendrix across the valley until dawn. He was the only person I knew who was equally happy in the sixteenth or twentieth centuries, though maybe the twenty-first was still a bridge too far.

Orla sped up as we got higher in the mountains. Her sense of a story was driving her forward. I had needed her to help me get to Nasib, but we wanted different things. And she was still holding too much back from me.

'Looking forward to this, Ed?'

'Orla, I'm just trying to get my family back. I need to find who killed Amina Joshi, for Emma. Whatever happens up there, we can't rush Nasib. He won't commit until he's worked out what's in it. Take it easy.'

If she was irritated, she didn't show it. 'You forget that I know more than you about how to get information out of people, Ed.'

We were waved through the final checkpoints and Orla pulled up to the stone steps that led up to the citadel. Nasib was there in person as always. Not for him the big man posturing and entourages of much of the Middle East. He was a scrupulous host, with impeccable manners. He shook hands weakly with both of us, as though his fingers were made of porcelain. He was certainly older, but still an indefinable age. His moustache and eyes were sadder, wearier. But the unmistakable twinkle of mischief and challenge was still there. His skinny legs were covered by his blue jeans. He wore a checked shirt, open at the neck. A gait like Mick Jagger. He led us up and onto the terrace, to the sweeping views down over the mountains, the air warm but thin.

'*Ahlan wa sahlan, bienvenue*, welcome.'

Like many Lebanese, Nasib used English, French and Arabic interchangeably, often in the same sentence. He looked me up and down slowly. The warrior's keen eye appraising me like a surgeon, probing for weakness. Nasib's success had been not his ability to understand human strength but human frailty. The white wine arrived – Nasib had at some point acquired a successful vineyard in the Bekaa Valley. He always claimed that the conflict years made the best wine – something about the anger of the soil.

'It is wonderful to see you, Nasib-*bayk*.' I added the honorific. There was no ego to Nasib, no protocol puff. But he was a man who inspired respect, and this was a place that demanded it. 'How have you been, my old friend?'

Nasib sighed long and wearily. 'Well, surviving, *cher* Edward. And for we Nasibs, you know, survival is success. This has been a better century than most so far, at least up here above the fray. But all around us the dreams we had for the Arabs are shattered. The naivety of the West. The tyranny of our leaders. The terrorising of Syrian civilians to save them from terror. The stupidity and greed of our politicians. So many brave people killed for nothing. We have lost the thinkers, the writers, the intellectuals, the idealists. And people wonder why we have so little soul left.' His shoulders sagged.

'How is Emma?' Nasib pretended he couldn't remember much of his own history, but he always remembered names.

I hesitated. The truth was that I had not really had any idea how Emma was for years. She was… well… surviving. Like all of us as we tried to slow our decay.

How was she surviving today? Was she drinking coffee with her bookseller by the Seine? Clearing out the apartment? Planning a new life? Did I even cross her mind? Or had my absence made me easier to forget?

'She's fine, Nasib. Just fine.' That look penetrating me again, through to the horoscope of my soul.

'And Amelie?' Nasib's wife was one of the most beautiful women I had ever seen. Tall, elegant, a regal Levantine grace allied with the curvy swagger of the night club diva. She had a Roman nose, long dark hair and the olive skin of the Mediterranean. A combination of nobility and sensuality. For millennia men had come to this abundant corner of the Middle East and been transfixed by women like her.

'She too is fine, Edward. She is in Paris this week. For the fashion, I think. Maybe you will see her when you return. For now I am alone up here.'

Alone with a hundred armed guards, the feudal lord's staff, the feudal lord's obligations to meet, fund, receive and protect his people. Alone with millennia of history. A burden the Nasibs had carried for centuries, however reluctantly.

A silence again. It was still too soon to discuss why I had travelled across continents and centuries to be here.

I shot Orla a look, worried that she might move us on too fast. But she sat back in her chair, chewing a cashew nut. 'And have you had many interesting visitors this summer, Nasib-*bayk*.'

Nasib smiled thinly. Everyone who was anyone came to the citadel. The new ambassadors, the returning ambassadors. Aspiring politicians needing his blessing and broken politicians needing his protection. Journalists and spies. Priests and imams. Crooks and saints. Nasib was a hub for history and geography. And a prisoner of history and geography.

'I just received some of your Northern Irish politicians. They wanted to talk to me about reconciliation. Two from the IRA, and two from the other side. They travel together now around the Middle East, helping us understand our weaknesses. They seemed very pleased with their courage and wisdom.'

Orla and I exchanged a furtive grin. The signs were already there that this would be one of those Nasib stories that we would tell again. We could hear the slight sarcasm creeping into his voice. The tiny glimmer of a smile at the edges of his thin lips, the slightest twitch of his grey moustache. I wanted to get him towards what I needed. But I bit my lip: this was a necessary part of the dance.

Nasib stretched back. His voice was weak but compelling. One knee shook almost constantly as though he needed to take a leak. 'After one hour of teaching me, what could I say? I had been honoured by their distinguished visit. Blessed by the generosity of their gifts – I had never before seen a Stormont Castle key ring: we don't have keys to my castle. They told me about the need to respect the rule of law. I suggested gently that Beirut had been known as the mother of laws when you British were in your difficult centuries.'

I tried to stay still. We needed to get to the Russians. The Americans would be shutting down any chance of getting to the truth about Tatham. I needed to know if it was really Crawford on that film. And yet Nasib wouldn't let that happen until he had set us up his way.

Nasib turned his head to look at the horizon. In the distance, there was a patch of the last snows on the mountain. This was the month when the gun runners and militias were freer to move across the high passes – a time of opportunity and threat.

'I told them that when they killed my father, I had twenty-four hours to assume the leadership, stop the retaliation massacres and go to Damascus to make peace with the man who had ordered the assassination. I told them how I sat at this table, suppressing my rage, my grief and my humiliation. But I could not take my right to vengeance: we were not strong enough. We are still not strong enough. And you know what that cruel bastard said to me when I went to make peace? He told me I looked like my father. A man not yet cold in his grave. I told that story to my guests from Belfast.'

Nasib gave a nonchalant shrug. Beneath heavy eyebrows his eyes laughed. The master of the weaponised anecdote.

'And then I showed them out. We had run out of reasons to talk of peace.'

## 43

The wine was topped up quietly. As always, Nasib was also drinking Mexican beer with a lime squeezed into the top of the bottle. The bottle was always discreetly replaced with a colder one before he had drained two thirds.

Nasib was relaxing, readying himself to plunge into the intrigue that had brought us here.

'I want to tell you another story.' I glanced at Orla. Her stare told me to sit it out. Be patient.

I smiled at Nasib, who was not going to stop talking for anyone. We were close now.

'During the war, I was running out of weapons. The fighting was brutal. Everyone left was a mercenary, everyone was a gun runner. The rest were dead. The Kalashnikov was our only currency. And I was sitting here, right here on this terrace, and a British diplomat arrived. Maybe it was you? I reminded him how the British had helped my people recently, during the 1842 war. They had given us weapons to fight the Ottoman oppressors, despite their treaty with the Turks. In those days, you British had a flexible attitude to allies. I learnt from the masters.' The wolfish grin again. This would all be a game if it wasn't so deadly serious.

I remembered coming. I had been eager, more naïve, even idealistic. It was a simpler time, even with the war around us. There were extra security checks and the sense that fighting could erupt at any moment. There were roadblocks, guns everywhere and the smell of death in the air. But there was also the dancing and the parties, even at the worst moments. Always on the tables. If the tables on planes were stronger, the Lebanese would dance on those too.

Nasib took a cashew nut, rolled it between his fingers, and continued. He was in raconteur mode. Not to be interrupted.

'Everyone was losing. No one could remember why we were fighting. But none of us knew how to stop. And nobody wanted to run out of weapons first. We all knew the retaliations would be vicious. And so I asked you for British help, *mon cher*, just like the old days. And do you remember what you offered?'

I struggled to recall, but Nasib wasn't waiting for answers. Maybe my response had long been polished into something more striking.

Nasib grinned. 'You said that you could send us some human rights advisers.'

He doubled over with laughter. His eyes sparkled. I chuckled. It had not seemed so ridiculous at the time. The sun had set by then on the empire on which the sun was never meant to set. But nobody had adjusted yet, least of all us. Human rights advisers. More with less.

Nasib was suddenly serious again. He fixed me with a wounded look. 'It was a betrayal, Edward, even if a benign one.'

I had learnt something in the last week about benign betrayal. And, in Crawford's case, the more hostile kind. As ever, Nasib had read me.

Nasib wasn't finished. 'That was the day I became a communist. As you left, I watched the convoy of lorries coming up through the valley. Syrian lorries, full of Syrian guns. All paid for by Moscow. Communism seemed like a wise life choice at that moment.'

He was laughing again. Orla and I smiled along. She was watching me closely, waiting for me to pick the moment. Nasib placed the cashew nut back on the table and took a swig of the cold Mexican lager.

My cue. A sudden breeze whipped a mat from the table. Nasib didn't notice.

Like everyone in the Middle East, Nasib still believed the Brits knew more than we did about everything that happened in the region. But I think he knew what was coming. Orla was impassive, but her eyebrow twitched. I turned back to Nasib, whose poker face was more practised.

'Thank you for your help with the Russians, Nasib. I had no one else to ask this time. I'm out of favour in London and Washington.'

Nasib nodded. 'That makes two of us.' He was silent for a few moments. Then a huge crocodile grin. There was something in this trade for him too.

'Edward, the man from Moscow who accompanied those guns was called Churkin. We became friends. He was often here during the war years, and beyond. He helped me out of many dark corners. When I told them about your request, I was pleased that it was Churkin who was on the next plane. I assume Moscow knows he is here, but who can say? I am old enough not to fear much, *mon cher*. We will eat now, and then you will make a new friend.'

Churkin. Pederson's handler in Paris, the man they called the Fat Russian. The man in Crawford's files. The Russians were taking me seriously.

We ate fast. Fresh fish drenched in lemon juice and eaten by hand. Okra in tomato sauce. Copious amounts of red wine, from the conflict years. Vine leaves filled with sticky rice. Meatballs rammed with herbs. Hummus. *Kibbeh* meatloaf. Aubergine. Raw goat meat with olive oil and more lemon juice. A riot of taste and colour. I hadn't realised how hungry I had been. The courses came and went. We were all meant to live on the Med.

As the plates were cleared, I watched Nasib expertly use his toothpick.

'You know, Nasib, my life until recently has been like a classic British banquet – ordered, structured, you know where to sit and which knife to use. But it seems now to have become more like a Lebanese meal – unpredictable, liberated chaos.'

Nasib slapped his leg with appreciation. The ringmaster celebrating the performance of one of his trapeze artists.

And then finally he placed a toothpick on the table and beckoned us to follow. At last.

'We will take our coffee in the armoury.'

We followed him through his study. There were books and press cuttings everywhere. Nasib had once told me that the problem with the region was not that they didn't read, but that they only read one book, again and again. There were scattered vinyl records from the Sixties and Seventies. Down the stairs to a cavernous stone wing, a series of alcoves.

'This was where we always stored the guns. We needed the space then. A few years ago, Amelie persuaded me to turn it into something less functional.'

There were huge Soviet-era paintings on the walls. Some muskets on simple display hooks. Nasib gestured at the largest one.

'That is the gun that killed my father. And over there, the gun that killed my grandfather. We got the man who killed my grandfather. My father's killer is, as you know, still in his Damascus palaces. An appeaser is someone who feeds the crocodile, hoping it will eat him last. Your Winston Churchill said that. I have been that appeaser for most of my life. But we have a more useful saying about crocodiles here, and we have more of them than Mr Churchill. We say that if you wait by the river long enough, the bodies of your enemies come floating by. We will use this space for the guns again, when the time comes. And then, once my sister ceases to wear black, I will invite your Northern Irish politicians back for more talk of reconciliation.'

We turned silently through an alcove and down some more stone steps. Always steps here. The mountain was ever present, shaping every decision. A refuge carved into the rock.

The small room had a simple wooden table, a traditional Arabic coffee pot with a long, curved spout like a heron's beak, some paperback books and a single bed. On it was a crumpled figure, a flabby grey face with deep sunken eyes. He was hunched and pale. He looked up at us and rose unsteadily to his feet. His legs seemed somehow too small for his body.

'You see, gentlemen...' Nasib's gesture took us both in as the Fat Russian waddled the few steps towards us. 'We in the Middle East also have a tradition of asylum.'

## 44

Churkin had a limp, wet handshake and the pallor of a man who has not seen sunlight in months, maybe ever. He was holding a small stubby cigar that wilted ash. He wore stained brown suit trousers, ill fitting, and a shirt that was much too large for him. There was a gun at his black belt. His black slip-on shoes were scuffed. He trundled to a chair and gestured to us to sit down on the sofa. Like him, it was saggy and flabby. We found ourselves at the height of Churkin's torso, almost his groin, looking up at him uncomfortably.

Round one to Russia.

Nasib pulled up a chair and turned it round so that he was sitting facing over the back. He was enjoying the moment.

We sat in silence for a few seconds, unsure where to begin.

Churkin's voice when it came was strangely high pitched and heavily accented. But there was a fluency and a pace to it. He was not a man for small talk. Nor putting people at ease.

'Excellency. I am glad to meet you. I want to know if I can trust you. And you want to know if you can trust me. Can we speak in private?'

He flicked a hand disdainfully in Orla's direction.

I glanced at Orla, who looked back through narrowed eyes, the bonhomie of the moment gone. The silence was awkward.

I was still unsure if I could trust her. But I couldn't let Churkin set the agenda. 'I don't have anything to hide from her.'

Churkin glowered. Nasib interjected.

'Dmitri, my old comrade. If we are seeking trust this is not the company to keep – a lost British diplomat, a rebel spy and a hack with no scruples. You almost make a semi-retired warlord feel a little honest.'

For a moment, Churkin looked angry. And then he and Nasib laughed. He rose and slapped his host on the back. 'Excellent, excellent, we all understand each other.' The moment had passed. Three short puffs on his cigar, more ash, back to the chair, towering over Orla and me as we sank further into the sofa.

Churkin told us, unnecessarily, that he had been a career KGB officer. 'Maybe no longer, but who ever really gives it up, eh, Excellency?' He had a nervous laugh, slightly forced.

'Indeed. You can check out anytime you like, but you can never leave.'

Nasib smiled at the quote. Churkin looked puzzled. He didn't like missing out. I would need that.

Churkin told us that the Levant had been his home patch for most of his career. 'This is home, though I preferred it when it had more weapons.' It was unclear whether he meant the room or the region. Both, probably. For the last decade though he had been taken off the Middle East. Time for new faces. 'So don't blame me for Syria, at least this time round.'

He made a melodramatic gesture, the hands held open to the ceiling and cigar ash falling down his sleeve. 'Excellency, we are both practical men. What is it you want, and what are you offering in return?'

I leant forward. 'I'm trying to find who killed Amina Joshi in my embassy in Paris. Now that your friend Magnus Pederson is dead, I think you may be one of the only ones who really know. I fear I was betrayed. But that maybe so were you. Perhaps we share an interest in the truth.'

Churkin smiled thinly as he nodded. 'I find the truth over-rated. Why do you not agree with the French that it was a suicide?' The nervous laugh again.

I chose not to smile. 'Too many people wanted her dead. And the knife that killed her was removed. But you know all that already from the video. Pederson told me he had shared it with you. Is my military adviser on it too?'

Churkin slowly looked at me, up and down. I wondered how much he would already know about me, which of my calls he had listened to, which of my reports he had read. I glanced towards the window so that he would not see my moment of naked vulnerability. He sighed deeply. 'Let's not get ahead of ourselves, Excellency. Nasib also mentioned that you might be helpful to us. In what way?'

I glanced at Orla. 'We have evidence of a new US-led data monitoring programme. I'm willing to share what we know.'

Orla gave Churkin a defiant look but said nothing. Churkin looked disappointed. 'Ah, Excellency. I'm afraid Pederson gave us all that.'

Orla did not want to lose the card. 'So you know how far Elizabeth Hoon is going?'

Churkin rolled his eyes. 'It must be hard for you to take. But Elizabeth Hoon is a character we recognise in Russia. Basic dictatorship is not complicated. Step one, an economic crash, blamed on elites, minorities and opponents. Step two, the promise of greatness, of bread and circuses. Step three, the gradual under-mining of national institutions; the intimidation of the media; and the reward of loyalty over competence. Holding enemies close. Step four, the personality cult. And the systematic removal of the remaining checks and balances on his power. At each moment, the dictator hopes that we all stay silent, argue among ourselves, or become distracted or frightened. And we do, time and time

242

again. All my life, Americans have told me that Russia will look more like America. They don't say it so much these days.'

I persisted. 'But don't you think Pederson might not have seen the full picture? He was blinded by his frailties. You of all people should know that: you discovered him. If I can understand who really killed Amina, then it will be easier to see who else wanted to conceal that programme, and why. I think that the research may have also been looking at the links between political views and vulnerability to pandemics. Amina Joshi may have been on to this. Pretty dangerous information in the wrong hands.'

Churkin cocked his head to one side as he processed this, looking at Nasib. 'The wrong hands indeed. You seem to have a lot of trust in Amina Joshi, Excellency. Pederson knew his Bible well enough. Too well, perhaps. He should have anticipated that every Samson has a Delilah. You don't think she wanted all these suicides? Why encourage weak-minded children to burn themselves?'

I had trusted her because Emma had trusted her. But I could not let him realise how far behind him I was, as regarded Amina Joshi. I decided to try a different tack as the bait settled, for both of us. 'Tell me about Pederson then. Didn't his leaks burn you too? I think Moscow shared the desire to silence him, and Amina Joshi. After all, he was your guy.'

Churkin narrowed his eyes, and then smiled. He was willing to raise his price. He hadn't decided how much. 'When they took me off the Middle East, Moscow asked me to develop their internet programme: playing offence not defence. This was the new Middle East. Also without rules. I worked on the information effort – your media call them troll factories – that coordinated social media attacks on Eastern European activists and anti-Russian politicians in the West. We developed the fake news operation through which internet users would be targeted with stories designed to shift their opinions of Russia's policies in Ukraine.'

'And Pederson was part of that?'

'Yes, an enthusiastic part. For us, you know, there was a delicious irony. How we chuckled every time an American talked about using the internet to spread American values, to open up the world, to spread democracy. We were once told that we should develop a Russian internet, which we could shape. But we didn't need to! We were beating the Americans on their version. When we played poker with Europe, we had already seen their cards. There are no rules on the web. A great invention. A driverless world.'

Churkin was a man who would know which confidences to share and which to hold back. I assumed this account was pretty well known in London and Washington. There had been a new Cold War with Moscow for several years already. He was hardwired to be transactional, and he could lie to himself without flinching. This was not yet the trade.

He lit another stubby cigar and continued. 'But we got over-ambitious, carried away. We wanted to go harder on the offensive. You remember how the CIA created the Taliban to fight us in Afghanistan? You know Afghanistan well, of course, Excellency.'

I avoided his eye.

Churkin continued. 'Well, we created our own internet Taliban. And that is when Magnus Pederson really took off. He was a lost soul when we found him. We took them, built them, programmed them. And then we set them loose. To seek out the information that would be most damaging to America and to Europe. And to get it out there where it could do most damage. Today's empires are tomorrow's refugees.'

'But, Churkin… why Pederson? Among the masses of hackers and misfits?'

'Because he was driven. He wanted to destroy the trust between your governments and your people. Put fog around everything until no one knew any more what or who to believe. And Pederson was perfect – he thought he was some sort of messiah. He was full of zeal, a wicked zeal. As you say, Excellency, he was driven by his own demons. That suited us. Because so are we.'

I leant forward. 'But he got out of control. Again, like the Taliban. Once they were unleashed they stopped listening to the CIA. They believed their own narrative. They became al-Qaida. And on 9/11 they bit the hand that had fed them.'

Nasib was nodding to himself. 'And how they bit it.'

He loved a good conspiracy. Orla was hanging on Churkin's every word. She did too.

Churkin shrugged. 'You're right. Moscow started to worry that Pederson was indeed our Bin Laden. His rhetoric was becoming more anti-authoritarian. Not just an assault on the corrupt institutions and hypocritical leaders of the West. But on us too. We had evidence of attacks from his people on our own systems. He was probing our business leaders – you call them oligarchs when they are Russian, but I've never heard any of you refer to a British oligarch. Do you not have any, Excellency?' A thin smile.

'No matter. He seemed not to care who he destroyed. He wanted to break everything. We enjoy the disorder when it is pointed in your direction. But not when it is pointed at us. We discovered that we no longer agreed with Pederson.'

'So you decided to end the relationship? Before or after he tried to convince Amina Joshi to kill herself?'

Churkin paused, scraping a fingernail into his ear. His eyes flickered towards the door and his hand to the gun at his waist.

'At first we tried to control it. We threatened him. One of his friends had an accident in Copenhagen. But Pederson seemed to think he himself was somehow invincible. The competition with Amina Joshi was starting to get destructive. She was also a growing problem for us. So, I gave him an ultimatum. He was obsessed with the idea of sacrifice. He told me he needed an Isaac, a sacrificial lamb offered up so that God would bless those he left behind.'

'And you had no problem with Joshi being that sacrifice.'

'I reported all this to Moscow, of course. She was not the gentle activist she liked to pretend.'

His tone was matter of fact, clinical. His voice didn't change at all. I avoided Orla's eye. I cut in. 'Why was Joshi such a threat?'

He ignored me. 'But then you join the story, Excellency. Joshi gets asylum at your embassy, out of our range. Well... further away from our range.' A grin, but he wasn't joking.

'We were furious. We thought you must have turned her in return for safety. We knew what she was capable of. Far worse than Pederson. Moscow became more anxious. She started quoting Einstein in her posts. *We don't know how the Third World War will be fought, but the Fourth World War will be fought with rocks.* Except she saw that as an opportunity. That's when I was told, suitably efficiently, that I was no longer in charge of the operation.'

Churkin looked pained, lost for a moment. I thought of my own moment, just days earlier, standing in Whitehall unsure which way to turn. Homeless.

But Moscow was not London. Churkin continued. 'I've been around long enough to know that this was more than a gentle retirement offer, with a nice clock. They wanted to clean up the programme, wipe our relationship with the Dissenters. Control-alt-delete.' His fat fingers mimed the action on a keyboard.

For the first time I could see his weakness. 'And you are the person with all the files. That's why you came here so fast when

I reached out, to take the excuse to stay with Nasib without alarming Moscow too much?'

'I have come to realise through painful experience that I prefer my intrigue offline.'

Orla seized the pause. 'And Moscow must know you're here?'

Churkin looked at her with disdain. 'Of course! How could they not? They know I flew to Beirut from Paris. There is only one place I could come. And if I do not go back soon, they may come for me. Another person suicided. For now, they may think I can still be useful. But that depends on His Excellency.'

He looked down at his hands for a moment, and then looked up at me once more, with steel in his eyes.

'And if they come for me, Nasib-*bayk* will do the right thing and trade me in for as much as he can get. He would be crazy not to. But once he has his price, he will pour me a large arak, and let me walk out onto that balcony there with my revolver. I always thought during the war that I would die in these mountains. A stray bullet. A hostile checkpoint. I have no fear of death and I have no wish to harm my country. At that point, I will be like Amina Joshi. Better off dead.'

'And so what is your price?' I needed more answers, not another death that was convenient for everyone but me. What was Churkin trading now?

Churkin fixed me with a stare. The avuncular raconteur was gone. The KGB interrogator was back. I was aware again of being at the height of his midriff.

But I persevered. I had come too far.

'I don't believe that Amina killed herself. Someone was with her on the film. Pederson told me that he had someone inside my embassy. Did he?'

Churkin sighed. Another long look out of the small window at the valley below. How many had died violently in these mountains, and how many more?

'Yes, Excellency. Amina Joshi did not act alone in her suicide. You think you want answers? I'm not sure you will like what you find.'

## 45

The mountain air in the armoury had chilled. Orla and Nasib had sat back in their chairs now, spectators not protagonists.

I had heard before the implicit threat on not liking what I would find, from Pederson. And I was determined not to let Churkin intimidate me either. 'I know already that someone in my embassy changed the knife, I assume to cover up his role. That another colleague got it to her.'

Nasib raised his eyebrows at Orla. This suggested even more of a conspiracy than he had anticipated.

But Churkin only shrugged. 'You Brits are too squeamish these days. All that matters is that Pederson's plan did not run to script. Amina Joshi backed out. And yet, she ended up dead. I think you care more about those answers than I do.'

'I'm sure I do. What's on the film?'

Churkin sighed. He was used to fewer questions. 'What matters much more now is that we show that the Dissenters are not as clever as they wanted us all to think. You Brits have always been more subtle than the Americans. They charged into that Copenhagen warehouse all guns blazing. They destroyed a building. But they have not destroyed the idea. Quite the opposite. Look at all these suicides, even in Russia now. *And here I make my sacrifice.* They have created a legend that could bring us all down. A new al-Qaida, living among us, destroying us from within.'

'All the more reason to get the truth out, however uncomfortable. But what is it you want from me? And who is on that film?'

'I started all this,' he said, firmly. 'And it got out of my control. You can help me cauterise the wound. You know that people in this part of the world somehow see a cunning British hand in everything. I always say to them that if you were that clever, that cunning, you would still be running the empire!'

Churkin sighed. He was enjoying the last power he still had.

'In my line of work, it is always worth assuming human frailty. Find the weakest link and start from there.'

I stood up, frustrated. Pederson had brought death into my house. Churkin had created Pederson. This Cold War relic with his cynicism, his world-weariness, his nervous laugh, his inability to cope with 1989. This was the enemy, just as Pederson was the enemy. And Hoon. The whole lot of them. The best of enemies.

I felt Nasib's gaze on me. Once again, it was his moment to calm and placate. He had the skills of a raw diplomacy that had existed in these mountains several centuries before the Brits had set out to charm and divide their opponents.

Nasib's voice was suddenly serious, firm. 'Edward, we've agreed that none of us trust anyone. But you will not be able to move on until you have found your answer. Just as I cannot move on until I have settled my accounts with the man who killed my father. And for that I too need help.' He looked at Churkin, who avoided his eye. Nasib could not make a move against Damascus without Russian acquiescence.

Nasib stood and leant against the stone wall. 'Maybe the answer you need is back in Paris. And maybe in the process you can help Churkin bury Pederson and all he stood for. This is a murder with too many fathers. I think you came here because deep down you're a rebel too. I just think you haven't worked out yet what you are rebelling against. Let alone what you are rebelling for.'

I tried not to show any sign that the jab had hurt.

Churkin pointed a fat finger at me. The offer was coming. 'Something else we understand better than you. Declining powers are more dangerous than rising powers. After all of this, do you really still trust America?'

I sighed. 'Look, future presidents will get back to putting fires out, not starting them. We can all see the damage being done by Hoon to our interests, our values. But I've not given up on the idea of America – reason, progress, tolerance, shared humanity. We haven't had a better idea. And you certainly haven't.'

Churkin was examining his fingernails carefully. But then he held my eye. His pupils were clear. There was deep weariness in his face. 'I think there's only one thing I can do to redeem myself in Moscow. And that's to convince you to be our friend. What is it the French call it? *Donnant, donnant.* We all give something.'

That was the offer: Betray your country for the truth. Nasib gets a clear run at Damascus. The Russians get a new source.

'What is it you are asking me?' To share what I knew about the Agonistes Programme was one thing. Some in my government might see that as betrayal, but I didn't think it was betraying my country.

But Churkin was asking for more. He looked grave. 'Pederson was indeed on to something much larger than Agonistes. You know that. Your station in Paris must have been bugging Amina Joshi. They knew what she had agreed with the Oxford professors. Get that for us and you get your film.'

Orla leant forward. 'You're saying Joshi was working with Peter Tatham?'

He stood. He was relishing my dilemma. What was the truth really worth to me? 'You know, Excellency, this was also hard for the others, for the Cambridge group.'

Enough. I thought of the Syrian dictator telling Nasib that he looked like his father. This extra humiliation was a step too far.

I gestured to Orla. 'Let's go.' The trade was too costly. 'I'll get there, Churkin. Just not this way. Clear up your own mess. And leave me to clean up mine.'

There was disappointment in his eyes, but it was brief. He stood. 'Very well, Excellency, I will try.'

I shook Churkin's cold and sweaty hand. I embraced Nasib, who felt brittle and tired – a sack of bones. 'You're sure, Edward?'

'Never more certain. Keep waiting by the river, old friend.'

As Nasib accompanied Orla to the top of the stone steps, Churkin called out to me. Every instinct told me to keep going, but I went back to him. 'What now?'

'One more thing, Excellency. Did you ever discover why Pederson so hated you? Your journalist friend must know by now. Ask her what she thinks the code on his door was.' His lip curled into a sallow smile. A look of victory like the one on Pederson's face as he died.

I imagined him standing there long after Orla had turned the car around and taken us back through the checkpoint.

We drove in silence for several minutes, me pensive, Orla with the window down to clear the heat from the car and the fog from her head.

I was not feeling the fog. Churkin needed me more than I needed him. My cooperation in providing evidence of Joshi and Tatham working together was his last lifeline. But I was not prepared to sell my soul to him. At least I knew that the Russians were looking for the answers on Tatham and Oxford too. One more country that needed Joshi out of the way. But not the hands on the knife. And I would find the answers without their film.

I still could not understand why my country had betrayed me, why Lynn Redwood had stuck the knife in. But more than that I needed to find out why Crawford and Lenny had betrayed me. Lenny was surely the weakest link Churkin had hinted at. Nasib was right: the answers lay back in Paris.

And now I needed Orla to trust me. After what Churkin had told me, I wanted to find a reason to trust her again too.

She switched on the car radio. A brief crackle and then the unmistakable voice of Magnus Pederson.

'...and I will be gone. But every generation must sacrifice its purest blood in order to gain liberty. And my blood will help many to find true freedom. Celebrate my life, and my sacrifice, through your freedom.'

I recoiled afresh at the unmistakable certainty, the unshakeable confidence in his own worldview. Orla was alert. She turned the volume up.

'We will signal a new Age of Distrust, that will replace the Age of Inequality. Technology will do to twenty-first-century weapons what it did to the bayonet. As the world bakes, tens of millions of the angriest, hungriest people will head North and West. They will be joined by millions more whose jobs will be automated or outsourced. These millions will be coming online in the years to come, and better able to understand the privileges that have been denied them. When that tide of humanity finally loses the last fragments of trust for the world you have built, their revenge will spread through your halls like a wildfire, burning everything in its path. The ultimate disruption, not just of your cities but your ideas. I will soon die knowing that I did my part. And now I end my pilgrimage. I encourage you to do the same. Until we bring down their palaces around them.'

I switched it off. Enough of that voice. The valley was being quarried. No doubt Nasib had a piece of that. There was a thick chalky dust in the air. I felt it in my nose and throat.

It was Orla who spoke first. 'Listen to Pederson's farewell message. He's talking about trust, too. One more devalued currency. We're always fighting the last war. We couldn't save Syria because Iraq destroyed confidence in the foreign policy establishment. People rejected the European Union and all its nonsense because MPs' expenses, banking crises and EU misman- agement had destroyed confidence in Westminster, the Square Mile and Brussels. Hoon is a rejection by the public of the estab- lishment. Of all of us. And now these Amina Joshi suicides. It is going to get harder and harder for anyone to govern.'

'Orla, that's why I think this case matters, beyond protecting my family. Everyone is about disruption now. It's not just the Kodaks that get swept away. It's more than that. It's ideas, states, values that get broken up. We've come to place such a premium on moving fast and breaking things. Where are the people prepared to move slowly and fix things?'

She continued as she drove the car round tight bends and out of the way of minibuses full of militia. 'It still doesn't make sense. You have the Americans and Russians wary of Amina Joshi, and worried about what was coming next. Also fed up with Magnus Pederson and worried what he might do next. You have Pederson needing Joshi to die an attention-grabbing death. And yet none with the ability to help her kill herself? Not when she was locked up with you? So Crawford had to kill her?'

I was silent. Pensive. Watching the Lebanese sky. If Amina Joshi was really working with Tatham, then the Agonistes Programme had gone way beyond our or US control. This was why Crawford had to take her out. Not to make a martyr of her. But to prevent her and Tatham turning their weapon against the US. If Pederson was a Frankenstein's monster for Moscow, Tatham was becoming one for Washington. And Amina Joshi was not Magnus Pederson's useful idiot. He was hers.

'So, Ed, where are you going next?'

I wound my own window down and inhaled a deep gulp of grit and mountain air. I could still taste oil, aniseed, tomato and wine. I was feeling a sense of trepidation through the fatigue and horror of the last three days.

'I'm still going where I've been going since someone cut Amina's throat. Where I've been going since someone drove another nail into the coffin of my marriage. Where I've been going since someone took from me the one job, the one world I have ever known. Where I've been going since I too lost my refuge.'

Below us, the late afternoon light danced on the Mediterranean. Had any country been given such a measure of beauty? And paid for it with such a measure of sorrow?

I looked across at Orla as she squinted into the sun and swung the car between the potholes. What progress was ever possible if we never coloured outside the lines?

'I'm going after the truth. Pull over.'

Orla stopped the car by the side of the road and cocked her head. We both knew then that we were about to cross a point of no return, it was just that I did not yet know what it was. She sighed and got out of the car. I followed. We looked down the valley at the sea.

'It's time for some truth, Orla.'

'I think this is a mistake.'

'Let me decide that. Churkin said that you knew why Pederson hated me so much, why it was personal.'

She was silent for a moment.

'No more lies, Orla.'

'I only pieced it together when I was back in Paris, Ed. The Russians must have known for some time, probably used it against Pederson.'

'What do you mean *against* Pederson? What do he and I have in common?'

She choked back a sob.

'Orla, you need to tell me. What was the code Pederson would have used on his door? Were you still together? Was it your name?

255

Have you been working for him all this time? Was I wrong to trust you too?'

I prepared myself for another betrayal.

She fixed her eyes on the horizon and sighed deeply.

'No, Ed, it's not that.'

I was exasperated. 'Then what, Orla?'

Orla composed herself. She turned slowly towards me, appraising me as she spoke.

'Ed. The code would have been Steph's name.'

'Don't be ridiculous. He didn't know her.'

She held my eye. The wind from the Mediterranean felt colder. Civilisations had risen and fallen below us. Orla was surely confused, wrong. The adrenalin of the mountains had worn off and I felt a deep sense of exhaustion.

'Ed, Steph doesn't want you to know this. But Pederson hated you because you were her father. Because you failed to protect her. The only girl he ever loved.'

'Loved?'

'You were too busy at the embassy to know what was happening in her life, to care about who she saw, to understand the risks. You were not there to save her when she needed it most. She was the girl Pederson could not protect. That's what drove him to you. Pederson wanted to destroy you for hate. He also wanted to destroy you out of love.'

## 46

To an insider, or someone able to imagine themselves an insider for a weekend, Paris is like no other place on earth.

But when you are an outsider, Paris can be an unforgiving city.

I had messaged Emma and Steph to let them know I was coming. Both, in their different ways, had been worrying that I was behaving erratically. They were not wrong.

The hours after Orla's revelation were the hardest. I had felt briefly strengthened by my decision not to take Churkin's deal. But the flight from Beirut seemed painfully slow. I agonised over what had happened to Steph. How had I not known? How had she relied on someone like Magnus Pederson to protect her? Why hadn't she told me she knew him? Had Emma known? I was ready to drop everything else and get back to her. Try to start to make things right. They could never be the same again.

Nothing would be the same again.

Just before departure I had received another text message from an anonymous phone. It said simply:

Keep an eye on the news.

Surely there was nothing worse now that they could hurt me with. I wondered if they had something on Emma and the bookseller. I had been ready to confront them both to find out how long and how far my wife had gone from me. But nothing seemed to matter any more, compared to the knowledge of this attack on my girl.

I had been unable to speak any more to Orla. We sat in silence at the airport, as the televisions carried news of more teenage suicides. In Europe, North America, Asia, South America, Australia. The numbers rising every day. An epidemic of pain and confusion. More distraught parents spoke of the loss and confusion. More families destroyed. More politicians despaired. Amina Joshi's face was everywhere. And Magnus Pederson's leaks. For a plan that had gone wrong it seemed to be working pretty well.

On the flight, I tried through my grief to process what I had learnt from Churkin in the mountains. Whatever Pederson's motivation for coming after me, we still needed to prove that Amina Joshi had been killed. I did not believe that the Russians could have been responsible, however much they wanted to create the conditions for it. They had the video, but they were looking for answers too. The Americans on the other hand had more reach inside my embassy than I would have known. And Crawford must have been their man. If Joshi had access to Tatham's data, then she had become much more of a threat to them than she seemed when she was just an idealistic campaigner. She could tailor her message to have maximum impact on those she needed to reach. Was Tatham playing both sides? And how did Suzanne Morley fit in?

I had fallen into a fitful sleep, and the recurrent dream of Steph's body covered by green moss in the mountains.

Once I got a Wi-Fi connection on arrival at the Charles de Gaulle airport, the latest leaks from the Dissenters were breaking. More suicides. And there were several missed calls from Jack Fleming.

I sat down in the baggage terminal and drew a deep breath. Orla found the story first. The BBC weren't yet running any detail. They had been burnt by fake leaks. But Sky had it. And I knew immediately that this one was not fake. An Abingdon clinic's medical record from thirty years earlier. The leak was simply a list of abortions, listed unsentimentally like a shopping list or the football scores. I didn't need her to read on, but she continued, unaware of why I knew what she would find. Lynn Redwood's was the third name on the page, her signature recognisable.

I didn't have to ask the year. I thought of Lynn's shoulders slumping in the car when Fleming had warned something was imminent. The question I had never been able to ask was now laid bare. And the answer lay in a cold lonely hospital on the Abingdon Road. That night – our moment – was the last time she had sacrificed self-control. I wondered if she had wanted me with her at the clinic that day, or anyone but me. But she had faced it alone. And then a lifetime of soldiering on.

I thought about calling or messaging her. But my dismissal had been her answer to that. A revenge served ice cold.

As we came into the Arrivals area, my phone vibrated again. Another anonymous number. I clicked on the message, my stomach tight.

Barnes, keep watching.

I did not have much time. How many more lives of those closest to me could still be ruined? I felt a growing fear that it was only a matter of time before the death in the mountains would be used against me. Could Crawford have set me up? Until I was able to show the link to Amina and the wider context I had no decent explanation. And if the world chose to agree the convenient explanation that Amina had killed herself? That now left me with a growing problem.

I returned to Paris a different person. I was no longer looking for the horizon I had once loved. I was looking for survival.

Orla put her hand on my arm as we parted. 'Are you sure you're okay?'

'Just write your story. You work it out. Find the link between Amina Joshi and those Oxford scientists. Tell people about who Max Crawford was. I don't care any more.'

I took a taxi to the embassy. I had decided to confront Lenny first. I needed to understand why he had been helping Amina Joshi, and what he knew about Crawford. Nothing happened in that house without Lenny knowing.

I rang the bell at the service entrance. I didn't want Sheriff, Alem or – worst of all – Parkinson to know I was there. Luckily it was Lenny who answered it. He froze in the doorway, unsure whether to run, laugh or cry. And then the professional top-to-toe appraisal. I was suddenly conscious of what a mess I must look. I was crumpled, jet-lagged and bereft. But behind this I wondered if he could also see that I had changed more fundamentally.

He didn't look so good himself. He had lost weight, and the skin sagged forward off his face.

He ushered me through the corridor and into his private rooms. Then bustled off efficiently to find me a gin. I wondered if he would come back. Or whether security would be with him. We didn't have long.

From upstairs in the kitchen, I could smell croissants and bacon. My old breakfast. Today it turned my stomach.

Lenny's room was downstairs below the kitchen, in the corridor where the staff slept when they stayed overnight. Lenny was normally here during the week. It was not worth heading back to his apartment between a late-night dinner and an early-morning breakfast.

And there he was again. Sheepish but still himself. Brandishing my drink.

'Are you all right, Ambassador?' He had checked himself. I couldn't tell whether it was because he no longer knew what to call me, or because he thought I was far from all right.

I tried to hold it together. The ambassadorial face he knew well.

'Is Steph safe, Lenny?'

'She's been staying in her room a lot. Orla Fitzgerald was around. But the French police came looking for her, and she's not been back since.'

They must know now that Orla had more on Pederson. Or maybe on me.

'How's your new ambassador, Lenny?'

A pause. He was being careful with his choice of words. Loyal as ever.

'He's settling in. Mrs Sheriff is trying hard.' He glanced at me awkwardly. I moved on. Time was short.

'Lenny, I need to know what was really going on with Amina Joshi. I'm worried that you could be in danger.'

His shoulders crumpled forward. 'I wish she had never come.'

'We all do, Lenny. But I have to understand what happened. Can you promise me you didn't help her kill herself?'

His eyes were hooded. He glanced down at his phone and at the door.

'No, Ambassador... Sir Edward. I told those detectives I didn't know that would happen. But I was helping her get stuff she needed. She was so kind. And so alone. She was a different person when the others weren't around. I like that in people. She asked me to bring her things. To pass messages to her friends. I wanted to help. Lady Barnes said I shouldn't bother you with it all.'

'Emma? What did this have to do with her?'

He swallowed, looked again at the door. I stood and moved between him and the exit.

'You know how close they were, boss. She said not to bother you with it all.'

I had been happy to see Emma and Amina rekindling their old friendship. But something in Lenny's awkwardness wasn't right. I put it down to his discomfort – he must have heard that we had separated. It would have been obvious when she was packing the apartment. There were no secrets in an embassy residence.

Except there clearly were.

'Lenny, what did Amina ask you to bring her?'

'Messages. But also recording equipment. They said she planned to make more videos, political videos.'

'They? Who said that?'

He sighed deeply. I wondered if he might try to push past me. I would not be able to stop him.

I thought back to Pederson's sneer. Someone closer to home.

'Lenny, was it Magnus Pederson who made you get her the knife? What did he have on you?'

Lenny looked weary. He rubbed his temples.

'I never knew what it was for.' He choked.

Footsteps in the kitchen above. Someone called his name. I didn't have any more time.

'Why, Lenny?'

He looked at me. Remorse, regret. He glanced across at the side table. And then he flinched. There were more footsteps above us. Had he called security? I could not get back out through the service entrance without a key. But I could get up the fire escape to my old apartment. Sheriff's apartment. And out from there.

I listened intently to the voices upstairs in the kitchen. One had an American accent, the other more familiar. Parkinson. What was he doing in the kitchen? There was a noise like a man choking as the coffee machine dispensed its usual half a cup of dark black tar.

I could hear footsteps again now, descending the stairs. I motioned at Lenny to be quiet, opened the drawer and picked out a knife small enough to conceal in my hand. I moved behind the door, clenched, waiting.

But the footsteps went past. I listened as several doors opened and closed. They were lifting something heavy.

I breathed out deeply, keeping my eyes on Lenny. While I waited for a chance to move, I looked around his room.

The room smelt stale. There was not much natural light down here. It was still all a bit upstairs/downstairs, like some period drama. Just now with more drama.

On the side table were Lenny's glasses and his notebook. On the notebook he had written 'Genesis 22'. I was intrigued. I didn't have him down as a bible basher.

As Lenny slumped into a chair, I rattled the drawers under the side table. In the first was a handwritten, signed copy of Amina Joshi's now famous 'Beatitudes for Diplomats'.

*Where there is outrage, let me be a voice of calm;*
*Where there is division, let me advocate tolerance;*
*Where there is post-truth politics, let me strive for honesty;*
*Where there is too much certainty, let me remain curious;*
*Where there are soundbites, fake news and echo chambers, let me strive*
   *for expertise, patience and judgement;*
*Where there are closed minds, let me make the case to be open to the*
   *world;*
*Where there are dividing lines, let me seek common ground;*
*Where there are walls, let me build bridges.*

'You believed in her, Lenny. But was that enough reason to help Magnus Pederson? Who else were you passing messages to?'

He looked up, a flash of anger in his eyes. And then his shoulders slumped. 'Only one other person. Some Oxford professor.'

'Was Amina working with him?' Tatham's tentacles had reached even here.

'Not *him*, boss. It was a woman. They were sending each other three or four notes every week. Never emails or calls. Amina would always ask me if I had new ones from her.'

'Do you still have any?'

'No. She would always rip them up.'

The second drawer was locked. I asked Lenny for the key, but he simply looked at the floor. I tried to jam it open with the knife. For a moment I felt guilty. Had it come to this? Rummaging through the butler's possessions? But there was too much at stake. There had been too much blood.

The lock didn't budge.

'Lenny, what about Genesis 22?' He was silent so I looked it up on my phone.

The story of Abraham and Isaac again. Churkin and Orla had spoken of Pederson's obsession with it. The jealous God, goading Abraham to sacrifice his son as a test of loyalty. Had I sacrificed my daughter out of distraction?

I turned to face him. 'Was Pederson giving you some sort of test? To choose between loyalty to me and to your family?'

Lenny rose slowly from the chair and moved towards me. I wasn't sure whether he would hug me or attack me. Instead, he turned and stumbled out of the door.

Whatever Pederson had done had worked. The small betrayals are often the hardest. This was just a quick trip to pick up a digital camera.

And a sharp knife on the silver food tray. As large as Lenny could risk taking from the kitchen without the chef noticing.

Sharpened, if that was not too much extra trouble.

The disloyalty must have torn Lenny in half.

As Pederson had warned me, it was someone closer to home. I now knew it had been two of them: Lenny and Crawford.

## 47

I had often used the fire escape from the basement to the apartment in the evenings if we needed something from the kitchen. I messaged Penny to check that there was no one around and climbed the three flights as quickly as possible. I went straight to Steph's room, but she was not there, so I let myself into the main flat.

The Sheriffs had not started to move in properly. Their heavy baggage would still be on the way. Our possessions were in piles, much of it already boxed and ready to be sent on. But to where? I flinched as I noticed the separate stacks. The unsentimental practicality of two lives diverging.

I looked down at the street outside. It was quiet. The remnants of the pilgrims had now gone. So much for Amina and Pederson's revolution. There was an extra police presence but nothing intrusive. It felt strange to be on the inside of the residence and yet an outsider. They were no longer there to protect me. Maybe now they were there to protect against me.

I wondered whether to take any of my stuff. But I didn't want to leave any sense I had been there. I hoped that Lenny would not say anything yet, give me more time. His last act of loyalty.

This space was dead to me now.

I thought again of Amina's body. Lenny had provided the knife and the recording equipment, but how had Pederson convinced him? He had initially helped Amina out of a sense of duty and kindness, but – as with Orla – Pederson had found a way to twist and corrode this.

I did not believe that Lenny could have been capable of helping Amina kill herself, let alone done it himself. His horror outside the room had been genuine. It had to have been Crawford, working with the Americans to silence her. Following orders, presumably. And once he had covered it up, he had then gone to Copenhagen to silence Pederson, with me as a useful distraction. Only then the Americans had found a way to silence them all.

Pederson had taught me one thing: trust no one.

As I looked out into the street, I knew that I would need to move fast to release much of what I knew to the public. It was incomplete but we had to get ahead of the next leaks. I would ask Orla to spare Lenny, but name Max Crawford, showing that he had acted on behalf of the US. She could reveal that Pederson had been working with the Russians. This was enough to undermine his credibility. Maybe that was all that Churkin had really wanted me to do. The Russians would officially deny it, but the damage would be done.

I didn't have enough yet on whatever Tatham and Joshi – or maybe more importantly Suzanne Morley and Joshi – were doing together. Orla might encourage others to share what they knew. This was her story now.

There would be fury in government, and the Americans would be livid. But it was the right thing to do. I would write to Angus Green first, to warn him. As Churkin had said, you never really leave.

I looked around the room for my stationery. I also wanted to find my favourite photo of Steph. The one with the sun in her hair, her summer dress, the Kent coast, a miniature railway. It had sat on our piano.

I rummaged through the boxes and put an envelope of photos marked 'national day' in my pocket: perhaps there would be further clues on when Crawford had been in the garden. But I couldn't find the family albums. I went through to our bedroom. My clothes had already been boxed. Would I ever need to wear a suit again?

Emma's cupboards were empty. I checked her study. There were more piles of books. And then under a table I found the box marked 'photos'. Emma's writing was on the side. A good place to start.

Once in Paris I had borrowed Em's phone to look for a photo she had taken of a piece of art she liked. She took wonderful shots. Thoughtful, simple and somehow kind. She found beauty in the unexpected and the mundane. But there were also evocative photos of Steph, of Paris, of home, of nieces and nephews, of furniture, of horizons, of strangers. Years of memories. It was an autobiography in pictures.

It took me several minutes to realise that the only person she didn't photograph was me.

This was now what I was. The ex-husband. 'The father of my daughter.' But no longer 'the love of my life'.

On top of the box of Emma's photos was a draft of one of Amina's blogs. The manuscript was annotated in Emma's writing.

I started to sift through the box, but these photos were unfamiliar. University photos. Blurred student shots. Drinks, youth, laughter, teeth and hair.

And in every photo, Amina Joshi. Close-ups, posed, unposed. Lingering shots of her eyes, hands, face, arms, skin.

And this was not a record of a casual friendship at university. The photos didn't stop. Together on a ship in their twenties. On a beach in their thirties. In hammocks in their forties. An autobiography in pictures.

Almost a love story.

It was only then that it finally hit me.

Was I the last to know that I had never been the love of her life?

## 48

Disorientated and distraught, I slipped quietly through the ball-room and out of the back gate. There was no sign of Lenny or the other staff. The residence was strangely quiet. I passed the back of the US embassy. What secrets did that building still hold? Kane must have relished my sacking. But this was now the least of my worries.

I walked quickly past the Hôtel de Crillon, ducking my head so as not to be recognised by the porter, and crossed Place de la Concorde, with its huge Egyptian obelisk amid a chaos of mopeds. This was where the French revolution had executed Louis XVI and Marie Antoinette. Thousands of tourists crossed the square every day for the Champs-Élysées without realising how much blood had stained that ground for centuries.

Into Tuileries park, with its candy floss and fairground, and the straight lines all the way to the glass pyramid of the Louvre. I wanted to walk and to think. There had been times when Emma had travelled, when she needed to be alone. She had always returned so vital, so refreshed. Did Steph know? How many secrets had my family kept from me? It was time to confront Em.

I was struck by how neutral I had felt towards the residence. It had never really been home. And yet this was the pinnacle of my career. I thought of Lenny, carrying his secrets and burdens. He could still help me confirm the truth about Amina. With Orla and Crawford gone, he was the last person before the killer to have seen Amina alive.

Stopping abruptly, I turned back towards the square where the guillotine had stood. Back towards my embassy where Amina had been killed. Back towards the American embassy.

I started to run, but then stopped and pulled out my phone. I couldn't simply turn up at the front gate, and Lenny would not let me in again. They would think I was deranged. I couldn't give Sheriff that satisfaction. Let alone Kane or Harry Parkinson. I couldn't ask Orla to take the risk of returning to the embassy.

Lacking options, I called Alem. I was surprised that she picked up on the second ring.

'Edward, where are you? They said that you had disappeared.'

'I don't have time to explain. Lenny is in real danger. Can you meet me by the Rodin?'

'You're back in Paris?'

I rang off. I knew she would come.

I got to the statue first. Tourists in sandals wandered past, heads in guidebooks and smartphones. An old couple sat in green chairs. Paris continued, oblivious as always to the death in its midst. It had seen much worse.

*The Kiss*. Rodin's hands had somehow imagined and then found these lovers deep in the bronze. An aristocratic woman in love with her husband's brother. It was a love that led to two murders, and an eternity in hell.

When she arrived, Alem was brisk, businesslike. She appraised me with a brief look of concern but was too professional to let that delay her. I knew that she would write this up later for the record.

'Edward. I shouldn't be here. What's going on?'

'I'm worried for Lenny. He knows too much about what really happened to Amina. And he's being set up.'

Alem sighed. 'But you need to be rational. Calm down. The situation is under control. Sheriff has confirmed the French account of the suicide. We have the autopsy with Amina's prints on the knife. He is urging us all to move on, even if he had the decency to look awkward when he was telling the staff how closely you were both working together on the transition.'

'But it's not as simple as they want. You surely know that, Alem?'

'We're not detectives. Surely you know that by now? You should never have tried to be. We've had the two Northern Irish cops here since you left. They've put the screws on all of us. Everyone wants to put this behind us. The Americans have shared all the intel too. Amina was working with Pederson to coordinate the leaks with her suicide. She had wanted to use the moment to launch global protests. All these grim suicides.'

'The Americans seem to know a hell of a lot about what was happening inside my... our embassy.'

Alem didn't pause. 'The French have also agreed we need a quick and clean resolution. And in any case, the media are elsewhere now, watching re-runs of Liz Hoon bombing the Dissenters and fretting over the world's teens having a collective rebellion.'

'But I know that the knife was changed for one that didn't bear the embassy crest. That matters. And why do you think Crawford has disappeared? Is no one asking these questions?'

'Edward, the question the Americans are asking us is why *you* disappeared. There are rumours you went to Lebanon. Rumours you are talking to the Russians. Kane even hinted that you were in contact with Pederson. The French think you took evidence of a suicide note from Amina's room. And Harry Parkinson says the police now want to talk to Orla Fitzgerald. They're gossiping about how close the two of you have become. Now she's disappeared. It's all getting hard to defend. Why is anyone going to listen to you about a crest on the knife?'

She paused as a German couple passed too close. Sandals and socks.

'And then you pitch up here, looking like this? Yes, Lenny does seem to have been too helpful to Amina. But no one is suggesting he was part of her death. A useful idiot, Parkinson says.' She scowled. 'As for Crawford, I'm sure he'll help us clear it all up once he gets back from leave.'

'I'm telling you, Lenny is not safe. He's the last link to the truth. Too many people need him dead. And Crawford isn't coming back. He betrayed all of us.'

She shook her head. 'This has been a traumatic period for all of us. And I know it's tough with Emma. But it's behind us now. Get some rest and some fresh clothes. We'll be okay, and so will you. But you need to straighten yourself out. Now if you don't mind, I have a job to do.'

I winced. She was back in ultra-efficient mode. Settling in a new ambassador. Keeping the old one on-piste. Rallying the staff. Keeping the show on the road. If Lenny had helped Amina, or Crawford had killed her, the FCO didn't want to know. Better for Lenny. Better for the embassy. Clarity trumped truth.

'Alem, one last question then. Did you know about Emma and Amina?'

She stared down at the gravel. There was a siren in the distance, slow and lamenting. And then she was gone. I put my head in my hands. I tried Lenny's number, but there was no reply.

I turned and started to walk towards the bookshop.

Before I had reached it, Alem called me – distraught and broken – to tell me she had gone straight to see Harry Parkinson. No doubt to report my presence in Paris.

The box was the mission's secure area. Most UK embassies had one. Mobile phones had to be left in a locker outside. The most secret files and communication equipment was stored there, and the room housed the main intelligence liaisons. It was small and stuffy, cramped and untidy. Normally she and I avoided it as much as we could but came in to read the 'red jackets' every week or so. For me it had been Parkinson's den, his lair. It even smelt of Harry. Booze, sweat and unwashed underwear.

Alem told me that Parkinson had eventually hauled himself to the door. He was dishevelled, more so than usual. She had tried to reassert authority, asked him about Lenny's safety. Parkinson had looked hunted but was holding it together. He had refused to share anything more, claiming that the Americans had massively restricted access. Urged her to trust him. Told her that Amina Joshi was a wolf in sheep's clothing.

He had passed her a folder marked 'UK/US Eyes Only'. In it was a transcript of Amina Joshi's last conversation. It was then that the call had come through. She had run to the residence basement.

'I remember Parkinson struggling to keep up, red faced and sweating. I called out for Lenny, but there was silence. I pushed open the bathroom door. He had a leather belt around his neck. His shirt was drenched in perspiration.'

Her voice caught. I slumped on to the nearest bench.

Another suicide at the British embassy in Paris. Another crime with no culprit. The press would put it down to the stress of having found Amina Joshi's body.

'And you believe me now?'

'Ed, I don't know what to believe. But you have to keep going. You owe it to Lenny now. And all of us.'

'Too right. But you owe it to us too. You can start by telling me what was in Parkinson's report.'

She hesitated, composed herself. 'Amina Joshi's last conversation was with someone she knew. Their words are not transcribed.

UK citizens don't have their words documented. After all, we're not the ones being spied on, are we? But which Brit?'

'Crawford, I assume. But I need one more thing, Alem. Or they're going to pin this on Lenny. Pederson had something on him. Get into the bottom drawer by his bed. Do it fast.'

Lenny had never really been called a butler in life, not that he would have minded. It had seemed out of kilter with our more egalitarian mind set. Now in death, when the story broke, he would be a butler again.

The butler who had seen too much. The butler who had tried too hard to please. The butler who could not help anyone any more. Not even the man who most needed him.

Churkin was right. The weakest link. Before Alem called me back, I knew that was why Lenny had been Pederson's target.

She was clipped, efficient as ever. But this time there was more complicity. We were on the same side again.

'Inside the bedroom drawer was a folder of grainy photos, taken from a distance. They were shots of a man in his twenties, in a park or forest. From the backdrop it was probably Bois de Vincennes or Bois de Boulogne. There were a series of other figures, some dishevelled, some suited.'

In a city of secrets, they were waiting for the man, getting their fix.

For a moment I wondered if this was how Lenny had really procured my weed.

She knew I didn't need to ask, but I wanted to hear her say it. Another Abraham, another Isaac. 'His son?'

She was silent.

I wondered if she would be the one to break it to the boy. And whether she would say what his father had sacrificed to protect him.

## 49

Hemingway and Company looked straight out onto the Seine. It had rickety bookshelf passageways and floors that you felt you could put a foot through. If there had ever been a twisted logic to the anarchic layout, it was long forgotten. Artists and writers had long used it as a place to write, sleep and love. It smelt of nostalgia. *Souvenirs*. Every day, hundreds of tourists now passed through its crammed corridors.

It was a great place to get lost and a great place to hide.

The bookshop manager looked at me with a mixture of surprise and gentle solidarity as I arrived. If I had not found the photos, I would have confronted him, blamed him for taking her from me. But it was not the bookseller who had stolen her. He was just the refuge, a comrade for Emma. It was Amina Joshi who had always been there.

Emma hadn't seen me at first, lurking in the American Beat poets section with Kerouac as my alibi. I had misquoted for years the line about seeing the people in your life recede in the rear view mirror as you drive away.

She smiled genuinely as I came towards her, but there was disappointment too. Not because I had come. But because she could see I still hoped.

We embraced, longer and harder than I had expected. She didn't need to say how awful I looked. I was hunched, in need of a shower and some sleep. I was trying not to think about the call I had just had from Alem. Of Steph's assault. Or of Emma and

Amina. Another betrayal. Another person I had been wrong to trust.

I had no diplomatic platitudes left. 'Lenny is dead.'

She froze. Em had always seen Lenny as different to the rest of the embassy, somehow on her side. And having worked for five ambassadorial couples, Lenny had long understood that it was the wife to whom he most needed to stay close, even one – maybe especially one – as detached as mine.

'How?'

'A phrase I've heard too much these last few days: he was suicided.'

She wept gently. 'None of this was Lenny's fault.' We stood in silent grief for several moments. For Lenny. And for everything we had lost in a week.

I forced the words out. 'Did you know about Steph?'

'What a question, Ed.' She was defensive.

I had nothing to put into the words. My voice was catching. 'An assault. Here. In Paris. Her friendship. With…' I broke off.

Emma sighed hard. Her lip quivered. 'We. Managed.' She tried to continue but no words came. I could not feel angry. We held each other.

After several minutes I pulled away. I had thought hard since getting her message in the mountains about what to say to her about us. Her relationship with Amina, whatever it was, might still just be the symptom, not the cause. If we agreed that, we had something to build from. After all, Amina was gone now. I could show her that my search for the answers was a return to what she might have once loved in me. Stripped of all the diplomacy and insincerity, we could rebuild.

And yet when it came to it, I had few words left. 'You say you want to move on. I get that. I know it's not easy. But I'll fight to get you back. Bit by bit. For Steph. But for us too.'

She was sympathetic but firm. 'Marriage isn't another of your peace processes, Ed. This has long been coming. But Amina dying made me realise it was time. We just want different things now. Maybe we have done for longer than we realise. It doesn't need to be hard any more. We'll always share memories. And Steph.'

I felt the anger rising again. 'Enough secrets. Does Steph know about you and Amina?'

Sadness crossed Em's face as she looked up at me. We examined each other in grim silence. She chewed her lip. She didn't need to ask me how I knew.

Lynn Redwood had said sometimes you had to pick a side. I wondered whether Steph would feel she had to choose between us.

'Steph knows, Ed. I don't think she will ever forgive me. I don't know if she should. If you should.' She looked at the floor, suppressing a sob.

I waited for her to look back up. 'Do you remember that night in Oxford? We had walked through the Parks and down by the river. We got sunburnt and drank too much cheap white wine. Then we found ourselves on the bridge. It was all so easy.'

She smiled. 'That was the last time we were spontaneous.'

Em looked at me tenderly. But she seemed torn. She could see I needed her to be there for me.

Yet every instinct told her that being there for me would make it harder for me when she was gone.

These were the quiet gear changes of a marriage. Lust had become love. Love had become affection. Affection had become coexistence. Coexistence had become tolerance. Tolerance had become ambivalence. It was the oldest story, and it was no longer enough for her.

It should never have been enough for me.

Amina had not stolen Emma. She was never mine to begin with.

'Emma, I need to understand. Were you running *towards* Amina? Or away from me?'

She looked beyond me, lost briefly and then she was there again. She took my hands. There was regret, maybe. Loss, certainly. But something more – relief.

'Amina was always there, Ed. But I now know it was this other life calling her, maybe even this other death? We drifted apart at times. But then there she was, on our doorstep. In our house. These two lives that I had hoped could be kept apart. At first, I was furious with her. Furious with you for having a job that allowed this to happen. But then we started to fall into the old patterns again.'

I wondered about the deception. The logistics of betrayal. How many people knew, connived in it? I had always assumed Lenny's looks of sympathy were only because of an unsupportive wife.

Emma composed herself but was a long way away.

'In the hours after she died, I had a brief glimpse of an alternative life, where Amina and I were travelling Europe in a Volkswagen campervan. A horde of unkempt kids, some old cassette tapes, bottles of plonk and a guitar.'

'How did you stay so calm when she was killed? You were the only one who did. Are you not more curious about what happened?'

She flinched. I watched the wave of sadness wash through her. I understood for the first time how Amina's death had broken her.

She breathed deeply, composing herself. 'What else could I have done?'

Somehow, in the midst of the dust of the bookshop and the debris of our lives, I could not find hate or anger. I had spent a life compiling my set of souvenirs. Filed them away for those moments of transcendence. On a roof, in a forest, in the sea.

Hers were filed away too. And we were packing separate boxes.

We hugged again and walked out of the bookshop together.

In the street, I turned to her, held her wrists. 'Em, Max Crawford killed Amina. I had thought it was because she was working with Magnus Pederson, coordinating these damaging leaks. Pederson hated me, for failing to protect Steph. But I now realise all this was something more even than that. Amina was working with an Oxford professor – something to do with sentiment mining and viral immunity. Lenny confirmed this to me. Their work became a threat to the US. Max was following orders as always. It was just that they were American orders, not mine. I'm going public.'

She had frozen at the mention of Oxford. 'I didn't know Magnus Pederson was the friend who couldn't protect Steph. I was too swept up in the fact that we had failed to.'

Silence again. I couldn't go there. 'I know. But, Em, this could be important. Did Amina ever mention a Suzanne Morley?'

Em looked out towards the Seine as she spoke. Until now her words had been deliberate. Now she was thinking as she spoke. 'They had become close. I couldn't really understand it, but she was always picking up these crackpots. Amina once told me that Suzanne Morley had taught her that activism alone was worthless, you had to weaponise it.'

'Weaponise it with what?'

'I don't know, Edward, but you need to move on. For our family's sake, let all this go. Maybe it was just Amina's time. Maybe she was ready.' And then with greater urgency, 'Please, Ed, let this go.'

'Let it go? Max is either dead or still a threat to us. Either way, the world needs to know what he did, and on whose orders. I've risked everything, lost so much, to do this. For you.'

'We need to move on.'

'Move on from what? From your affair with Amina? From the murder? From us? I'm just trying to move us forward.' I faltered. 'It's all I've ever really done.'

She pulled her face away from me for a few moments. She seemed to be wrestling with herself.

When she turned back, her voice was barely audible. 'Ed, it wasn't Max Crawford.'

I gripped her shoulders. 'What?'

Her eyes flashed. 'You say you want the truth for Amina's sake, for mine. But you never heard me. I said again and again to let it go. You want some answers? Would it help you if I said it was me? That I was the one who helped my friend through her final moments when her courage faltered? Would that be enough for you to stop all this while you still can?'

I stood stunned, speechless.

She needed to walk. Always her defence mechanism. I stood in the middle of the pavement, the mopeds and tourists suddenly silent around me, and watched her walk away.

There was everything to say. And we had nothing left to say.

Disorientated, I turned left up the Seine, passing the *bouquinistes* of the Left Bank, with their postcards and first editions. I reached a bridge covered with the padlocks left by the lost lovers of Paris, and stood there, looking down at the river below.

But was it true? Had she really helped Amina to kill herself, as some kind of act of love? She must have been the unrecorded voice on Parkinson's recording, the accomplice in the video Pederson had wanted to show me, and Churkin had sought to buy me with. Being at the bookshop that night, with its chaos and crowds, was no great alibi. I remembered her in the hours after the death. Efficient and on top of things, emotional but not distraught. Pederson had spat out the words with such relish and triumph: closer to home. I could never have imagined how close.

Had her hand trembled as she pressed the cold steel blade down, feeling the strength collapse as she completed for Amina Joshi what she could not herself complete?

If Amina Joshi had been working with Suzanne Morley, Lenny's hint was right. She had chosen Peter Tatham. She was indeed the Delilah to Pederson's Samson. Amina had discovered that Tatham had found a way of predicting people's wants in a way that could be used proactively by governments as a tool of control, which was what the US government was planning to do. This was what Orla was on to, which was why she had been targeted. But the key to the saga wasn't really about predicting political sentiment, it was about viral immunity, the work of Suzanne Morley. Amina Joshi was working with, not against her. Tatham's sentiment mining was just cover for their real work, which was why he could be so casual about it. Amina Joshi wanted to ensure that future pandemics were more likely to kill those less likely to share her worldview: older white men, the obese, Hoon supporters. She, Tatham and Morley were using his data to make it easier to influence people against governments, and to map this with vulnerability to the likeliest pandemics.

This was motive enough for the Americans to use Crawford to kill her. But why then had he turned up in Snowdonia to save Orla?

And now Emma had given Crawford a potential reprieve with her confession.

I could not believe her capable. I had seen the depth of her grief.

But if she was capable, this truth would rip our family apart forever.

And if I didn't share what I knew about Amina Joshi, the Agonistes Programme and now Emma with the police, then my old tutor was right: the shits do always win. The wrong people had won again: Hoon, Tatham, Pederson, Churkin, Amina Joshi. With their useful idiots: Lenny, Emma, Sheriff, Angus, Crawford.

And, if I stayed silent, me.

If I had learnt anything about myself in these days of loss, fear and purpose, it was that if I was to defend truth and protect my daughter this time, I had to be as zealous as them.

Even if that now meant accepting that my wife was a killer.

## 50

Paris was sticky and humid. The shops were being boarded up for the night and the chefs and waiters were opening up the restaurants. The city had a glint of expectation in its eye. In the distance there was a haze around Sacré-Coeur. Notre-Dame was as forbidding as ever, casting a shadow over the inky blue Seine below. This was the time of the afternoon the French called *entre chien et loup*, between the dog and the wolf. On good days, it was about horizon and hope.

Today, I didn't see the horizon and I didn't feel the hope. I felt my hand cold against the beer glass.

Stephanie and I had arranged to meet for an early supper in Les Philosophes, her favourite restaurant, where the vibrant Marais district with its falafel and queerness met the tourist quarter behind Notre-Dame.

I arrived first. I was desperate to see her. The one pure thing I could cling to in the midst of all this upheaval. If everything else was broken, I could at least be a good ancestor. Stephanie would be there for Emma, I knew. Even if I could not.

There was birdsong from a Marais balcony. I had started hearing birdsong soon after my father died. Today was the first time I had really understood the birdsong would go on without me. My daughter would still be there to hear it.

When she was twelve, a stray dog had bitten Steph. We had been walking on a beach near Hastings. Emma was worried, panicking about infection. She had wanted to get the bite checked at the hospital. But I had argued that it would clear, we should enjoy the rare family moments we had together. Later when the infection spread, and Stephanie was in a second week in hospital, I had spent sleepless nights by her bed. Holding her hand. Watching her chest rise and fall. Praying to a God I had quietly fallen out of touch with at some point. Cursing myself for having let this happen. Vowing never to expose her again to danger.

When she had recovered, she had insisted on going out to find the mongrel, and taken it in, nursing it, becoming devoted to it. Every time I had looked at that dog, I had felt reproached. Like I lacked the compassion she demanded, the courage she had.

I took a sip of the beer and looked out over the square, past the street performers on the corner. There were jugglers, an acrobat, a skiffle band.

I was ready to start processing again, through the fog of emotions. I needed to find pieces of wreckage to cling to.

Everyone had wanted Amina Joshi dead, even Amina herself, although she had wavered at the end. Pederson had blackmailed Lenny into helping prepare the suicide: a final, sick piece of performance art, designed to get maximum exposure for the release of the latest documents, and unleash the anger of people already incensed. Orla had been aware but had tried to talk Amina out of it.

And now I was confronted by the possibility that my wife, out of love, might have helped Amina to finish the job. The French and Brits had no interest in investigating any possibility it might not be a suicide. Not because they were involved but knowing that suggestions of a murder would launch more protests, more suicides. Someone had then come to the mountains to ensure Orla could not reveal Tatham's sentiment mining programme. They had clearly concluded that without her I wouldn't piece it together or would fall into line out of loyalty or fear.

But she, and they, had missed the bigger story: Amina had indeed weaponised her activism. She had found a way to even up the fight – to work the data and the epidemiology to make it likelier that conservatives died in future pandemics. Maybe in the end it was the prospect of breakthroughs with that effort that had made her reluctant to kill herself. Either way, she had needed Emma's help at the end. Meanwhile, Crawford had gone after Pederson, using me as bait. And someone had come for Lenny. His 'suicide' meant that he could be safely blamed for providing the weapon, and any other loose ends that complicated the story.

But those two pieces still did not make sense. Why had Crawford come to the mountains? And if Emma had been there at the end, why had Crawford changed the knife? Had he initially assumed an American assassination and wanted to help cover it up?

In the midst of it all, I still could not imagine Emma able to assist in Amina's suicide. But had I ever really known her?

I flicked open the envelope of photos that I had picked up in the residence. They were mainly guests at the embassy reception. The usual eclectic mix of the great and not so good. A strained photo of me with Peter Kane. Orla Fitzgerald looking stunning in her emerald dress. Vibrant and alive. The European ambassadors, their not-so-excellent excellencies gurning smugly. Alem surrounded by colleagues. Parkinson leering at the wife of a fellow spook: he had been in the garden all the time. Sophie fiddling with her smartphone to update the embassy's Instagram account.

There was a close-up of Max Crawford resplendent in his medals, holding court with some old story of derring-do.

He did not look like a man preparing to commit a murder. But I no longer believed in my instincts on who I should trust.

There was a great shot of Stephanie, early in the evening. She had always been photogenic. She had a faraway look in her eyes. The white dress, crisp and clean. A splash of bright red lipstick.

I felt it like a punch to my gut. I gasped, grasping the tablecloth, trying to steady myself as the world spun.

In her hand, resting at her side as she smiled at the camera, was her smartphone.

There was a heaviness deep in the pit of my stomach. The place where hope ends.

She had told me that when she had found Amina, it was because she had returned to her room to pick up her phone. Yet she had it with her all the time.

I heard Pederson's scar of a snarl. His joy in the suspense. 'Someone closer to home.' Churkin warning me that it was better not to know the truth. Emma trying to deflect the blame onto herself, knowing that the truth was even worse.

My daughter had been with Amina when she died.

Had I been so blinded by love? Could I have been so stupid? Was this a piece of art for her? An act of hate, of rebellion against a controlling parent? Revenge for my failure to protect her?

I had wept when I first read the story while cycling through Andalusia. As the Moors besieged the stronghold of Tarifa in 1296, Alonso Pérez de Guzmán was charged with defending the city. His enemies had captured his son in battle. They paraded him below the walls of his fortress and called up to the old man to open the gates and save the boy's life. Guzmán had wept alone for an hour in his private chambers, his sobs shaking the castle. And then he had put on his finest red cloak, taken up his favourite dagger, kissed the blade and thrown it down to his enemies. The boy had been killed. The city had stood.

But now there might need to be another betrayal. Only I was now the parent called on to make the ultimate sacrifice.

And then, there she was. Crossing the bridge towards me. Her light blue summer dress swirled around her knees. Her bare shoulders were brown and toned. That same splash of bright red lipstick. She was vibrant and alive. Below her the Seine was brown, washing away the sins of the city.

She waved across at me, beaming. She looked so radiant, so perfect.

So innocent.

## 51

Later she told me she knew as soon as she saw me. She had expected to find me weary, older. But she had never thought she would see the idealism gone. She understood even in that moment that she had done that.

We hugged long, trying to delay the conversation that would break us. In those moments I felt again the pain of loss at the school gates. She was there and yet somehow further away.

We sat. An uncharacteristic awkwardness as the waiter fussed with the napkins and put another carafe of water on the table. I nodded at the menu, but she shook her head. She took a piece of bread in her hands, toying with it. Specks of hard baguette fell onto the white linen cloth. I thought again of her white dress. The lightness of her that night in the garden.

Steph swallowed hard, took a long sip of water.

Where to begin.

A simple question yet the only one that really mattered any more. 'Are you okay, Steph?'

'Mum said she saw you, Dad. Said she talked to you about her and Amina. Said she wanted you to move on now. Let all this go?'

She spoke without emotion, with control. But her voice wobbled as it reached for the question.

I had been staring at my hands on the tablecloth. The hands that had buried the body on the mountain. What had my daughter made me? What had I made her?

I started to speak but choked. She took my hands across the table, and I forced my eyes up to look at her. She was weeping as she looked at me. At the moment when I felt weakest, it somehow gave me strength. She could still feel.

I tried again.

'Orla told me a story in the mountains. About why Pederson was who he was. But the story was really about you. I wasn't there when you most needed me. Forgive me.'

She breathed hard. 'That's not your fault, Pops. None of this is your fault. That's why I didn't want you to go to Magnus Pederson.'

'All my life I've dreaded losing you. I knew it would come but imagined a thousand small cuts, the distance between us growing. I lost you that night and I never even knew it.'

'You haven't lost me.'

I wished so much that I could believe that.

I grimaced. 'What happened to Amina?'

The waiter came back to take the order. Steph waved him away. She composed herself.

'When I found out about Mum and Amina, I argued with them both. I said they had to talk to you. Mum was clear they wouldn't, but I was working on Amina. I got to know her in those weeks. The more I saw, the more I realised that she was dangerous. And not just to us, our family. She was becoming more certain. This sense of destiny, of complete self-belief. This zeal.'

My hands were pressed hard together under the table now. I felt the nails dig into the palms. I had not only been the last in my house to know about Emma, but the last to see what Amina was becoming. I nodded at her to continue.

'Amina was torn. Between Mum and this image she was creating. The campaign. What she called her martyrdom. She was being wound up by the activists. By Magnus Pederson. He must have enjoyed the idea that her suicide would harm you. Maybe that it would harm me too. She started talking about the need to shock, to get people's attention. To stimulate a popular campaign.'

'I know now what she was doing. Maybe she was better off dead, like everyone keeps telling me. But Steph, what was this to do with you?'

'I started to see it as a way to save us, to protect you. Amina wanted death but lacked the courage. If she was gone, you and Mum could stay together. All I did...' Her voice faltered and stopped. The waiter loomed but did not need to be waved away this time.

'What did you do? I need to hear you say it.' I was surprised at the anger in my voice.

'I didn't need to do much. I just talked to her. Encouraged her. She needed someone with her at the end. I was worried about what she might become in death. But I was more worried by what she had become in life. She didn't care that she was destroying you, us.'

'But by helping her you have destroyed me. Where did I go wrong, Steph? Did you do this out of hate? Because I failed you?'

Her shoulders fell forward, and she steadied herself on the table. Her voice was almost silent. 'No, Dad.' A whisper now. 'Please understand me. I did it out of love.'

I looked out towards the square, trying to steady myself. A busker had started his act, covering Willie Nelson covering Elvis on regret and failing at the little things. The tourists continued to pass by, unbothered. The Seine continued to flow, uncaring.

Steph took a deep breath. 'I know what I did. But I never imagined that anyone would know I was there. I didn't know it was being recorded. I handed her the knife when she lost the strength to lift it. As she fell to the ground it dropped by her side, and I put it back by her hand.'

'Her right hand?' I remembered wondering why it was there, not by her stronger hand.

'I don't know. I wasn't thinking. Lenny had got it from the kitchen. I just wanted her gone. She tried a first time and stopped the cut. She just needed the encouragement. The second time she pressed the knife harder into her neck. She looked suddenly so sad. I couldn't watch any more, and yet I see it every time I close my eyes. Every time I look at the internet it's there again, like she's haunting me.'

This was why Pederson had not released the video. Maybe one last effort to protect Steph. And because the damage it would have done to me was outweighed by the lack of conviction in Amina's martyrdom. Better to let a thousand conspiracy theories fester.

'But you were just a witness, Steph; she would have killed herself without you there.'

I knew as I said it that neither of us believed it.

'I talked to her. Told her to be brave. Made her keep going. That's what Magnus Pederson saw on the film.'

The name brought me back to the table with a jolt. 'You spoke to him?'

She was pale. A girl again, waiting in the dentist's surgery. 'He called me the following day. Played me the tape of my voice, coaxing her to kill herself. Wanted to meet again.'

I thought of his relish as he had prepared to play it to me.

'Why didn't you come to me?'

'How could I, Pops? I was terrified. You were frantic. I didn't know what he wanted. I didn't want to break your heart. I knew telling you would...' She trailed off. We both knew what it had done.

'Did you tell Mum?'

'She worked it out. But no, I sorted it.'

'How?' I felt the fury surge through me. Another betrayal.

A sigh and then she sat up straighter, pushing herself through this final admission. 'I went to Max Crawford. Told him everything. Told him about Pederson's call. Told him that to tell you would destroy you. Asked him to protect you from what I had done.'

Crawford. The laughter lines and the jaw. My daughter's crime had been the grim truth from which he had tried to protect me. He had risked everything, lost everything, to do so, hiding the knife that killed Amina, the knife with Stephanie's prints. He had then even followed me to Snowdonia to protect me from the Americans. And then to Copenhagen to protect me from the risk that Pederson might share the truth. And to try to destroy the tape, the remaining evidence against my daughter.

His favourite story. Gelert, the faithful hound. The ultimate act of loyalty, never understood. In the legend, the king had come to understand too late what had been sacrificed, and his own treachery in not seeing it. I had been so convinced of his betrayal. And yet he had been on my side the whole time.

'I cursed him at the very moment he was saving me. And I've given Orla the material to blame all this on him.'

She tried to speak but I could hear nothing.

All I had ever wanted was to hold a mirror up to her so that she could see how beautiful she was. And to build a fortress around her to protect her from the world.

But she had been the one to build a fortress around me. To protect me, from the knowledge of Emma and Amina. She had decided that only she had the strength to save our marriage, to save our family. Whatever it took.

'My daughter.'

Maybe anyone can choose between truth and lies. I had already faced the choice between truth and friendship. Between truth and country. Between truth and values. Between truth and self-preservation. Between truth and my wife.

What happens when you face a choice between truth and love?

Had Abraham faltered as he sharpened the knife, trying to delay the moment? Had he struggled to compose himself as he piled the brushwood on the altar? Had he managed to ignore the growing fear in his son's voice, and felt the moment when the absolute trust started to break? Had Isaac ever *really* forgiven him, really forgiven God?

What cruel God asks you to sacrifice your child?

'I need to walk.'

I rose from my seat, pushing the table back. The couple on the next table broke off their conversation for a moment. I strode onto the square and stood in front of the busker. He was mid-twenties, Steph's age. He had a kind, open face, light brown eyes. A face untouched by cynicism, by experience. How fortunate it was to be untouched by experience. He grinned up at me.

I took a fifty-euro note from my pocket and threw it into the hat in front of him.

'Please, I beg you. Just stop.'

## 52

It would be several weeks after Max Crawford's apparent death in the US missile strike in Copenhagen before the letter was delivered. George Crawford knew that his younger brother would get one too.

> *Dear George,*
>
> *If you're reading this it is because I had one adventure too many.*
>
> *We talk a lot about valour and courage. But I've always fought for survival, and for the guy next to me. Loyalty matters, especially when they cannot see it.*
>
> *You'll often be told that individuals shape the world. Often you'll be told that we're all tossed along on the tide by much larger forces of history. Neither is really true, I think. The world is so much bigger than we can ever comprehend. But we can change it in small ways. You just have to choose where to put your effort. Don't leave your own song unsung.*
>
> *People are amazing. And infuriating. I hope that you seek out those who are both. Invest in the ones who are loyal, adventurous and pioneering, who are excited about life, who want to build things — ideas, societies, businesses, adventures — not knock them down. Find people who seek exhilaration but can also swing. I'll always remember us*

doing King of the Swingers. I'm sorry I won't be around to see you do it with your kids, my son.

Know your flaws but don't be blinded by them. As you get older, you come to love them a little bit, even if no one else does.

Don't take anything for granted. Don't believe anything without challenging it. Don't love anything without understanding it. If he deserves punching, punch him. If she deserves loving, love her. If it deserves conquering, conquer it. If not, let it pass you by. Don't pick someone else's fight.

Find what people love about you and be true to that. Trust your DNA – yours is good. Rebel against it, fight it, but find it. We owe it to our ancestors to hold onto the best of them. But never think that the advantages you inherit make you somehow better than those that don't have them.

At the end of the day, there is wine, olive oil, music, love, camaraderie, mountains, oceans, family, laughter, purpose, soul. Life really is beautiful. And we're here for a good time, not a long time.

That's enough of all that. If there is one last thing I have learnt, it is to choose your own epitaph. I hope mine is easy enough to agree.

We spend all our lives trying to make our parents proud. They mostly just want us to be happy. You've always made me proud and happy.

Proceed until apprehended.

Dad

# Epilogue

Two years later, Emma Kendall looked up from a Keats early edition as her partner entered the bookstore. She would take her to the Spanish bar on the corner for some dry sherry and Iberian ham. They would sit together quietly. Emma had never truly forgiven her daughter for helping Amina Joshi kill herself, but she had never stopped loving her either. She had never truly forgiven her ex-husband for having let time and the Foreign Office knock him off course, but she had never really stopped loving him either. She might take a book to lose herself in. There was no need to plan. We become what we pay attention to. It was freedom she had always wanted, more than love. And how did the song go? It was just another word for having nothing left to lose. The bookseller smiled at her as she left, and then watched her for too long as she walked away.

Lynn Redwood was being driven home after a statement in parliament. The car paused at a traffic light, and she looked up for a moment from her red box, peering over her glasses into the soupy gloom of one more late London night. A couple in a cafe were kissing, oblivious to the world around them. There was a bottle of Southern Comfort on their table. She watched them for a few seconds, a reluctant voyeur, and then returned to her papers as the car pulled away again. She smelt for a second the faint smell of disinfectant, and she was miles away, her coat pulled tight around her, alone and weeping. Walking away from an over-lit surgery with its functional equipment laid out in neat rows of metal and plastic. The staff whose names she had never wanted to know. Walking away from the sacrifice and loss. Walking away from another man who couldn't clear up his own mess. Too much weakness leads to failure. Too much freedom leads to pain. Too much truth leads to despair.

James Sheriff looked with satisfaction across the residence garden. An Englishman's home is his castle, and what a castle this one was. Beside him, Peter Kane sucked loudly at his champagne as he ogled the retreating calves of the new senior residence manager. They were no longer called butlers, though he had just admired with as much sincerity as he could muster the small plaque to the last one. Washington was still melting down over the continued Dissenters' revelations, but Kane's shares in the arms company would do just fine, and another generation of Kanes would get a decent head start. That was a decent legacy. His father might finally be proud. Sheriff teased him that he now had more Twitter followers than the American. 'You were the future once, Kane.' Kane grinned back with the certainty and confidence of one of history's winners. In the end, and when the bullets were flying, people would always choose security over liberty. Paris of all cities could tell you that.

In Washington, President Hoon glowered at the television. Why did she still seem to inspire such unfair hatred and derision? Even the cable channels now seemed to be ignoring her. Why did no one come to brief her any more? And where was her chief of staff these days? She needed a new target. The market for entertainment was infinite. The market for bold leadership was infinite. The threats from those who hated her were threats against America. And she alone could fix it. Beyond the gates of the White House, new movements were emerging to challenge the cheap politics of polarisation. The real America, restless and hopeful, would soon be on the march again.

Sir Angus Green groaned as he sat in his Whitehall corner office, the lights of St James's Park glowing dimly outside the window. In front of him the long and unpalatable list of possible embassy closures. Who to spare, who to condemn, who to leave in purdah for another day? The sword of Damocles was heavy today. The new foreign secretary had now said again that they must do 'much more with much less'. Ugh. The world needed more diplomacy than ever, but what did he have to work with? In the end, much less. He remembered the words of a previous foreign secretary, looking out at the same view on the eve of the First World War. 'The lamps are going out, we may not see them lit again in our lifetime.' He took out his green pen and started to rearrange the deckchairs on the *Titanic*. Always one job too many.

In the mountains above Beirut, Nasib-*bayk* finished another bottle of arak, and put on a Rolling Stones LP. The devil's story of treachery and greed echoed out over the valley. As he walked back across the terrace of the thirteenth-century citadel he sashayed his snake-like hips mischievously and chuckled out loud. Survival, that was all that mattered. He had carried the name on for another generation. It would soon be someone else's turn to take on that heavy burden. And one day, if he waited long enough by the river, the dead body of his enemy would come floating by. There would be one more musket on the wall and his sister could wear flowers in her hair again. He did not hear the sound of the single bullet from the armoury downstairs. One more assisted suicide. Leave nothing behind.

Alem Nigusie straightened her tight black leather skirt and walked up to the microphone. It was a hot Madrid night. She was carrying no notes. Her hijab combined the colours of the British and Spanish flags. She looked around her at a more diverse group of invitees than the usual diplomatic receptions. Sophie was there, smiling back confidently. There were more wheelchairs, more rainbow flags, more life, more creativity and ingenuity. Britain was in safe hands. Fewer dead carp, fewer sharks. 'Ladies and gentlemen, welcome to this celebration of Britain and Spain, and of what unites us rather than divides us. More than ever today we need expertise and judgement against fake news and echo chambers. Honesty and curiosity against intolerance and post-truth politics. These values are hard to march for, hard to articulate. But all of a sudden it feels like we need to fight a bit harder for them. In the end, what else do we have?' A smile crossed her lips briefly. She paused for effect. 'Winston Churchill once told a story...'

Professor Peter Tatham kicked off his expensive flip-flops and tucked into his light chicken salad as his super yacht cruised into St Tropez. The chef had done his usual excellent job. He casually tapped open the encrypted app. A couple of swipes and he had the locations of every attractive woman in the town who had that week told a friend that she wanted a new man, within the recording range of an average smartphone. He scrolled through their photos and picked a bar where a few seemed to be gathered. Why make it hard for yourself? Assumed consent. Technology was a playground for those with ambition. Agonistes had been officially mothballed by the Americans, and Amina's followers were less focused than she had been and had become bad for the brand. But he and Suzanne Morley had found others eager to take up their expertise. Mortality was for mortals. Not for a man of wealth and taste. Why did liberty have to be strenuous?

In a warehouse in Geneva, hundreds of Dissenters worked through the night, preparing the next release of government data. On the wall, two large portraits hung menacingly over them, spurring them on to new frontiers. The first was the *Time* magazine shot of Amina Joshi crucified, using the iconic image of her pale face in its death throes. The second was a black and white shot of a glowering Magnus Pederson looking like Che Guevara. There was graffiti with his most famous lines – 'all truth is lies', 'destroy to build', 'permanent outrage', 'trust no one'. The new Dissenters had their prophets and their martyrs, their gods and their devils. The suicides continued to strike terror into parents and governments. Others would step forward, eyes blazing with zeal, to make the ultimate sacrifice. Pederson had not died in vain. He had been the first to see the coastline of the Age of Distrust.

In the Paris HQ of *Le Monde*, the editor looked once again at the Pulitzer on the shelf. She had picked it up on behalf of Orla Fitzgerald. The extraordinary, groundbreaking article had told the story of Magnus Pederson and Amina Joshi, leading up to her death in Paris and his death in Copenhagen. There were hints of cover-ups by the governments of the US, France and UK. But there were no winners in the story: Amina was an ambitious narcissist and Pederson a twisted manipulator with delusions of grandeur. As well as scooping every award, there were enough hints in the article for the Hoon administration to quietly shut down the Agonistes Programme. But Orla never emerged to claim her prize. From the same anonymous account that she had emailed the article she had asked for all royalties to be sent to a foundation for reconciliation between former combatants, set up by a former SAS general called Max Crawford. No one had heard anything else from her, and the police had long since called off their investigation into her disappearance. Perhaps she was working on her next big piece.

At Hereford's memorial of valour, a young SAS trainee polished the newest plaque, to General Max Crawford. There were no medals left to win. No adventures left to run. The simple words were engraved on a small rectangle of copper – 'We are the Pilgrims. We shall go. Always a little further.' So many kills, for queen and country, and then they had said that he died in a routine training accident in Hereford. No one on the base believed the story about the training accident. Few really believed he was dead. Max didn't do routine. Or training. Or suffer accidents. The short epitaph left by his sons read simply 'Proceed until apprehended.' Only a few people knew how he had been in Copenhagen when the American strike hit the building, and they would take the secret to their graves. Only one man alive knew that Crawford had been there out of personal loyalty, maybe even friendship. The truth is that you fight for the guy fighting next to you.

And in the early afternoon of a perfect spring day, Sir Edward Barnes looked out across the lawn of his Sussex home. An Englishman's home is his castle. This was less of a castle than the residence in Paris. But it was more of a home. In the end it had been easier for everyone in government to turn the page while he took what Angus had called 'an indefinite period of gardening leave'. Everyone but Ed Barnes. But he'd be back. The shits might win most of the time, but you could sometimes make it a bit harder for them.

He took a long drag on his spliff and looked across at his daughter. She squeezed his hand. So many nights standing outside her door, listening to the sobbing and trying to find the courage to knock. One day he might find the words for the bond that their secret had created. And the shared fear that someone in Moscow still had Pederson's tape. One day he might sleep a full night. She had sacrificed what was left of her innocence to hold the family together. But she had failed. He had sacrificed what was left of the truth to hold the family together. And he had failed too.

The easiest betrayals to make are the ones where we betray ourselves.

But sometimes you have to pick a side.

They listened on in silence to the low notes of the jazz clarinet. A breeze caught the branches of the poplars at the foot of the garden.

The silences between the notes and the wind between the leaves.

Now wasn't that the truth.

## Acknowledgements

This was my agent Ed Victor's idea, hence the dedication. I'd been to see him to discuss what to write next. I suggested something on the history of coexistence or migration, developing the themes and tensions of *The Naked Diplomat*? I was curious about shifting boundaries: liberty versus security; coexistence versus wall building; global versus local; trust versus distrust; truth versus lies; moderation versus zeal; technology versus tradition; certainty versus curiosity.

Ed was gently but firmly discouraging, as only he could be. 'I think you need to write a detective novel.' At the time I assumed he was joking.

Ed died in early June 2017. My extraordinary wife, Louise, said that if I had a song, I should have a crack at singing it. By the end of the month I'd written the guts of this story. I based at Civitella Ranieri, a fifteenth-century Umbrian castle now a haven for artists, musicians and poets. I'm hugely grateful to the staff and benefactors of Civitella – what a place, and what an idea. And to the proper authors and artists there, who helped an imposter think about how to write dialogue, conjure a memory or appreciate a clarinet solo.

The draft then languished until the year of the coronavirus, when I was once again able to give it some time. The world had moved on so much by then that everything far-fetched now seemed quite tame.

I loved writing this book. I tried not to stray too close to reality, and none of the characters are *firmly* based on people I have actually met. The most outrageous parts of the book are the real ones. The more boring I invented.

Thanks to those who provided vital feedback on the drafts, especially Guy Winter, Charlie Brotherstone, Jon Sampson, Matt and Becca Norbury, Alex Hammond, Debbie Dalzell, Mark Wilkinson, Sarah Zaid, Gareth McLean and Chris Wheeler. Bill Massey and Russel McLean's expertise and patience were indispensable.

We must defend the progress and freedoms we take for granted. Against people like Pederson, Tatham and Hoon. Against people who tell us not just what we should think, but how we should think. The real dividing line of the period ahead is between two basic human instincts – to fight for resource or negotiate for it. We need to retain our restless curiosity to seek out the unexplored spaces. We don't need less politics, just better politics. A politics that gets us back to the basics – to hope, aspiration and opportunity.

My first Foreign Office appraisal suggested that I might make a decent diplomat if I managed to contain my zeal.

I'm still trying.